The Worsted House

The Collected Stories of Ramsbolt

Jennifer M. Lane

Cover design by Al Hess – cultofsasha.com

Copyright © 2021

Published by Pen and Key Publishing

jennifermlanewrites.com

ISBN: 978-1-7334068-9-5

For Roscoe and Ann, though we never met.

ACKNOWLEDGEMENTS

Special thank you to Shelly and Al, without whom my words would be fewer and my life less full.

Old walls are noisy things.
Radiators ping and gurgling pipes
The unspoken lyrics are loudest.

November morning light making quilts on the walls.
Bumps and bruises and strange little welts.
What it was. What happened.
What it meant to someone else.

And the orange halo of spring
Hanging over the kitchen.
Early tomatoes from Victory Gardens.
Crisp snaps from summer cucumbers.

Someone stained a wall.
A boy who left his bike beneath a giant oak perhaps,
When it was very small.
And he was not so tall.

They are all around us now.
Noisy.
In the here.

CHAPTER ONE

Helen's Tavern smelled like beer. The floor was sticky, and the air saturated with the grumbled snarls of agitated farm workers and Arvil's sputtered drink requests. Logan fielded them one by one, strange as they ever were, as they spilled from the darkened corner where he sat behind the morning paper. In between, it was nothing but beer orders from men who dragged their hands through their hair, the grayed remains of their youth. Bern pounding one after the other, and Dan picking farm life from under his nails with a pocketknife. She dragged out the night, avoiding the chatter from her husband, Grey, who'd been stuck on repeat for weeks. He wanted to buy a house. Logan knew they couldn't afford it.

Lucky for Logan, Penny and Adelle gave her margin, sitting on either side of him and indulging his real estate whims by gushing about the potential hiding in pixels of run-down properties.

At Dan's nod, Logan grabbed a six-pack from the cooler and shook open a paper bag.

"We got a new cooler when we rebuilt the place. You know you don't have to order six packs from the to-go fridge anymore." She dropped the bag in front of him and held out her hand for his cash.

"I got my habits. Don't like change." He forked over a twenty. "Keep it."

"Lo!" Grey waved her over and slapped cash on the bar, waving his phone with an incoming call. "I gotta run. I still think we should consider getting a place. I have to do something with all this cash from after-hours emergency plumbing problems."

Logan took his money and glowered. Every time he mentioned buying a house, the world tilted on its axis, and the room spun. She lost her stable, happy home once when it was forcibly taken from her parents by the government, and she had no desire to get close to real estate again. Especially if she wasn't the one in control of it.

She tugged her ponytail and brushed dark-brown strays from her eyes. "Who is it this time?"

Grey shrugged into his jacket. "Kyle. It's poo water this time."

Adelle swallowed a sip of wine. "That downstairs bathroom again. It's such a pain."

"Mmm. Expensive." She rang up Grey's tab and shoved the change in her tip jar.

"Exactly," Grey said. "I want to come home to my own place. I'm tired of that cramped little house. It doesn't have a porch, and I have to kick off my boots in the truck." He pulled his knit cap down over his ears and gave her a broad grin. "Sick of giving my money to Warren for rent when we could be buying our own place. Catch ya at home. Might be a late one."

Grey trudged out the door and was gone.

"Guess I'm better off hanging here for another round. Kyle is not going to be in a good mood." Adelle ordered another with a nod. "Grey's really hung up on getting a house, huh?"

Logan yanked the cork from a bottle of pinot grigio and filled Adelle's glass to the top. "Grey is convincing himself that he hates our house, because he'd rather live in something much more decrepit. It's some checklist he has. Work. Wife. Hovel."

Penny's eyes grew wide. "If Nate wanted to buy a house, I'd be thrilled. I'd love to get out of the loft and stretch my legs."

"Well, Nate would probably spend within his limits." Logan sighed and took out her frustration by wiping down the bar. "We can't afford a house. That's all there is to it. And this is definitely not the right time."

Logan dropped another drink in front of Penny.

"Thanks." Penny pulled it close. "I think it's sweet he wants a house."

"It would be sweet if we could afford it. Debt we can't afford to pay back isn't much of a romantic gesture."

A pit of boiling acid rolled in her stomach; a burning that had become familiar since Grey started talking about real estate with every meal. She wasn't sure why it made her upset. She grew up around real estate, immersed in the strategic maneuvering of apartment complexes and office building renovations, walls being valued and swapped in highly charged games of real-life Monopoly. People in suits had marched through her life, their personalities surgically removed, dampened by tailored jackets and pants. They cast aside everyone who couldn't do something for them in return, building their reputations with escalating zip codes. She'd set down her father's baggage a long time ago, after he went to prison for laundering money through his own empire, and she had no desire to pick it up again.

Penny tipped a glass Logan's way. "What's the worst that could happen?"

"I don't know." Logan slammed Grey's empty glass into the dishwasher rack. It felt good, but she regretted that it didn't break. "I just don't know. Okay? Maybe it's the permanence of it. Buying a house isn't like playing chess with office buildings. It's not a business decision for him. It's all emotional. He wants to live there forever and make some white-picket-fence fairy tale, but he doesn't know how much work it is."

"Permanence, huh?" Adelle and Penny swapped looks.

Logan bristled. She didn't have time for their snark. "What?"

Adelle shrugged. "We've heard this from you before, that's all. That you don't want to be tied down."

Their words hit her like stinging arrows. She turned her face to hide her wince. "It's not like the wedding."

But Adelle wasn't wrong. If she owned a house, she wouldn't be able to jump and run. The idea stirred all those unsettled feelings she thought she'd resolved ages ago, when she gave up the anonymity that protected her from death threats in the fallout from her father's crimes. She'd unmasked herself in front of the world to save Helen's Tavern and the soul of the town. She'd dug herself into the soil when she married Grey, but clearly, she hadn't put down the roots she thought she had.

She leaned back against the bar, arms folded, hoping one of them would diagnose her condition, because she didn't understand it herself.

Barely a syllable escaped Adelle's lips when Logan changed her mind. She threw up a hand and shut her friends down. "It's not a good financial decision right now. Period. I don't want to fight about it. Not with Grey, and not with the two of you. And definitely not while I'm at work."

"No argument from me." Adelle settled back on her stool. "I always wanted a little house, but it's not really practical when I can live above the shop without a mortgage."

"That's what I mean." Logan threw her bar rag in the sink. "Our place isn't free, but it's cheap. Our mortgage would be twice what we pay in rent. I just don't want this to destroy our marriage." She grabbed a new rag from the stack and wound it around her hand. "I'm just not interested in buying a house. Period."

Penny made a little wet ring on her napkin with condensation from her beer. "I can't believe this would destroy your relationship. You guys compromise really well. Remember your wedding day?"

"I know. I chose Ramsbolt."

"Those are pretty deep roots you have going on already."

"Yeah, but Grey is portable. There's a whole big world out there, and it's full of shady plumbing and people who need a drink. We could go anywhere."

"You could always buy a house on wheels." Adelle slid her empty glass across the bar. "One more before I have to go pry Kyle off the ceiling when he sees the bill from Grey?"

"See? Bills like that are why I don't want to be tied down."

CHAPTER TWO

"What you need is a vacation." Logan squeezed between Grey and the fridge, opened the door enough to grab the salad dressing, and banged her funny bone on the fridge door trying to put it on her salad. She rubbed her elbow on her way to the table. "Why don't we go on an adventure. Something to break up the humdrums. You liked Montreal."

She'd drag him anywhere to keep him from showing her pictures of run-down houses all over town, doom scrolling on his phone through shacks he swore he could fix.

Falling into her chair, she stared out the window to the field beyond. It hadn't been mowed, and the late summer grasses had grown two feet high, tipped with purple wisps that bowed and swirled in the breeze. It had been winter when she moved into the house Grey rented from Warren. The single-story Cape Cod was tucked on a back street behind her old apartment above the post office. Like everything in Ramsbolt, it was close to everything else, only a few minutes' walk to Adelle's and Penny's. And she loved it. What it lacked in space, it gained in being cozy. Unlike her old apartment with everything crammed together in one room, it had a separate kitchen and dining room, a living room with a fireplace that didn't work, and maybe they had to share a bathroom, but they did have separate closets. And it had a back patio that looked out over their sunny yard, even though it didn't have a roof. They even had a detached garage where Grey kept his truck and tools.

It had taken a while to fit her stuff into the house he'd lived in alone for so long, despite how little she owned. It had taken even longer before her heart settled there. That house felt like the home she'd always wanted, even if it looked nothing like the places she'd dreamt of as a kid. She didn't want to throw it away by moving, yet again, into a place she couldn't afford.

"Don't you feel cramped in here?" Grey sat across from her and waved a radish at the end of his fork.

"No. Is it my stuff? I know I leave my work bag in the dining room. I could put it in the closet."

Grey shook his head, eyes pinned on his salad. "It's not your bag."

"I heard you cussing at it when you tripped over it yesterday morning. I'll find another place for it."

"I didn't mean to wake you up." Grey sipped his iced tea. "If we had a bigger place, me leaving for work wouldn't interrupt your sleep."

"You'd still have to get out of bed, though. I don't want a place so big we have separate bedrooms. My parents tried that. It didn't make them fight any less."

"Who said anything about separate bedrooms?" He dropped his fork and threw up his hands. "I'm not fighting."

"Neither am I!" Logan's voice went up an octave.

"Then why are we yelling?"

"I don't know. I don't want to move. It upsets me talking about it all the time."

A crouton shattered when Grey speared it, crumbs shooting across the table. "It's cheaper than paying rent. That's all I'm saying. We could own something instead of paying someone else."

"Where are you going to find a house for sale that's less than the seven hundred bucks we pay for this place?"

"All over Ramsbolt." He jabbed at his phone, pushing it across the table. "I keep trying to show them to you, but you're all *meh, meh, meh* about it."

She willed her slowing breath to calm her insides. "Wet cardboard boxes cost less than this place, but that doesn't mean I want to live in one. That's all you've been showing me. Why would you want to choose between something with a hole in the roof, a rotting pile of asbestos, or something with a giant crack in the foundation?"

His eyes widened. "We can fix it up."

"Why waste all that time and money when you can stay where you are and have money in your pocket to live a little? Like, I don't know…" She rubbed her eyes with the heels of her hands, pressing so tight that fireworks exploded in the dark. "Portland. Let's go to Portland for a weekend."

She lowered her hands, and Grey grabbed them across the table. "Lo. I don't want to fight. I don't want to waste money on a vacation either. Boredom isn't my problem. It's space. And I don't want to pay rent to someone else anymore. No matter how much room we have, I'll always want to own my own slice of land."

That was the opposite of what she wanted, but her thought was interrupted by a text alert on Grey's phone. He unlocked it. "I have to run. Parts are in. If I hurry, I can pick them up before they close."

Filling his mouth with a last bite of salad, he shoved his phone in his pocket and dropped his plate in the sink.

"For Kyle's place?" Logan squeezed past him and scraped her plate into the trash. Her appetite was spoiled. It was only lettuce anyway.

"Yeah. Grogan's has the parts in. I'll get this knocked out, and I'll take a nap so when you get home, we can finish watching that show."

"Sounds good. I have a Skype with my mom in a few minutes anyway."

"Tell her I said something in French." He rolled his keyring around his finger, and his keys lassoed into his palm. "We good?"

She pulled him into a hug. His shirt smelled like metal and solder. It was a comforting smell, the one she came home to every day. The one he always brought home to her. "Of course, we're good."

"Great. I gotta get this job done so Kyle's customers have somewhere to pee, and Jacques can have a toilet to drink from. Poor dog." She let him go, and he slipped out the door, waving over his shoulder. "See you when you get in."

It would be well after three when she'd get home from work, but she loved the nights he set an alarm and greeted her when she came in the door. It had been weeks since he'd done that.

On the off chance her mom was around a few minutes early, she rang her on Skype, propped her phone against her water glass, and slipped back into her seat. The grainy screen pixelated, fading from white to reveal the kitchen of her mother's tiny cottage in France.

"Hi, Mom." The room behind her came into view. Ivory cabinets with blue and white tile backsplashes. A row of little copper pots hung from beneath a cabinet. Logan folded her arms and squinted at the small screen. "How are Aunt and Uncle?"

"They're fine. He runs five miles a day or something like that. She's into chickens now. Dirty beasts. They'll eat each other. Did you know that? Little cannibals. I used to love the chicken piccata at the country club in Connecticut. Never again."

"Sorry to hear that. Any news?"

"About what? Chickens? She brings me their eggs like it's some sort of gift. Stands in the doorway like she wants a Nobel Peace Prize. What am I supposed to say?" Her mother's eyes widened, and she shook her head, soft gray waves skimming her shoulders. "I have no desire to eat your cannibalized chicken babies?" Her nostrils flared with disgust, as if someone suggested she wear flannel.

Logan held in a laugh. "I meant about life, but the chickens are entertaining."

"They smell like death. Cackling all day. You should hear it. Anyway. Have you heard from He You Will Not Name?" Her mother cocked one eyebrow, lips curled in a curious sneer.

"I have not heard from Dad." She'd been blocking every incoming call from every correctional services phone number for so long that none even showed up anymore. She couldn't remember the last time she didn't answer his call. If he really wanted to see his family, he wouldn't have laundered money with foreign investors and made illegal campaign contributions and put everything at risk. He'd have taken care of her, not left her homeless with ten grand in her pocket to last her the rest of eternity. "I doubt I'll ever want to hear from him, to be honest."

"You may feel differently one day."

"Won't. What else is going on?"

Her mother rolled her eyes around the kitchen. "I'm learning to make bread. It's tiring, but it smells nice. What about you? I want to hear how you and your carpenter are doing."

"He's a plumber. We're good. He wants to buy a house, and I don't. I'm trying to convince him to go on a long weekend and get away for a while. I don't know, Mom. He's really digging in his heels. It looks like the only compromise will be the one I make."

"Listen to me." Her mother wagged a finger at her laptop's camera. "Take my advice. Do both. Go on vacation, blow off some steam. Wear a cute little bikini and make him realize what he'll be missing if he pisses you off."

"That's not my style…"

"Then wear a one-piece. I'm serious. When you get back, go look at real estate with him. Property is always a good investment."

A laugh escaped, and Logan didn't resist it. "That's bullshit. Do you remember when Dad bought that apartment building and put that LLC in your name? He lost so much money on that project."

"Only because people sued. If they'd just accepted that rent control isn't eternal and moved on peacefully, we could have…" The shine faded from her eyes. Logan knew the look. Those moments were fewer and farther between, but every once in a while, some fleck of the past, of how easy life once was, would fall in front of the lens. Her focus would shift for a moment too long, and she'd grow sad, missing what she once had.

"I know what you mean," Logan said. "More space would be nice. He's always tripping over my bag, and he wakes me up in the morning when he makes coffee before work."

"I may not know my way around a good marriage, but I know you have to compromise. You think you compromise, but you're a stubborn human, Logan Cole."

"Don't say that. I'm not."

"You are. You moved to Ringworm, Maine, and married an electrician just to spite your parents. Flexible, well-adjusted daughters don't do that."

"Plumber. Ramsbolt." She threw her head back and enjoyed the head rush. "It doesn't matter."

"At least Greg isn't laundering your money and selling out the country to the highest bidder."

"Grey, Mom. His name is Grey." She raised her voice and spoke in staccato. "Grey. Plumber. Ramsbolt."

"Fine, dear. I believe you."

"It's not a belief. They're nouns."

Logan's mother sneered to her right, nose twitching at an off-screen window. She leaned in and whispered at the camera. "That woman is on her way with those eggs again."

"You should compromise, Mom. Tell her you don't need quite so many."

"Shush." A distant tap of a door knocker made Logan's mother sneer again. Her finger hovered near the screen. "I have to go. Do yourself a favor. Go on vacation and let the man buy a damn house. If you hold him back, he'll only resent you. I recommend vacationing on the Cape. It's lovely this time of year."

CHAPTER THREE

"My mother was right. We should have gone to the Cape." Logan slipped her feet from her sandals. The porch at their bed-and-breakfast had white painted floorboards, and the heat had made it glossy and gummy. She curled her toes. "Bar Harbor is boring."

Grey topped off her glass of wine. "Want to walk down to Main Street after this? We could get ice cream?"

"Tourist trap. And we had ice cream for lunch." She wrinkled her nose, then thought better of her disdain. It might not be the emotional getaway she'd been hoping for, but it was better than anything she thought they could afford. That was the only downside to keeping their money separate. She knew how much money she had to spend on Grey but refused to accept he'd spend any on her.

Bar Harbor hadn't been that bad. It had been great if she stopped to admit it. The weather had been unseasonably warm, the evenings were cool, and she'd had plenty of time to dip her toes in the water. The glider on that painted porch had been a great place to cozy up as the sun went down. Why didn't she feel relaxed?

Grey pushed to his feet, and the glider rocked. "Let's carry these down to the water, then." He held out a hand. "Come on."

One hand in his, the other wrapped around her glass, she wiggled her toes into her sandals and scampered in his wake. "We're not supposed to take the glasses off the porch. The sign in our room said so."

"When did you start following the rules?"

Down a side street, they turned onto a narrow, gravel alley bordered by wildflowers and stray lupines. It dumped them out onto the Shore Path that edged the town on the east. They climbed a short wall and crawled down to reach the rocky shore where the water of Frenchman Bay splashed and pooled, dragging in eelgrass. Logan plopped down on the rocks, balancing her drink as she sat.

Grey pulled his buzzing phone from his pocket and scowled.

"No plumbing emergencies. I thought you changed your voicemail message." She held her glass up, leveling her wine with the horizon.

"This isn't work. I gotta take it."

Weather-worn pebbles scraped together beneath his feet like anchored wind chimes as he paced. Logan scanned the horizon, searching the bay for elusive puffins as ships rolled by. Birds called overhead. It wasn't Bar Harbor's fault she wasn't at ease. She put a lot of pressure on the trip to ease her mind and put them back on solid ground, but she brought more stress than luggage. They hadn't talked about house hunting since their fight over salad, though, if you could call it a fight. They hadn't spoken at all for a day after that. Neither had apologized, and the tension strung between them like a tightrope about to snap.

Logan balanced her glass on a flattened rock, planted her palms, and twisted to face him. As soon as he hung up, she'd apologize. There was no doubt her mother was right, and she was being stubborn. Either the perfect house was out there somewhere, and she was just being negative, or it wasn't, and he would get it out of his system.

But Grey faced the wall and the houses beyond, phone pressed to his ear.

"Uh huh." He nodded, kicking at pebbles. "Yeah. I can't today, we're not home. We can…I can tour it on Tuesday."

"God damn it, Grey." She spun back to the water and kicked back her glass, letting the wine dry out her throat. "I should have known."

He landed beside her, soundless. "Should have known what?"

"Don't bullshit me. It's obviously about a house."

"I'm not hiding things from you, I swear. I didn't ask for that call. It just happened." He put his hands in the air.

"I was about to apologize to you." She tossed a rock at the sea. Under her breath, she said, "You can forget it now."

Grey's eyes narrowed. "You knew you were being stubborn and mean about it and came to your senses and decided to apologize but changed your mind because my phone rang? Thanks for the confidence, Lo."

"That's not what I said." But it was what she meant. He hit the nail on the head. Her mind raced, picking at straws, hoping for one that would validate her flush of anger, but there was none. She let her shoulders fall, a pit hollowing in her stomach. "I just feel totally out of control all over again. I finally have a home I like, and I feel like I'm going to be forced to move into something without a floor, and I'll have to use a bucket as a toilet."

Grey grasped her shoulders. "That's not going to happen. I am really good at toilet repair. I even deleted that stupid real estate app for you. I wouldn't make you live like that. If we found the perfect thing together, it would be great. If we didn't, then the right thing would come along eventually. I just want to have something that's all mine. Feeling like a good provider is icing on the cake. I know that your whole life you were set to be the breadwinner, and everything fell apart." He tilted her chin. She looked him in the eye. "It's easier said than done, but you could let me make something easy for a change."

"That's kinda what I was going to say." She offered him a weak smile. "I'm sorry. If you want to look for a house, I will look at them with you. But only if you agree that we don't have to settle for something crappy."

His eyes lit up. "I promise. No crappy."

"Who called?"

"Don't get mad."

Logan shoved her hands in her hoodie pocket and lowered her head. The tide was coming in. Water lapped at her sandals. "Why do you think I'll be angry?"

"Because it was Arvil."

She threw her head back and rolled her eyes. Arvil, for all the redemption he'd raked in over the last few years, was still a selfish man. He was the last person she'd buy a house from. "There is no way he has your best interest at heart."

"It's a real estate transaction, not a mentorship. He heard us talking at the bar, and he has a property he wants to put up for sale. It's not even on the market yet."

"And he wants to cut you a deal, right?"

Grey stepped back. "Something like that."

"What property is it? Or should I ask what run-down shed?"

"It's so good, Lo." He stepped back and grasped his glass from its place in the rocks just as the tide wrapped around its stem. He downed the contents and nodded toward their bed and breakfast.

Stem between her fingers, she carried her empty glass upside down, remnants dripping on her ankles as they trod the path back to the porch. Too bad wine glasses couldn't fill themselves.

"I know you've seen the house," he said. "It's on the street past the library on a corner lot. It's not just any house. It's *the* house."

"What do you mean *the* house?" She held the glass right-side up as they walked up the drive to the bed-and-breakfast.

They climbed the stairs to their room. Logan fought the key into the lock and pushed the door open with her hip.

"I wanted to live there when I was a kid." Grey unearthed more wine from their little fridge and filled their glasses again. "It's such a cool house. It's three stories, and there's this rounded turret castle thing."

Logan accepted her glass back and took a sip. "The one that's all drippy Victorian looking with the peeling paint?"

"That's the one. I used to break into it when I was a kid."

"You broke into someone's house?" Logan barked in a harsh

whisper.

"No, it wasn't occupied at the time. There was an older lady there when I was young. Then she died. Arvil's owned it forever. I didn't know he owned it at the time. Anyway, it has this galley kitchen and a butler's pantry with real wood cabinets. It would need some new appliances, but that's easy to do. The dining room has those built-in corner cabinets with old glass doors. There's an ironing board that slides out of the wall. Upstairs has huge rooms with cool closets, and there are fireplaces everywhere. Logan, you would love it."

"It sounds like a lot."

"It could use a good cleaning, but it wouldn't be that bad. I just want to see it. Arvil heard us talking about a house, and he knows I love the place. It's a small town. He probably knows I used to play around in there. He was just giving me a heads-up and a chance to bid first."

It's a small town. He didn't have to tell her that. Every town had its official way of doing things and at least one unofficial and much easier way. Since Adelle became town manager, the official way of doing things had been getting easier, but the easy way of doing things was still only available to natives. And Logan didn't need to be reminded that no matter how hard she worked, no matter how much she contributed to the town by saving its only bar, she'd never be a native. It was one rule for people like her and another for people like Grey. Being married to him made it easier sometimes. She did get shuffled to the front of the line when she needed someone to come fix their stove. But it wasn't her clout that got the response, and sometimes it was a reminder of everything she'd lost. All the old paths had been paved with gold. Now the gates were locked shut.

Logan sat on the edge of the bed and swirled wine in her glass. "Were you going to tell me?"

"About the house?" He sat beside her. "Of course."

"When?"

"Like, right then? I don't know. I hung up the phone, and you were mad already." He put up a hand. "Don't get mad again. Please. I don't want to fight. I just want to dream about this house for, like, three minutes."

She leaned and nudged him with her shoulder, a slow smile setting in. "Have you ever been to the Thousand Islands?"

"No, where are they?"

"New York. West of the Adirondacks. Anyway, it's a bunch of islands on the St. Lawrence River. Canada on one side, New York on the other. There's a house there on a private island owned by some rich Canadian guy my dad knew. I was probably fifteen years old, wearing some hideous taffeta dress. We climbed on a boat and went out to this island, and it was the most amazing thing I'd ever seen. The sun was setting behind it, and these lights were glittering out over the water. The party was stupid. One of those political fundraisers that usually sent us kids sneaking off with a bottle of whatever, hoping we didn't get caught. Half the people didn't speak English. But that house was my ideal. I swore if that house ever came up for sale, I'd buy it."

"You're saying you understand how bad I want to see this house?"

Logan held her glass between her knees and took his face in her hands. He hadn't shaved, and two days of scruff made him look younger somehow. Rougher. A little more rustic. "Yes. I don't want to deny you this. And I'm sorry. Where I come from, couples talk to each other. Most of the time, anyway."

The corners of his eyes lifted with his smile. "I'm sorry I didn't communicate better. I never meant to sound like I'd go behind your back and buy some house you didn't approve of."

The flutter that rose in her stomach was tempered by the undercurrent. She wouldn't say it out loud, but the weight of everything she'd lost was an anchor that tied her to the shore. As much as she wanted to set sail and drift away with him, the fact that she would never be able to pay her fair share kept her feeling like an outsider.

She gave him a kiss, and he caught her glass before it slipped from her lap.

"Thanks." She held it steady.

"Did your parents talk about real estate? I can't picture your mom being savvy about stuff like that. No offense, but on Skype she comes off a little…"

"Distracted?"

"Good word."

"Well, she was in the loop. Most of the time. Some of that air of hers is a game. She never wanted to give the impression she had any influence or knowledge. It's a lot easier in that world to pretend you only care about the drapes. But there's a big difference between a business deal and our home."

Grey took her glass away and set it on the floor. He slipped a hand behind her back. "Do I get any bonus points if I promise to keep you in the loop about everything?"

Logan giggled as she lay back. "I don't need to know every time you clean up someone's floor, but I expect to be in the loop on the finances, yeah."

"We're not fighting anymore?"

Logan rolled him onto his back. "Nah. I think we're making up."

CHAPTER FOUR

"I can't believe he lied to me. He went to see that house without me, and he promised he wouldn't." Logan thanked Adelle for the tea with a grin that didn't budge the anger lining her face. She pulled a stool up to the counter in Adelle's flower shop and settled in next to Penny among the petals and stems. "I'm glad you're here because I'm about to lose it. I know it's stupid to be this pissed."

Her cheeks burned, and she couldn't look her friends in the eye. The words coming from her own mouth sounded childish. She couldn't put her finger on Grey's exact offense, on what specific button he'd pushed by omitting her from touring the house, but the anger blistered within her, and she had to let it out.

"What did he promise, exactly?" Penny reached past Logan for a cookie, extras from a baby shower that Marissa, the town baker, bartered for some daisies.

"He swore to me that he wouldn't look at houses without me. I woke up, and there was this stupid note taped to the fridge." Logan pulled it from her pocket and smoothed it on the counter. The admission was notable for what it omitted—there was no hint at apology. "What the hell is this? *Went to see house. Laters.* He didn't even wake me. Laters? What is he, twelve?"

Yellow flakes of frosting scattered the table as Adelle broke the handle off a baby rattle cookie. "Maybe that's it? He didn't want to wake you up?"

"We fought about this. Bad fight. We barely spoke. He knows how hard it was for me to even arrive at a place where I would entertain the idea of a house, and he promised me that we would do this together." The plate of cookies danced as she pounded the heel of her hand on the counter. "I don't know if I can deal with all this sneaking around and secrecy and being kept out of things."

Penny put a hand on Logan's arm. "Okay. Don't say anything you might regret. Say it to us not him."

"I don't want to keep him from what he wants. I told him that." Tears pooled, threatening to fall. She rubbed them away with the heels of her hands. "I'm sorry I'm unloading on you guys. It's just…I'm so afraid we're going in different directions."

The reassurances came at once.

"No, that's not it," Adelle said, laying down her cookie.

"Definitely not." Penny rubbed an eyebrow. "There could be a thousand reasons he didn't wake you up. Maybe he only had a few minutes to get there."

"Maybe he tried to wake you," offered Adelle.

"This whole thing has sucked from start to finish." Logan took in a deep breath and let it out, shaky and staggered. "I don't even know why I feel this way. I'm sure it goes back to feeling helpless, like I can't pull my own financial weight because he makes more than me."

She waved her hands. "All of this is a mess. Like I have no control over the situation because I can't afford to have a say."

Penny gave her a sad smile. "Is he really excluding you from the whole process, though? Like you said, this could just be plucking some old string. You went through a lot of trauma."

Logan rubbed at her temples. "I'm over all that, though?"

"Are you, though?" Adelle cleared her throat. "I wouldn't be. Everyone experiences change, but you *really* experienced change."

Dropping her hands to her lap, plucking at the sharp edge of a nail that could use some filing, Logan gave weight to the idea that past trauma could be kicking up dust. It wouldn't be the first time the past showed up, trying to ruin the future. Her voice was small. "Part of it is…I don't know. I'm not equipped for this. I don't mean to be offensive about it. I love my life here, but I had a whole different set of expectations for the way things would be. Sometimes it's hard to live in my own skin. It's all uncharted territory."

Adelle pulled cookie crumbs into a pile and brushed her hands over the trash. "We get that. I think we all wage war with our expectations. I wanted a little house with a yard where I could put a ton of flowers. The reality? I can afford to look at pictures of that on the internet by stealing Penny's Wi-Fi."

Penny held up her glass of tea. "Cheers. You're welcome."

"And thank you!" Adelle clinked their glasses. "When Grey comes home, try not to blow up at him? Tell him the truth. That you're disappointed you didn't get to go and ask if you can see it. Hey, what if he didn't want to waste your time? What if he thought it would be crap? That could be it."

"I doubt that's it. He was excited." Calm was starting to settle in. That, or exhaustion. She clasped her hands together, squeezing them tight to gain some focus.

"Even if it isn't exactly what you want, there may be something about it you love," Penny chimed in. "Do you know what house he went to see?"

The conjured memory of Grey so animated, dreaming about the gingerbread house, chipped away her anger, exposing the soft sadness beneath. How could he not want to share that with her? Had she been cruel in her hesitation and pushed him away? She cleared her throat. "He excluded me. It's his dream house. The only house in Ramsbolt he ever drooled over, and he was so excited. And then he didn't share it with me. It's on a corner lot way down the street behind the library. Some tall thing with a rounded tower. I'm not going to divorce him because he wants to buy a house, but it really hurts. I was upset about it, and then I convinced myself to get on board. He promised to include me, and now he's excluding me. Why?"

Adelle leaned in, eyes wide and sparkling. "No freakin' way." She grabbed a piece of paper and a pencil from a drawer and drew a rough sketch of the intersection and the house at the corner with its rounded turret and its front porch. "This place? I know this place. Everybody does. I would love to get my hands on that garden. It's all overgrown now. But can't you imagine it with hollyhocks and foxgloves and lupine in the summer?"

Penny pulled up the house on her phone, looking up the address on a map. Logan pinched and zoomed, looking at the street view.

Adelle had a hand on her heart. "Hydrangea on either side of the steps and hollyhocks…"

"What's a hollyhock?" Logan squinted, but she couldn't picture anything Adelle saw.

"Tall spikes with flowers. Kind of papery petals like a hibiscus or a Rose of Sharon but smaller. Here." She grabbed a catalog off a stack and thumbed through the pages. "They grow in all kinds of colors."

"That's pretty. I like the ones that look like carnations."

Adelle flipped a few pages ahead. "See this? It's a cottage garden. They can be some work, but you could learn as you go. I'd love to help."

Logan forced a smile and flipped a page. "I like these, too. Foxgloves."

Adelle tapped her shoulder. "We could have a lot of fun with this. Come on. There's a silver lining here. There could be a lot to look forward to."

"Fake it till you feel it, right?" If she bought into their enthusiasm, the worst thing that could happen would be a better mood. "Maybe we'd get bigger closets out of the deal." She closed the catalog. "I like the flowers. They're pretty. I don't know if it's my thing, but you're right. I was just shocked and upset. There's probably a perfectly good reason he didn't wake me."

"Oh, thank God." Penny leaned back and gripped the edge of the counter. "I wasn't sure if this was a *change my mind* talk or a *commiserate with me* thing, and I always get the two mixed up."

Logan patted her knee, allowing herself the lightness. "I appreciate both sentiments."

"If it's reassurance you're looking for, it's pretty obvious, I think." Adelle put the catalog back on the stack. "The love of your life wants to buy you a house. Go with it."

Logan's phone chirped. She swiped the screen. "Picture. From Grey." She held up her phone.

The photo was taken from inside the top turret room. Exposed buttresses of dark wood curved toward the ceiling where they met at a tiffany-style glass lamp, all covered with a layer of Gaussian dust. It was lined with windows and bench seats below, and a fireplace nested in the wall on the right, surrounded by stone with a deep wood mantle. Her stomach went hollow and her throat dry. She set her phone down and spun it.

"Whoa," said Penny. "How is this in Ramsbolt?"

"It's been empty long as I can remember. An older woman lived there years ago." Adelle tilted her head. "I always wanted to see inside that turret. Damn."

"It looks like it could use some cleaning." Logan pinched and zoomed the picture, off and dreaming. Some crisp, light paint and some classic window shades. Pillows and a painting above the fireplace. Few rooms looked as perfect for every season as that one. She could picture having coffee there as winter bloomed to spring and summer faded to fall. "I could sit there forever."

"You're the luckiest girl in the world," Penny said, lost in dreams of her own.

Tipping her head back, eyes closed, Logan said, "I feel like I am. And I feel like the world's biggest jerk. I don't know how we could afford it, though."

"It's okay to have feelings. It's normal." Adelle gave her a playful punch to the shoulder. "And it wouldn't be so bad to have a house, would it?"

"Especially this one." Logan zoomed in on Grey's picture again. The tower's windows were filthy, and the camera's focus didn't allow for a good view, but she was willing to bet that view of Ramsbolt was the best in town. "It wouldn't be bad to have this one. Might be nice, actually."

She closed the pic and sent a reply. *That's amazing!*

A second text came through. A beautiful kitchen with a slate backsplash and dark-gray cabinets. It was much nicer than she expected. Arvil must have been doing some improvements. "Look at this kitchen. There's so much counter space. And all those cabinets. I could put things away. We wouldn't have boxes of cereal on the counter. We wouldn't have to store our bowls on top of our plates."

She sent a reply. *This must be really expensive.*

His reply was fast. "Arvil will negotiate."

Her heart pounded, blood rushing and warming her skin. She let out a long, thin breath, her pulse throbbing in her ears. "Okay."

Adelle's eyes widened. "Okay? What does that mean?"

"It means I'm ready. Trust, right? I have to trust him." She replied. *Give it a shot.*

Penny grabbed her hand, nearly knocking her phone to the ground. "What? What did he say? What did you say? What's happening?"

Logan swallowed hard to unstick her throat. "I told him to do it. Make an offer."

Adelle leapt to her feet and reached across the counter to pull Logan into a hug. Returning it was halfhearted. They weren't wrong. The house had plenty to offer. Space, a larger kitchen, room to spread out. It would need a deep cleaning, but she'd done it before when she cleaned years of Helen's cigarette film from the bar's old office. So many things hadn't turned out as she'd planned. Her future was less travel and comfort than she expected, more vagabond and lackluster, but so far, things had always worked out for the better. She even looked back on her tiny apartment above the post office as the good old days. Ramsbolt wasn't the dreary layover she expected it to be. It had become a sunny town full of wild blueberries. The plumber who teased her all night at work became her husband. The women she met had become her best friends. And the short-term job to hold her over turned into a career she really loved. Maybe, just maybe, this house would become a home. It was worth a shot.

She pulled away from the hug. "Calm down. Don't get too excited. I'm just leaving the door open for some good things to come in. If it works out, it'll be great."

"And if it doesn't," said Penny, "Then it's fate saying the time's not right."

"Exactly." Logan tucked her phone back into her pocket and grabbed a cookie off the plate. "Either way, I'll know I didn't stand between Grey and what he wants."

CHAPTER FIVE

Grey sifted through papers on the kitchen table, stacks of forms and old tax folders making a foundation for cereal bowls and coffee cups. Logan carried hers to the sink and ran water into the bowl, slumping over the small pile of dishes and drowning out the last half of Grey's question.

The tempered excitement she'd felt the day before while talking to Adelle and Penny had cooled overnight. She'd never been thrilled, but as the hours wore on and reality set in, her elevated mood dipped.

Adelle and Penny were right. It was a blessing that Grey was able to buy a house. She couldn't entertain the idea of one on her own. Embarrassed by her outburst the day before and fully aware that her shifting mood wouldn't help things, she'd closed in on herself. It was the only way to keep the floodgates shut, so she didn't make a fool of herself a second time by unloading feelings on Grey that she might not feel in another two weeks. She'd only be ashamed of herself, anyway. Hunching over the sink and zoning out at the stream of water running soaking their dishrag was about all she had the emotional energy for.

"It's like you're not even hearing me." Grey flailed his arms. "Logan. Hello?"

She shut off the water. "What? I'm sorry."

"How many years of tax forms do you have?"

"Seven?" She squirted dish soap into her coffee cup, the brown and green soap swirling in a nose-curling potion. "The ones since I moved here."

"What about the ones before that?"

The dish rag dripped when she lifted it from the sink. "I could get them, I guess. I'd have to call my dad's old tax people. I'd rather not, though."

"Did you work, though? Was there, like, income?"

She let go of the rag, and it splatted into the cup. "Investment income."

"You didn't have a job?"

Turning from the sink to face him, she squeezed the rag into the cup and flicked her soapy fingers at her bowl. "What is this for? Do you need it to fill out a form or something?"

His deep dive into her employment history hit rock bottom at the first question, and he wasn't getting the hint. She didn't have the employment history he was looking for. She didn't have the income background the bank wanted. And if he thought her income from the bar would help him buy the house of his dreams, he had a looser understanding of money than she'd given him credit for.

He tapped a pencil on the table, foot bouncing on the floor beneath his seat. "Taxes are on this application, and I'm just trying to get the papers together. It's cool if you didn't. I just figured you did."

"I was at Yale." She scrubbed harder at the mug than she needed to, then turned on the water. It hit her spoon, and soapy water splashed over the counter onto the floor and all over her shirt. Grabbing the dish towel off the stove, she dried her hands and ran it across the floor with her socked foot. "I didn't have a job."

He blinked back at her. "Not even work study?"

"Billionaires don't qualify for work study. Even at Yale. Can you stop? Please?"

"Okay, well." He pushed one paper to the side and fished another from beneath a green folder. Running his finger down a list of boxes, he squinted at the fine print. "What about tips and reported income from the bar? You have that, don't you? You have your current taxes, right?"

"I just said I did." She grabbed an empty coffee mug and gripped it so hard she thought it might shatter. What did Grey know about filing taxes? He kept his receipts in an old ammo can.

"I don't know what you're suggesting, Grey, but I'm pretty sure I don't like it. You think I don't know how to pay taxes? Are you implying that I didn't file my taxes because my father wasn't great about doing his? Or do you think grifting is genetic?"

Grey's face turned red, and his eyes widened. He turned from her. "That's not what I meant. I know it's a sore subject. That's why we keep our finances separate, and I'm not trying to get in your shit. It's just, the application is asking for these things. Maybe we should sit down and make a list of what we need?"

The only alternative to throwing the mug across the room was putting it back in the sink. "Let's try this a different way. I really don't have enough money to include in this process. It's not worth the effort. Let's just consider my income icing on the cake and use yours for the mortgage. Okay?"

Grey nodded, his cheeks even redder than before. She could tell that he was rummaging through his brain for some way to defuse the tension, but she didn't need it. It was her own short temper causing the upheaval. If she was going to make it through a long night at work, she was going to need an antacid.

She let him off the hook. "I'm sorry. The whole tax thing might always be a little raw for me. I'll try not to take every mention of taxes personally." She kissed the top of his head as she passed, but flipped the green folder over for good measure, so she didn't have to see that stupid bank logo. Ramsbolt Rural Lending didn't give her warm fuzzies. It killed her appetite and made her stomach hurt thinking that the people who worked there, the same people she saw in the market, knew how little she made. Giving them access to her tax history would only rip open the scar tissue that protected her once-wounded pride.

She slipped down the hall, short as it was, and grabbed her work bag and a handful of antacids from the closet. Being a few minutes early for work never hurt. Besides, she'd rather cut lemons than sit in this acid bath.

"You're leaving?" Grey twisted in his seat to face her. "Can we look at this real quick? Two minutes."

She chewed a chalky tablet, paused, bag in one hand, the other on the closet door, fighting the urge to slam it. Lashing out would be childish. She chose honesty instead.

"I don't know how you guys do it. I'm just not emotionally cut out for opening my life like that."

"Like what? It's a mortgage application? The whole world does it."

"The whole world doesn't bank with Ramsbolt Rumors and Lending." She threw her bag over her shoulder and grabbed her water bottle from the top of the fridge. "Besides, you promised that my money wouldn't be involved in this."

"Come on, Lo. It's not like that. They can't blab your business. And when did I promise that? I don't mean…"

"In bed. In Bar Harbor. You promised me. Or don't you remember?"

He turned away, and she went for the door.

"Okay. We won't involve your money." He stacked papers into little piles and flipped the folder open. "But can we sit down tomorrow and figure out what a budget might look like? If the house pans out, we will need to manage things better."

"Fine." Her bag grew about ten pounds heavier. She hoisted it on her shoulder.

"Just a suggestion here." Grey put both hands in the air but still didn't look her in the eye. "We might even want to consider getting a joint bank account or putting all our money together instead of keeping it separate."

Her blood boiled, and she popped another antacid. Despite her stiffening shoulders and straightened back, her bag slipped to the floor. It landed on her foot with a thud, and she sucked in a breath.

How could one pair of work shoes and an empty water bottle weight so much?

She'd never been at someone else's mercy for money. She had an expense account as a kid. Her father taught her how to manage it, keeping track of debits and credits. Not that it was lavish; her mother had insisted her childhood be normal, but she had enough money to buy toys and birthday gifts for friends. She learned to make charitable donations. There was some irony in having been raised to manage money someone else gave her, and now that she was earning her own, someone wanted to take it away.

"Hell no." She bent and grabbed the strap to her bag and heaved it back up on her shoulder again. "I'm not going to be given an allowance or have to report to you every time I need to buy something."

She was supposed to be a decision maker. An independent thinker who made her own way. She was a breadwinner, not a scavenger.

"You don't have to report what you buy to me. This isn't 1854. I'm not trying to run your life or take anything away. I'm just trying to..."

"Great." Her voice was shaking and almost at a yell. "If you're not trying to, then don't."

She gritted her teeth.

Grey stood, anger lining his face. "Look. This isn't complicated stuff. We're supposed to be a team, and you're acting like you're the only one being impacted here. I'm scared to death. A mortgage is a big deal. A house that needs work is a big deal. But I don't want to live on top of each other in this little house anymore. I want something of my own, and you made it sound like you were on board with that. You told me to negotiate with Arvil. Now you're all…" He waved his hands in the air. "Don't inconvenience me."

Logan clutched the strap of her bag and glared back at him. The anger between them could spark a storm. Part of her wanted to part the clouds, but she was also done with caring. Tired, hungry, she'd rather flee.

"I like the way things are," she said. "Separate. Ever since we got married, every little thing I can control has been taken away from me. Where I keep my shoes. How much sleep I get."

He threw his hands up. "Exactly. With a bigger place, I won't be on your nerves all the time."

"Oh, so I won't hear you making coffee in the morning, but I lose my bank account in the trade? You say this isn't 1854, but your wife is used to a little autonomy. I don't know if this is a small-town thing or what, but I'm not ready to be someone else's property."

"Property?" Grey slapped his palms on the table, face red. "You can be in control of all of it, for all I care. Here. Take it."

Her anger swelled and shook the ground she stood on. All the emotions fractured. Anger and sadness broke into little islands. Fear for the future swelled into a volcano and hot tears threatened to fall. Pieces of who she used to be and who she thought she'd become had been chiseled away. For every bit of ground she gained—new friends, a soul mate—she lost a chunk of herself. She turned her head, needing just a moment to pull it all together.

Grey swept a hand across the table and papers fluttered across the floor. The green folder slammed into a cabinet and landed face up in front of the stove. "Take it. Take all of it. Burn it to keep yourself warm."

"Grey. Come on." She bent, picking up the folder, and a single tear spilled over the gate, staining an unsigned form. "That's not what I'm saying. You want the house, don't you? I just don't want to lose control of everything in the process."

"What are you losing here? What?"

"I like the way things are." She rubbed her eyes with the heel of her hand. "I don't know. I'm just tired and frustrated."

He grabbed a paper and crumpled it into a ball. Turning from her, he lobbed it at the sofa where it rested on a brown plaid cushion. "I won't put your finances in the application. I'll build a budget on only my income, and you don't have to be involved at all. If you want to move in with me, that's great. And if you don't, you can stay here. Or get your old apartment back from Warren. Whatever."

"Grey? I don't want to—"

"What?" He spun to face her, eyes red. "You don't want me to control your life? You don't trust anybody. I don't know why I thought I'd be any different."

"I do trust you." She gripped the edge of the counter. "I just have a really bad relationship with change right now."

Grey fell onto the sofa and flattened the paper on the coffee table. "I'm tired too, Lo. I get it. You've been through a lot of shit. I guess I just thought you'd eventually think of me as your equal."

"You are my equal." She wiped her eyes with the back of her hand and wiped hot tears on her jeans. "I don't think I'm better than anybody else."

"I don't mean it like that. You always walk around like you don't belong. Maybe you don't see it, but I do."

She blinked up at the light, at the bugs that collected in the fixture. "I don't belong anywhere."

"Well, you can put down roots here or you can keep everyone around you at arm's length. If you think it's always easy for me to be married to someone who acts like she's about to jump and run, you're wrong."

"Is that what this house is to you? A yoke?"

"You're not cattle, Lo. You're my best friend. My soul mate. I just want us to have a really cool house to live in, but I feel like you won't be happy unless you're the one who pays for it."

"That's not true." Her voice was tiny, her words barely audible, because she knew it was a lie. He was right. "No, you're right."

"What?" He blinked across the room at her.

"You're right. I just need to be in control of something."

"Then we can split the bills. Keep your own bank account. It's not that big of a deal. None of this is."

She nudged the folder with her foot. "Okay. I trust you. I don't mean to seem like I don't. It's hard sometimes. Everything is always hanging on by a thread."

"Then that's something we can fix." Grey got up and brushed his palms on his pants. He stopped at the intersection of carpet and linoleum, her in the kitchen and him in the living room.

She bent to pick up the papers.

"Stop. It's not your mess to clean up," he said. "I'm the one who lost my temper."

"Not really, though. I got mad first."

He faked a smile. It was obvious. "I couldn't tell."

"I don't want to use my income on the application. We can share the bills. But I want to see the house. If I'm going to set down roots, I want to know what it looks like."

Her phone buzzed in her pocket. She took it out and glanced. "It's Mom, and I'm going to be late."

She crossed the divide and gave Grey a kiss. "I'll talk while I walk."

"You want a ride?"

"Nah." She shook her head as her phone buzzed. "I like the walk. Keeps me in shape."

"Wake me when you get in?"

"I will. Love you." She slipped out the door, and his echoed sentiment followed.

Her mother was settled at her table, the same kitchen background as always. Logan said hi as she turned from the driveway and hopped a buckled kink in the sidewalk. The neighborhood was quiet, but for Mrs. Lanford screaming at her husband about lemonade because he was deaf. Logan kept her voice down to steer clear of nosy neighbors.

"What's up, Mom?"

"Just checking in to see how things are going. Did you go on vacation?"

Logan rolled her eyes. "We went to Bar Harbor. I hated it."

"You should have gone to the Cape. How is house hunting?"

The last thing she needed was for her mother to get involved, but she didn't want to lie. She was a terrible liar. "Grey found a place that he loves. I'm going to look at it soon."

Her mother leaned in and squinted. Logan winced at the close-up of her mother's forehead.

"Logan, have you been crying? You're all puffy."

"It's allergies, Mom."

"No, you had a fight. I know that look."

She sighed and picked up the pace. "Fine. We fought about the house. I don't want my money tangled up in it."

Her mother's snort echoed across the line. "Your father hated co-mingling funds, too. Until he didn't, apparently. You do take after him. But you should try not to."

"It's not a financial thing. I just don't want…"

Her mother talked over her, patting herself on the shoulder. "We taught you well. Keep your money to yourself. Always have an escape plan."

"I don't know if that's the best marriage advice." But it was the best advice her mother would give. For her own reasons, she'd always had one foot at the threshold, adopting the paranoia of every upper-echelon housewife she lunched with. One day she worried Lorne was cheating, the next she was certain he'd paid someone to follow her. None of it was true. For a fleeting moment, Logan wondered if that's where her restless spirit came from, but she brushed it aside. Her own traumas were real enough without taking on her mother's delusions.

"The best marriage advice is the kind you hope you'll never need. Take it from me. Take it from France. Always have an escape plan."

CHAPTER SIX

"This was my favorite episode." Helen juiced lemons by hand at the bar, squeezing them into a strainer over a pitcher, one eye fixed on reruns of *The Wonder Years*. "That Winnie. She's a genius, you know. In real life."

The bar was always slow just after opening unless there were sports to watch or the weather was bad. On a crisp late summer day like this one, though, it would be hours before Dan and Bern would stumble in from the farm, making it the perfect day for Logan to do inventory. She estimated the volume in a bottle of Jim Beam, made a note of it on the laptop. "Never saw it. I've heard of her though."

"Reminds me of you. I think it's the hair."

"Thanks, Edith Bunker. It's early for Dan and Bern. Wonder who this is." Logan huffed and shook her head, returning the Jim Beam to its place. The outside door opened, and boots stomped on the mat in the vestibule. She wiped her hands on a rag looped through her belt loop, preparing to greet a customer, and shot Helen a friendly smirk.

She expected a weary traveler or someone who lost their

electricity just before their favorite TV show, but Grey stopped just inside the doorway, dangling his keys with a come-hither look that said he was up to something. She rubbed at the back of her neck and turned away, grabbing the next bottle on the shelf. Renewing their argument in front of Helen was not how she wanted to start the day.

"It's not a good time, Grey." She estimated sixty ounces left in the bottle and typed it into the laptop. The argument replayed in her mind, him throwing the papers, the folder landing at her feet. "Can whatever it is wait until tomorrow?"

"It can't." He jingled the keys.

"I still have the gins and vodkas to count."

Helen looked up from her limes, knife poised. "Go on ahead. Nobody's coming in here anytime soon. I'll finish inventory."

Helen was notorious for overestimating bottle volume and sorting a spreadsheet wasn't her forte. Logan shook her head at the idea of Helen taking over the monthly count. She'd only have to do it over again. "I'm so close to finishing."

"Half hour. Tops. It's important."

Helen patted the bar. "Put the laptop here. I'll do it. Just like you showed me."

"It's only the vodka and gin." She looked between Helen and Grey, who dangled his keys. "It'll be a slow night. I can do it when I get back."

"Half hour. I promise," he said.

Logan saved the spreadsheet, adjusted her ponytail, and ripped the bar rag from her belt loop. "Where are we going?

Grey pushed the door open and held it with his foot. "It's a surprise. Come on."

"Wait a second."

She shot a glance at Helen who waved her away with a smile. Helen had always been like a grandmother to her, making sure she had home-cooked meals and places to be for holidays. Logan and Grey spent every Christmas with Helen. The woman had a history of being kind to a fault, and Logan was protective of both Helen and the tavern. And she hated to impose.

"You're sure?" she asked.

Helen pushed the cutting board away and blinked at the empty room. "With all these customers? I'm sure. I've survived busier nights than this."

"Okay. But we can't be gone long." Logan slipped from behind the counter. She scampered across the gravel lot in Grey's wake. "Is this about the house? I hate leaving Helen to do the inventory."

"She'll do it right. Have faith." Grey held the truck door open for her.

"She shouldn't have to do it at all. It's my job."

The door shut with a hollow metal thud. Grey leaned in the open window. "We won't be gone long."

"Where are we going? The house?"

Grey hopped in, threw the truck in reverse, and steered onto the road back toward town. "You'll see."

"It better not be the bank." She wagged a finger at him, and her voice was light and jesting.

He smiled at the road ahead. "Indulge me. I know you hate surprises, but just let me surprise you this time."

She'd taken a leap of faith when she told him to chase his dream and negotiate for the house, drawn in by the beauty beneath all the dust, but her heart wasn't with her when it came to the financial implications. She wasn't ready to see any forms or watch Grey sign any papers. The closer they got to the turning circle, the less certain she was that she wanted to see the house either. It was clearly his destination. They navigated the circle and passed the street to the library, then turned left onto a residential road, aiming for Grey's dream house. The lump in Logan's throat grew larger with every turn.

The homes were set back with large front yards. Long driveways were cut into islands by crabgrass, dotted with ant hills. Mailboxes leaned on wooden posts. The houses were largely the same, single story with a detached garage, a front door that opened to a small porch, and another on the side. One had a skylight, another a curved drive, but all of them spoke to the simple housing preferred by the town in the post-war years.

They slowed at the edge of a row of pines and pulled past them, turning onto a driveway that swept uphill. The house was unlike any other in Ramsbolt. Set further back than its neighbors, it seemed to tower above the town. Two and a half stories with peaks and a tower, a painted porch shaded the double front door. The wild front yard had overtaken the garden beds with tall grasses reaching into massive dead shrubs that encroached on the porch. Ivy climbed the railings and licked at the windows.

Logan hopped out of the truck and stood at the edge, where the sea of weeds met the driveway. Grey strode past her, toeing at the weeds and finding pavers in the grass.

He reached back for her hand. "Come on. It's safe. I promise."

She took his hand and inched to the porch. The remnants of garden beds with white painted bricks set into the ground at angles were visible on either side of the walk, edging the house. The wood stairs leading up the porch didn't budge under Grey's feet, so Logan took them with confidence.

Whatever colors the porch once wore had faded to pink, peach, and flaking grayed white. Spider webs clung to the roof beams and dangled from light fixtures.

"All of this just needs a good coat of paint and some cleaning." Grey dug a key from his pocket and shoved it in the door. Logan hugged her elbows, willing herself to be smaller, out of the reach of anything with legs.

The windows looked good but old. The panes of glass were all intact. She tapped one.

"None of them are broke. I don't think they're original, but they're in good shape." Grey pushed the door open. "Wouldn't have to replace them for a few years. Buddy of mine from high school does windows."

A warm blast of musty wood air hit her like a freight train. It wrapped around her and pulled her in despite her better judgement.

Inside, the entrance narrowed to a long hall, rooms branching off. Stairs ascended to the right from a carved newel post. Every visible inch was crafted simply: solid and wood and just ornate enough. Egg and dart trim bordered the ceiling, and thick baseboards lined the walls. Were it polished and furnished, the entrance would have put some of her New York friends' digs to shame.

A piece of plywood stretched across two sawhorses at the bottom of the stairs, a paper cup stained with old coffee leaving a visible ring.

"Has Arvil been doing work in here?"

"Not for a long time. As is." Grey grabbed her hand and squeezed. "Let me show you around."

To the left was a room with green wallpaper and dark wood built-in bookshelves. It would make an impressive study for people who needed a study. Windows in the curved corner looked out onto the porch. Dust motes swarmed in streams of light that limned the darkness and streaked the floor. She dragged the toe of her sneaker across dust and shiny, dark wood peeked through.

Grey jumped, testing his weight. "It's a good floor. Solid. Squeaks in places."

Beyond lay a dining room with peeling red paper and built-in corner cabinets. It would take a massive table to fill the room and more friends than she could count to occupy it. But the fireplace gave it a cozy feel, and she could picture the room broken up into smaller spaces.

Grey was steps ahead. "You have to see this," he called back to her, waving her on.

Across the room, the deep doorway to the butler's pantry was lined with cabinets. There was more storage in the pantry than she'd seen in years. A radiator under the window had a box set into it with a cast iron door. She swung it open.

"Arvil said it's for plates. To keep them warm."

The door creaked closed. "What luxury."

"The kitchen's through here."

The wide galley kitchen stretched across the back of the house. The appliances weren't much, old and rusting at the dinged places, but the counters were made of gray and white granite, and there was so much space an army of chefs would fit comfortably. At the far end, a sliding panel separated the kitchen from another room, like her own private bar.

"Arvil said it's an old game room. They'd go there after dinner. It would make a neat room to hang out in. That door over there goes to a bathroom." Grey pointed to a door that disappeared in the wainscoting.

"That's under the stairs, right?" Logan tested her mental map of the house.

"Yeah. It's a nice bathroom. Modern. Needs some cleaning and paint."

"And God knows what else." Logan muttered to herself. She squeezed his hand. "At least we wouldn't have to worry about paying a plumber."

Back into the hall, they nudged the sawhorses aside and climbed the stairs. Bedrooms and bathrooms, showers and clawfoot tubs, Logan couldn't picture herself living in those spaces, though she liked the idea of separate bathrooms.

Grey picked up the pace on the stairs, moving with the confident demeanor of someone who felt at home. She shrunk a little in his wake.

They stepped into the master bedroom and into the sunny corner tower. It was just as cozy as it appeared in Grey's picture, but it didn't warm her to the idea of owning a house. In fact, it made things worse.

The light and airy room in Grey's photo was full of mortgage rates, insurance loopholes, and maintenance costs.

"This is kind of big for us, isn't it?" Logan winced as she looked out over the town. "It would take forever to clean something like this. And it's been sitting for a while. I'm sure it needs a lot more than just aesthetic stuff."

"Arvil's done some work. The boiler will need to be replaced within the next five years or so. The basement needs sealing and parging. It's gross down there."

"I imagine so." Logan turned to the fireplace. She ran her finger along the mantle, and it came away dirty. And that was just the outside. "Don't get mad at me. I'm just playing devil's advocate. These fireplaces will need cleaning and probably repaired. How old is this roof? Cleaning is one thing, but the cost of upkeep will be huge. Oil heat will cost a fortune."

Grey put up a hand to silence her. She hadn't pissed him off. Rather, the look on his face said he'd thought of all that, and he was rather pleased with himself. "The radiators all work. You can filter heat where you need it. Plus..." He jabbed his thumb at his chest. "Plumber."

"Okay. The appliances in the kitchen will need to be replaced eventually. Now, if they don't work. And the garage?"

"It's fine. Plenty of room for my truck and my stuff. It's even got a lofted space, so I have room for pipe and extra tools and stuff."

He grabbed her by the shoulders and spun her to face the windows. He wrapped his arms around her and rested his chin on her shoulder. His breath on her ear was warm.

"This view of Ramsbolt is…"

He sighed, and her heart skipped a beat. Her arms tingled, and she chewed her bottom lip. It would be a great view to wake up to, the best view from any bedroom window she'd ever had, in fact.

Grey squeezed her in a hug. "Come on. Admit it. It's perfect."

"It's not perfect. Nothing's perfect."

"But it's great. And you know it."

"Fine. You're right." She lowered her arms to her sides and slumped. "It looks like a fairy tale."

"And in the winter? Picture this bench with cushions and curtains."

Logan grinned. "Since when do you care about cushions and curtains?"

"Since I stood with my best friend in an old house with really good bones and knew that this is what I want to do with the rest of my life."

She turned to face him. "Are you sure it has good bones, though? Once you start digging around, you never know what you'll find."

Grey tucked in his lower lip and looked down at the floor, a telltale sign that there was more going on than he'd been letting on.

"What?" Logan asked. "What's that look?"

"The inspector said the house was great. The porch needs a few floorboards. Nothing major or structural. The roof has another ten to fifteen."

"Inspection report?" Logan had seen her fair share of them lying around. Her father ordered them all the time to look at properties he was interested in. Any smart buyer would do that. It wasn't something you did unless you were serious. "That was fast. I didn't know you hired an inspector."

"Yeah, it's a guy I run into sometimes. I trust him to tell me the truth. I didn't want to take a credit check hit if the inspection wasn't good enough."

"And this just fell into place over the last twenty-four hours?" She folded her arms and unfolded them, not knowing how to come across half as critical as she sounded. She trusted him, and he was checking all the boxes, but the storm cloud within her was making her short of breath and a little shaky. She had to defuse the ticking bomb before another argument erupted. "I'm just asking. I don't mean it like that."

"No, I know. It happened fast. I feel bad about not telling you. I texted the guy, and he wasn't far away. It only took him about two hours to run through the place. He hasn't sent the full report yet, but he gave me the bullet points."

He grabbed her by the hand. She had no choice but to follow him across the room. "Can you picture waking up here? I'm thinking we make this our room. Bed over here. A new one. King size bed, big enough to swim in. These closets need some airing out, but they'll be great. There are two more rooms down the hall. We can make a little sitting room with a desk and that old metal filing cabinet of yours. And someday I want to retile the bathrooms so they're a little more modern—"

"Slow down. You're going to wear yourself out." Logan grabbed his chin and kissed him. "All of this sounds exciting, but I don't want you to get too wrapped up in this yet. What if you don't get the house? You'll be crushed."

And she would be relieved.

Grey grabbed her hand and pulled her close. He flipped her hand over and placed the key in her palm, folding her fingers around it.

"Too late. It's already ours. Welcome home."

CHAPTER SEVEN

Logan squeezed the key so hard she was sure it would break the skin, slip between the bones of her hand, and fall to the floor. It cut into her palm, gratifying.

"You bought this? Wait a minute." Logan turned away from Grey, too many questions bursting like fireworks for her to grab just one, and each of them too explosive to handle. It hadn't even been twelve hours since he tried to make a budget at the kitchen table. She pressed one hand against her forehead, the other still gripping the key. "There is no damn way you got a loan that fast. That bank moves slower than Congress."

"Not really. I guess it's who you know. I texted the inspector, and he came by. While he was here, I went in and talked to Emily at the bank. I already had enough for the down payment in savings. I drank a cup of coffee and talked to Carol for a bit while Emily did her thing. Oh, I ran into Carol. She's working on a new sign for the hardware store. It's going to look great. Oh, and the bank got new coffee. It's that New England stuff you like. Better than what they used to have with those pouches—"

She grabbed his shoulders. "Grey. The house?"

"Emily gave me a preapproval letter. It just means I'm good for it. She showed me a range of what my interest rates would look like, and I'm happy with it. I stopped at Marissa's for a blueberry muffin. I was going to stop over at the pub, but I got a call from the inspector, so I finished my muffin and took the letter over to Arvil. He stared at it for, like, two minutes. We negotiated a price, and he handed me the keys. It was that fast. We haven't signed the paperwork yet, but it's ours in theory. He said we could get started cleaning it up."

She cleared her throat and planted her feet, folding her arms across the tightness in her chest.

"When I said negotiate, I thought we'd at least get to talk about it. I mean, I have to pack up my stuff. It's going to be a lot of work to clean all this. When am I supposed to be ready to move?"

Fireworks blasted off within her. It wasn't easy to keep them from lighting up her face with anger and fear, but she did her best to soften her expression without coming across as sarcastic. "And this deal with Arvil? It doesn't make sense to me. Arvil is not that nice."

"He said he wanted it off his hands, and he needs the cash right away. I wrote him a check for the down payment, and it's ours. Almost. Emily's going to call me when the papers are ready to sign."

"You gave him money?" Logan's pulse went from slightly elevated to breakneck speed so quickly that she reeled in the lightheaded rush. She let out a slow breath and planted her feet to ground herself, grabbing the railing for support. "I just want to make sure I understand. You gave Arvil money."

"Yeah. He threw out a number. I threw out a lower number because the place needs work."

She started to sweat with an adrenaline rush. "And you gave him cash."

"It was a check but yeah. It's a down payment."

"Okay. Is there an escrow account? Did you write down the number that you agreed to? Have you signed anything?" She couldn't picture Arvil negotiating in anyone's favor but his own. The man was greed incarnate. She could clearly picture him scamming Grey, though, and draining their savings in the process.

Grey threw his fists on his hips, head tilted. "We had a little back and forth, yeah. I thought you didn't want to be involved in this. I used my savings. Yes, Arvil and I wrote down the terms, and we both signed it."

"Can I…How much did you—" She stopped short of asking how much they agreed to. She wanted to see the agreement on paper, to hold it in her hand and read between every line and figure out what inevitable fine print swayed this deal in Arvil's favor, but Grey would only say she was being mistrustful. And the key digging into her hand was a constant reminder not to start the second argument of the day. She trusted him. She had to. And she had to get back to work. "When the deal is done will you show me the paperwork?"

His chin lifted, and his back stiffened. All his angles sharpened. "Can't you just say thank you?"

"Really?" Her arms fell to her sides, and her hands clenched into fists. "I didn't ask for this. I specifically asked not for this. Yeah, I agreed to it, but I thought we were a team."

"We are a team. I'm just asking you to trust me."

She clenched her jaw and bit her tongue. Waiting for the pain to subside, she weighed the battle against the aftermath. He wanted it both ways. He wanted them to be a team and for his money to be her money, but he didn't want her to know what he spent on a house? Her mother's voice rattled around in her head. *Get a prenup. Squirrel money away. Protect your own future.* She slammed that door shut.

"I got a really good deal, Logan. An amazing deal. I just don't want to fight about it."

"I don't want to fight about it either. Never mind. I know you have it under control, and it isn't any of my business."

"It is your business, though. I just want you to trust me."

"I do. I'm just checking. What's next? You get the loan and sign the papers? When is that?"

He tugged his knit cap down over his ears. "Emily said less than thirty days. Could be as little as a week, since I qualified, and the paperwork was easy. I figure we can clean the house up a bit and work on packing up our place. It won't take long. We don't have that much stuff. Couple of trips in the truck."

"Did you give Warren notice yet that we're moving out?"

"I'm going to stop by there later and give him a heads-up. I don't have a date yet. I'm not making things final until the papers are signed, but Warren's a good guy. I just want to let him know."

One wave of uneasiness washed out like a tide, and a new one rushed behind it. They'd need oil to heat the place. More window air conditioning units. And furniture. The place was so empty. It would be cold in the winter. It would need rugs and curtains and more money than Logan had to spend.

"How old is this electrical wiring? Is it safe? What about air conditioners? Is this place insulated? What are the walls made of? Is it plaster and lath? I hate that stuff. You try to hang a picture and it crumbles. What about..."

Logan wiped her forehead with the back of her hand. The air was getting thicker and hotter. She left the room and gripped the banister, peering down the dusty stairs at the path of raw floor below that got bigger and closer the longer she stared. The floors needed sanding and staining. The world spun on its axis.

Swallowing hard to push the dry lump from her throat, she tried telling herself it would all work out. One hurdle at a time. In no time, the place would feel like home. She trusted Grey, and he wouldn't let them sink. But without a safety net, every molehill really was a mountain, and she wasn't sure how many she could climb.

Grey appeared beside her, draping an arm around her, and she fell into him. "The wiring is about twenty years old. It's fine. It's plaster and lath walls, but there's picture rail everywhere. Air conditioners are easy to come by. This place can be converted to HVAC easily. It might take a year to get to it, but we can afford it. This is a good thing, Lo. Scary, but good."

"Like a root canal." She chewed her bottom lip. Her heart raced, chased by an adversary she couldn't describe. "No, you're right. I have no idea how we can afford a house like this, but if you can make it work, this should be a dream come true."

It would be Grey's dream come true. She'd be packing her things and moving them into a home she hadn't chosen. It wasn't the cruel eviction that leaving New York had been. By most people's standards it would be an exciting step up from their tiny cottage. Sure, no one was seizing her assets and locking the doors. The air around her was still thick and hot, but she filled her lungs with it anyway and told herself it was just past her traumas and the memory of losing control of her life that were coming back to haunt her.

She forced a smile. If she faked it long enough, she'd come to see it as a solution and a blessing. For now, it felt nothing like a solution. It felt like a giant mistake.

Grey bumped her hip with his. "You're doing a really good job of pretending to trust me."

The breath from her sigh was cooler than the air. "I'm sorry. It's not you."

"You don't have to say anything. I just want you to know that I won't let you down. I might not think of everything, and I may have to prioritize stuff, but I will get this place cleaned up. You don't have to lift a finger."

"No. It's not all on you. I'll help." She unclenched her palm. The key had left its impression in her hand, and her knuckles ached from squeezing so hard. She held it up by its little ring. "I'm getting pretty good at cleaning out grimy places. Is this my key?"

"All yours." Grey pulled her into a hug. It wasn't the first time her hug was ahead of her heart. As he squeezed her back, she blinked in the dust kicked up in the sunlight that streamed through a stained-glass window. It looked out to a backyard she hadn't seen yet, to a place where they'd make memories with their friends. It dawned on her that Grey had a history there. It might be one he had to sneak in to make, but he loved that house, and she loved him. No matter what they faced, it couldn't be nearly as life changing as the day she stepped off that bus at the edge of town and sweet-talked her way into a job at Helen's Tavern. She would have welcomed an easy fix back then. Now it was time to accept one.

She pulled back from the hug. "I hate to do this, but you have to take me back to work. Helen's doing inventory, and there's no telling what that spreadsheet will look like when I get back."

CHAPTER EIGHT

Logan sat in Grey's idling truck next to the dumpster in the tavern parking lot. Penny's red Jeep was snuggled up against Helen's boat of a car with its broken suspension. At least there'd be friendly faces inside, and with any luck, Helen wouldn't have made a mess of her inventory spreadsheet, but they would have questions. They'd expect her to be excited, and a tiny, soft voice within her was, but a much louder voice was terrified for Grey that it wouldn't pan out, that Arvil would pull the plug, or that the financing wouldn't work in his favor. Even worse, Grey could get the loan he wanted, but they'd be mortgage poor and unable to feed themselves. There was no way to keep the news to herself. Her bones went to Jell-O, and she lacked the strength to reach through the truck window to open the door.

It took a few tries, but it creaked open like the soundtrack to an old Halloween movie.

"I'm going to get that fixed one day." Grey blinked at her. "I'll pop off that door panel in our garage."

"You don't need to. I'm just a little…"

"Flummoxed?" He beamed.

"Good word." She said goodbye, gave him a quick kiss, and reached out the window to open the truck door. She slammed it and leaned in the open window. "I'm sorry I'm not more giddy or whatever. Surprises aren't my thing."

"I know you hate surprises. I wish it hadn't happened so fast. I feel kind of bad about that. Then I got wrapped up in it." Grey chewed on his lower lip and gave his eyebrows a flirtatious waggle. "I'll make it up to you."

Logan laughed and slapped the side view mirror as she inched to the door. "Just no more surprises."

All eyes fell on her when she walked inside. Tying her hair back and slipping behind the bar, she tried to pretend like it was all normal, as if that would make the world stop spinning, but Adelle was onto her and Penny was hot on her heels.

"I heard a little rumor through the grapevine today." Adelle pushed her glass around on the bar, curiosity burning in her eyes.

Logan tied her apron on. "I knew I could count on the grapevine. I learned about the house about eighteen minutes ago. How about you?"

Helen looked between the two, confusion lining her face. Adelle hadn't spilled whatever she knew.

Penny gasped and gripped the edge of the bar. "Is there news? What's happening? Grey bought the house?"

Eyes fixed on the floor while she tightened the bow that held her apron around her waist, she put on the most nonchalant air she could, partly to diminish their expectations and partly to diminish her own.

"He has a handshake agreement with Arvil, yeah. He gave him a deposit."

Penny clasped a hand over her mouth, eyes wide, and Helen nearly knocked Logan over when she nudged her with her elbow.

"That's fantastic news. I'm happy for you two." Penny bounced on her stool and turned to Adelle. "How did you know? Why didn't you say anything?"

Adelle sipped her wine. "Not my news to tell."

"I'd kind of like to know, too. Who told you?" Logan swiped Penny's empty and replaced it with her favorite white wine.

"Marissa told me. She came by the shop. She was at the bank, and Emily told her."

Muttering under her breath about Ramsbolt Rumors and Lending, she didn't realize she'd been overheard until Adelle raised both hands in surrender.

"Marissa was complaining about Emily, not really gossiping about your house. She figured I already knew. Anyway, Emily can't keep her mouth shut."

"Typical small town." Helen was still counting the vodka, and bottles clanged as she put one back.

"What else did Marissa have to say?" Logan slid open the cooler door and let the cold air wash over here. They were running low on Corona. No one wanted it anyway.

"She just said she was happy for you. Especially after everything you've been through."

"Well, it's hardly a nice place." Logan slid bottles around, making a mental tally of what was missing. "There's dust an inch thick on everything. The lawn looks like a wheat farm. Lead paint chipping off everywhere. God only knows how bad the plumbing and roof and…"

She clenched her jaw and gritted her teeth to keep the thought of electrical wires from falling out onto the bar. Helen didn't need to hear it, and she didn't need to entertain it.

"Anyway, wallpaper is falling off the walls in sheets. And you know what that means. The hardest wallpaper to remove is the wallpaper that wants to fall on its own. Of course, I'm the one who'll be doing the cleaning. Grey will be doing the maintenance and heavy lifting to make it livable while the financing happens."

"Wait. You have the keys?" Penny leaned forward, anticipation sizzling off her.

"Yeah. Arvil let him…us get a head start on it, since it's not really in livable condition. Once the paperwork is done, we'll set a move-in date."

Adelle cleared her throat. "That shouldn't take very long. Emily told Marissa that everything was submitted. You should know fast. Week or two."

Logan huffed and tugged on the hem of her shirt. "Marissa knows more than Grey does. That seems fast for a loan, though." And it didn't feel right. Nothing about it felt right.

Helen picked up a bottle and peered through it, quizzical, at Adelle. "Didn't old lady what's-her-name die in that house?"

"God, yeah. Seems like a million years ago. She was a hermit, though. I don't think I ever saw her."

Helen gazed at the ceiling. "She had that blue Crosley station wagon that she'd park in the middle of Main Street when she went to the market. Took her forever to do her shopping, too. Blocked the whole road before church one day. Market stopped opening on Sundays after that."

Adelle snickered. "I thought the house was haunted when I was a kid. We wouldn't go down to the end of that street."

Penny watched their exchange like a tennis line judge. "I thought that was Arvil's house. Nate said Arvil owned it."

Helen shook her head. "Lord, no. He lives on some little house just down the street here. He owned it though."

"He was doing a lot of work in there." Adelle centered her wine glass on its napkin. "I assumed he was holding onto it to make a big profit."

Helen shook with a laugh. "That's his way. It is the biggest house in town."

Logan's stomach clenched, twisting itself around the fear that Grey had been taken for a ride. Everything about this deal stank to high heavens, and Grey was just blind with adoration over a big old house that wasn't even his style and couldn't be further from hers.

Penny tossed her curly red hair over her shoulder, and it bobbed back into place. She threw a hand on her hip. "Sounds like somebody's going to need more furniture. I'd be happy to cut you a deal on some nice things."

Adelle turned to her, and with a sharp inhale and a hand to her throat, launched into a matchmaking scheme, pairing rooms in Grey's new run-down house with pieces of furniture in Penny's store.

Grateful for the chance to slip away, she closed the cooler door and sidestepped Helen. In the backroom, she grabbed an empty case to fill with bottles and carried it to the dark back corner where cool air pooled. Clutching a bottle of merlot to her stomach, she breathed slow and deep, letting the stillness calm her racing thoughts. The last few days had been a whirlwind, tilting every inch of ground she stood on. Bombarded on all sides, nothing was stable except the bar.

Logan jumped when the light flipped on. She put the merlot bottle in the box and grabbed the closest bottle, inspecting the label for nothing at all.

"When I got divorced and moved into that little apartment, I was a mess for weeks. Wasn't just the divorce." Helen rummaged through boxes, tearing open flaps, and peering inside. "Couldn't find my stuff for days. Lost my keys more times than I can remember. There were days I opened the diner late. Couldn't find my shoes. Right now, I can't find that Tino's vodka."

Logan pointed. "Tito's. To your left."

"Ah." She grabbed a bottle and held it high. "Got it. Anyway, I still got boxes in my attic I didn't unpack. Just moved them from place to place. I still think of that old apartment over the post office as the good old days."

Logan carried her box with its bottle of merlot to the tower of beer bottles and ripped open a case of something domestic with a silver label. "I forgot you lived there, too. I think of it that way a lot. I'm just not sure I'm ready to think of the place I live in now as the good old days. They're still good days."

"Seems like every time I had to move it was because there was a disaster. Wasn't ever a good thing for me. Doesn't have to be a bad thing for you either."

"That obvious, huh?"

"From a mile away." Helen hooked the bottle in the crook of her arm and made for the door. "Take whatever boxes you want from here. Packing boxes are hard to find. You want me to leave this light on or you still trying to catch your breath?"

She had to hold her breath every time she flipped that switch. The memory of that fire was never far away.

Logan threw two more bottles of beer in the case. "You can leave it on. I'm right behind you."

CHAPTER NINE

Logan tore open the flaps of an old beer case, the neck of her T-shirt over her nose to stifle the old cigar smell in the yellow sitting room. Their last round trip took less than half an hour, and the clock was ticking if she was going to find the loan paperwork and Grey's copy of the deed before he got back with their last load of stuff. Inside were shoes and Halloween decorations. Keeping careful track of the boxes, she closed the lid and moved on to the next.

Cool air blasted in the open window, and on the horizon, a dark wall swept into Ramsbolt. Rain was moving in, the kind that pushed its way across the land, cold and clammy. It clung to her skin, and she shivered. Grey was probably moving fast, trying to get home before their stuff got wet.

She yanked on the flaps of another box. Pots and pans. No luck.

Part of her wished she'd gone with him and said a proper goodbye to their old house. It was the first place they lived in together. It was the place she put on her wedding dress before Penny drove her to the church in her Jeep. But Grey needed the space for their last bag of clothes in case the threatening skies opened. By the look of it, the choice was wise. She'd said her fair share of goodbyes to things anyway.

The unmistakable rumble of his truck engine preceded him up the drive. She restacked the boxes and rushed out the door, launching off the porch to give him a hand. They dodged the first of the rain drops, hauling the last of their belongings onto the porch and heaving bags of clothes and boxes of shoes through the front door and into the sitting room, then caught their breath as the thunder rolled overhead.

"What's that on your sleeve?" Grey pulled his hat off and tossed it on a box.

Logan twisted the sleeve of her rain-soaked T-shirt. "Ew. I don't know."

Grey pointed to a white splotch on the wall. "You're taking the paint off the place."

"No." She hunched and smelled it, wrinkling her nose. "It's smoke, I think. Nothing some good primer won't take care of. Carol has it. I used it at the tavern."

"Shame. I thought this was a nice yellow." Grey grimaced.

"Yeah, well. Appearances can be deceiving." Logan spun in place. Everything but their sofa and bed had ended up in that yellow room, soaking up cigar smoke filtered through people's lungs. Full as it was with their stuff, she couldn't believe she ever doubted they could fill the house, though. "Good motivation to get all this put away. We could always paint it yellow."

He wrapped an arm around her. "Or we could paint it blue. Or purple."

"No. Not purple. Anything but purple. Maybe something appropriate for the age of the house?"

"See?" He smiled down at her. "You do like this place."

She swatted him. "I never said I didn't. I just said it was terrifying. When was it built, anyway?"

"Nineteen twenties, I think. Forties? I don't remember. It might be in the deed. I have a copy around here somewhere." He spun on the spot and wiped his forehead with the heel of his hand. "No idea where it is. Who cares, anyway. Just look at this place."

Logan's heart skipped a beat. She cared. She wanted to read it. Asking him for it would only start a fight about why she didn't trust him and why she had to pick everything apart, though. She'd been walking on eggshells when it came to matters of trust, and the last thing she needed was to get cut by those shards. She'd believed him when he said that Arvil called out of the blue, and she'd believed him when he said the sale of the house just fell into place before she could see it. Now they were back with a vengeance, begging to be yelled about.

She tried to stuff them down, along with the missing paperwork, into that pit in her stomach where they could roil with everything else in her life she refused to let bother her, but it didn't sit as well as her father's money laundering and her mother's incessant fretting about paintings and social events. This was her money and her home, too. And it was her husband.

She started to ask about the paperwork, how could he lose track of it, with trying not to sound too eager about it, but Grey jumped and turned, scanning the room.

"This is cool. Logan, you're going to make this place look great. I don't think it's terrifying. Exciting, but not scary."

Terrifying wasn't even the tip of the iceberg. Boxes were stacked five and six high. Piles of bags with their linens and clothes were strewn everywhere. CDs and movies, dishes and glasses, dented tables, and their little collection of Christmas ornaments were all tangled together in a rushed packing job that made Logan's skin crawl. Unpacking it all was one thing. Replacing what they broke in the move, paying the mortgage, and keeping up with the bills would be something else. She still hadn't asked what all of this cost, and this new effort at trust was making her sick to her stomach.

Grey's phone rang, and she scratched at her shoulder. His hums and uh-huhs amplified into questions about water. Another plumbing problem in town. He shoved his phone back in his pocket and gave her a kiss.

"I have to run. The Outdoor Store has a leak in the employee bathroom."

She smiled. "Can't they just climb in a kayak and deal with it?"

"I wish. Sounds like a simple fix, though."

"Dinner first?" Peanut butter and jelly were all they had. "I can put a sandwich together for the road."

"I can wait. I'll be back in an hour." He smooched the top of her head and checked his pocket for his keys. "Be right back."

Her smile faded as he launched down the stairs. His truck rattled to a start and backed down the drive. Logan was left with a room full of boxes and piles of bags. And somehow Grey thought she was going to be a good interior decorator? This gingerbread Victorian whatever it was certainly wasn't her style.

The pain in her stomach twisted and churned. She'd always been independent and outspoken, never afraid to speak her mind, and this sudden effort to trust Grey was making her afraid to ask questions and rock the boat. It was also leaving her in the dark and turning her into a sneaky snoop, digging through boxes behind Grey's back. That was hardly the definition of trust. Also, how could he lose track of the paperwork for the house he just bought? Why wasn't it with the rest of the filing cabinet?

"All this stuff has to be sorted anyway," she said to convince herself. "If I just open a few boxes to look for some paperwork, and happen to find the bath towels, the ends justify the means, right?"

She ripped open box after box, churned through bags of clothes, and found the contents of their filing cabinet in milk crates at the bottom of a stack. Marking her place with an upturned folder, her ear poised for sounds of Grey's truck, she thumbed through every page they had, old taxes and receipts. Terrified he forgot something and would step through the door at any moment, she raced through the pages, but she reached the end before twenty minutes had passed and had to admit her defeat. Not only had she not found the house papers in anything they'd packed, but she'd also made herself feel like a fool for being so crazy. Standing and brushing paper dust from her hands, she couldn't kick the feeling, though, that if he weren't hiding the papers, she would have found them. And if she didn't clean up this mess, he would find out she'd been looking for them. Then he'd accuse her of not trusting him, and the whole thing would blow up again.

Besides, it had to be somewhere. The quicker she got their stuff sorted and unpacked, the faster she would stumble on it.

She picked a box and ripped open the flaps. "Dishes, utensils, and washcloths."

Shoving the linens into a bag of clothes to take upstairs later, she carried the rest across the hall and into the library. A wooden pop came from upstairs and a metallic creak from the dining room as the house settled. Raindrops pounded the porch outside. They were sounds she'd grow to know, but for now they were a foreign language, the soundtrack to someone else's life. Or no one's life, for as long as the house had been empty. Logan was just a transient, a traveler, a visitor to those walls. She'd settled into her fair share of guest rooms and suites, and she'd always felt at home. The age of the house papered and painted in someone else's taste, with Grey's name on the mortgage…all of it avalanched, burying her under its weight.

The box growing heavier in her hands, she wove through the dining room and pantry, leaving the dishes on the kitchen counter next to the groceries she picked up that morning. Her belly grumbled at the sight of them, and she threw together a peanut butter and jelly sandwich. They'd be eating a lot of that in the future until they got on their feet.

One by one, she pulled dishes from the box. At the bottom was her plate, the one she never let Grey touch. White porcelain with a yellow border and little pink flowers, its gold band worn and faded. It was the first thing she bought with her very own money when she moved to Ramsbolt. She got it from Penny's antique store before they were friends. Penny's Loft was a cluttered mess back then, just like

Logan had been. Furniture was stacked higher than her emotions, and everything had been covered in dust. A lot had changed since that day.

She ran her finger over the chipped edge of the plate. She'd hated that chip. It had been a constant reminder that everything good in her life was gone, that everything in this new life came at a high cost. She placed it on a high shelf by itself, away from the other plates.

Grabbing the jelly, she flung open the fridge. Aging and dented but cold inside, it wasn't pretty, but it wasn't broken. She left the jelly on the top shelf where it sat without company. No butter or eggs or orange juice. Grey loved orange juice. It was just like her first days in Ramsbolt all over again, starting with nothing.

One unpacked box would have to do. They couldn't starve for the sake of a tidy house. She texted Grey with her plan, snagged her purse from the newel post at the bottom of the stairs, and checked the sky. Nodding at the departing clouds, she aimed for the market, taking a shortcut between houses. She slipped past the library, making a mental shopping list to get them through the next few days. Toilet paper, a light bulb for the upstairs bathroom, some paper towels. Pasta and cereal. Apples. Lunch meat.

Her mental list mostly complete, she shuffled down the alley between buildings and stomped her muddy sneakers clean on the sidewalk. Slipping into the market without making eye contact, mildly ashamed of the muddy footprints in her wake, she regretted more than her shortcut through yards.. All the progress she'd made earning a living and managing her income, and she was back to buying generic toilet paper. But there wasn't room for resentment. It would only slow her down. Things would be tight for a while, just until the bills leveled out, and their savings stabilized. The house was a good thing, she told herself. If she had to live off leftovers and peanut butter for a few weeks, it wouldn't be the end of the world. It was a small trade for having a nice home and a good roof over their heads. But it still felt like backsliding. And her stomach was still in knots over her lack of financial control. She just had to hide it.

She dropped her items on the belt and paid in cash. Plastic bags draped over her arms, she rushed out the door and ran straight into Adelle.

"Whoa!" Adelle greeted her with a wide grin, her hands on Logan's shoulders. "Housewarming supplies, I hope. How is the house?"

Logan stepped away from the door and rested her bags on a bench. "A mess, to be honest." She wiped a hand across her forehead, but the muggy air offered her no relief. "We got the last truckload of stuff in while it was raining. We packed in a hurry to save on rent and nothing is labeled or organized. We had some nonperishables but nothing cold to drink. Figured I'd risk the weather to hit the market."

"It must be fun to spread out in a new house. I'm jealous of the blank slate. I sometimes wish I could just start over. Throw everything out, paint the place."

Logan's eyes widened. "You're welcome to come paint mine. I have one room covered in cigar film, a lot of peeling wallpaper, and a bathroom covered in pink tile."

Adelle's face lit up with excitement. "We could have a painting day. We could all come over and help. It would be fun."

"That would be fun." She didn't want to hurt Adelle's feelings, but the idea of making apologies for the state of the house didn't fill her with the kind of warm fuzzies that usually went along with throwing a party. "Once we figure out what we're doing. I'll let you know."

"The look on your face doesn't say fun. Stressful move?"

Logan probed a tooth with her tongue. Honesty wasn't always the best policy. Spilling her guts would only lead to saying things she might regret and, hopefully, wouldn't mean come tomorrow. She might not be able to shake the feeling that something was wrong about this house, but that didn't mean she needed to say it out loud.

She brushed it off with a shrug. "Just overwhelmed, that's all. There's so much to do."

Adelle's eyes widened, and she grabbed Logan's arm, excitement spreading across her face. Logan braced herself for the incoming suggestion. Whatever it would be, Logan knew it wouldn't be a stress reliever.

"Hey, a housewarming party could take the edge off. Tell us what you need! Penny was just saying she could use a good party. We haven't had a celebration around here since the two of you got married."

"I don't know. The place isn't perfect, and…"

"It doesn't have to be. That's the point."

Logan had been to plenty of bad apartment warmings in her time as friends moved into new digs. None of them had been perfect. A party might be just the thing to lift her spirits, anyway. "You're right. It's just friends. We deserve a little fun. Let's do it."

"Yeah?" Adelle grabbed her hand. "Set a date! Let us know what food to bring. I can't wait to see the place. I've wanted to go inside forever. Is it cool in there?"

"It won't be in the summer." She simpered at her own bad joke. "It probably just feels that way because it's been closed up for so long. It has some neat rooms, though. There's a butler's pantry with tons of cabinets and a really cool old plate warmer that's part of the radiator."

"That sounds awesome. I've always admired the garden beds. You can tell they used to be grand. I'd be happy to help you clear it all out when you're ready. Just don't go pulling at that ivy without gloves. It can irritate your skin."

The idea of tackling the ivy was laughable. "When you see the inside, you'll know how low on my priority list that ivy falls. I did see a spider crawl out of there the size of my hand, though. I definitely won't touch it until at least winter."

"That's a good time to pull it out, actually." Adelle glanced down at Logan's bags. "I should let you go. If you'd like company, just give me a ring. And pick a date for that housewarming."

Logan strung the bags on her arm. "I will. Looking forward to it."

She spent the walk back to the house trying to convince herself that she would look forward to it eventually. They could string some lights up in the library, put on some music. She would dance, even if her feet didn't want to.

Pausing at the end of the driveway, she checked the mail. Nothing but junk. An ad from a used car place in Colby. A bunch of coupons in their address forwarding kit from the post office. She tucked them in with her groceries.

Adelle was right. Pulling out all that ivy would be a chore, but without it creeping up the railings, the porch would look inviting. She wasn't much of a plant person, but some kind of floofy shrub with flowers would be pretty. It did have the potential for some curb appeal.

Bags growing heavy in her arms, she marched up the drive. Movement in the overgrown grasses caught her attention, and she jumped, heart pounding.

A cat pounced from beneath the porch and took off after its prey. She thanked him for his public service with colorful choice words, and she climbed the stairs.

A little paint and this place will look okay, she thought. *Plants can't be that expensive. Adelle said she would help.*

And the place was hers. It was a home. No shared walls, and no nosy neighbors. It was better than the hollow life she thought she'd live running some charitable foundation for her father, dragging business contacts to sterile clubs and restaurants. Looking up at the double front doors with their warbled glass, it was hard not to see the years in the layers of peeling paint. It might be old, and even after a deep cleaning, it might still be dusty in some spots, but it was theirs. It was their blank slate, and it came with a lot of cozy, old charm. And it deserved a celebration, even if she didn't feel like it.

She avoided looking in the sitting room with the piles of boxes yet to be sorted and made her way to the kitchen. While she unloaded the groceries, she filled a mug with water to make some tea.

A little caffeine, and I'll be ready to jump right in.

The microwave whirred as her mug did a pirouette. She opened a cabinet to stack boxes of pasta.

This kitchen's so dark. Why did he paint the inside of the cabinets, too? You can't see anything.

She flipped a light switch, and the microwave crashed to a halt. Sparks spit from the outlet, and the lights went out.

CHAPTER TEN

Logan paced the dining room, static under her skin and a wad of horror hot and tightly wound in her chest. She never talked about it, but the night the tavern caught on fire had replayed in her mind every day since it happened. Sometimes it was the sound of Grey's voice beneath the screaming alarm, telling her to run. Sometimes she was frozen in the hotel parking lot across the street, knowing the night was cold, though she couldn't feel it on her skin because the fire burned so fast and so hot that it scorched the air. Every time she'd flipped that light switch in the stockroom, something sparked. She'd taken for granted that it was just old wiring, but the fire rewired her. She couldn't see the threads snaking through the walls, but the fact that it could kill her was never far from her mind. At least once a day since that fire she'd told herself she was afraid of nothing and being silly.

Shaking the electricity from her hands, she flexed her fists to put some feeling back in her fingers, and she found her phone sitting on a windowsill.

She could text Grey, but he would only tell her not to worry. So much was on his plate already. He hadn't said as much, but she knew he kept his concerns to himself and her out of the loop because she hadn't wanted to move. There was no reason why she couldn't handle this herself. But it would be Grey's money paying for it. He should decide.

Her feet moved beneath her without her consent. Facing the kitchen, phone in her hand, she could hear Grey's voice in her ear. *You're just on edge, that's all. The wiring is fine. Are you sure you didn't imagine it?*

She opened their text messages. *I'm calling Martin. Microwave tripped when I turned on the light. Sparks.*

He didn't say no or offer to take it on as she thought he would. And he didn't criticize her for her fears. *Tell Martin to call me w/ the bill. Scary.*

Leaning her back against the wall, her eyes closed tight, she waited for the thoughts to settle like the plastic beads in a snow globe. He hadn't teased her, but he hadn't put her at ease either. He hadn't stopped her from texting Martin, but he also hadn't said that it would all be okay. She cracked her knuckles and rolled the tension from her shoulders. Why did she need validation?

"You're an adult, Logan Cole. Call the damn electrician."

She found Martin in her phone and relayed the story and the interrupted microwave and the sparks from the switch.

Luckily, he wasn't far. He breezed through the house and into the kitchen with his bag of tools, scattered them across the counter. He squinted in the dark at the fabric-coated wires that he dug from the wall and ambled between the fuse box and the wall, running new wires, and turning things off and on.

While he worked, she silenced the part of her that yearned to apologize for wasting his time over something so frivolous.

She leaned in the doorway. "Thanks for coming so soon."

He muttered, peering into the wall with a flashlight. "Don't mention it. I owed Grey a favor, anyway."

The door slammed, and Grey's voice echoed through the house. "Martin?"

"We're in the kitchen," Logan called back.

Covered in dried sludge and silver flecks of solder, Grey paused in the dining room. "I'm a disgusting mess. Gonna take a shower. Everything good?"

"You gotta make a map of your wiring here, buddy." Martin tapped a screwdriver against his palm. "Mark it down on your electrical panel over there. Have you plugged something into every outlet?"

"Nope. I'll do that in a second." Grey waved socks and took off up the stairs. "Soon as I'm out of the shower."

"Must have been a tough job." Martin pulled the plate off the last kitchen outlet and loosened the screws that held it in place. He wiggled it and inspected the wiring.

"Seems like most of them are." Logan cringed at the old wiring.

The water turned on and cut off with Grey's shower, and his footsteps moved through the upstairs. Logan hovered and avoided eye contact, her senses alert for the smell of singeing wires, while Martin put the outlets back together and gathered tools, his hands black with the sticky remnants of old electrical tape. He formed the black strips into a gummy snowball and lobbed it at the trash can. It skittered across the kitchen floor when he missed, coming to a stop at Logan's foot.

"I'll get that," he said.

She toed it toward the can. "Don't worry about it. Are you sure the wiring is okay?"

He grabbed his tool bag by the handles and leaned, listing against its weight. "You had too many things on that circuit. Lights and a stove and a fridge. Then the microwave. I ran new lines to separate the big things. You should have plenty of juice now."

"Should have?" She pasted on a smile and jumped, overreacting to Grey moving around upstairs. She swallowed hard against the dryness in her mouth. "Is there a way to be sure?"

"Pay someone else for a second opinion."

She'd offended him. She could tell by the way his forehead lined and the way he clutched his bag. He was doing Grey a favor, and she wasn't making it easy.

"I didn't mean it like that. I'm sorry. After the tavern fire, I get jumpy about electricity."

Martin pushed past her, through the doorway, patting her arm on the way by. "I would be worried, too. You're good now. Just don't overload the circuits."

She trailed him into the dining room. "How do you know if you're overloading a circuit?"

"You blow a fuse. Then you go to the box and reset it. And then you don't do it again. Grey!" Martin stepped into the hall. He craned his neck, peering up the stairs. "Grey?"

"Sorry I'm asking so many questions." She had a million boxes to unpack anyway. "Thanks for coming on such short notice. New homeowners, right? I don't mean to be a pain."

Martin scratched under the brim of his hat, his face softening. "It won't always be like this. Home ownership ain't always about maintenance."

She snapped her mouth shut, keeping her disagreement to herself. Her father's whole life had been stacks of bills and complex accounting and property management nightmares. Every time he bought a building, he spent months ironing out the problems just in time for more to crop up. And for as long as the house had been unoccupied, Martin's attempt to make her feel better fell flat. There was plenty of room for problems to lurk beneath the surface.

Grey bounded down the stairs, a lamp in his hand. He shook it, and the shade wobbled. "I tested every outlet."

Martin nodded. "Don't forget to double check the fuse box and label where everything goes. I got a pair of walkie-talkies if you want to borrow them. Makes the job easier."

"I might take you up on that." Grey stuck out his free hand. "Appreciate it. I'll swing by tomorrow to check out that soil pipe."

"There's a hell of a hole in the front yard. It's got to be that pipe." Martin scratched at his hairline. "No idea when it happened. Had a good laugh when the wife freaked out. She thought a sinkhole opened up and was going to eat her old Ford."

"Sinkholes? Like they have in Florida, where the ground just opens up and swallows a whole house?" Logan put her hands behind her back and leaned, pressing them against the dry, cracked wallpaper. "Does Maine have those?"

Grey rubbed at his earlobe. "I don't think so. But this is probably just a cracked pipe."

"What causes it?"

He tapped the lamp against his leg and shrugged. "Lots of things. Tree roots. Age. Inactivity. If no one flushes the toilet or sends water through it for a long time, sudden water pressure can find a weak spot, and it can fail and leak. Then it washes the soil away, and you get a hole in the yard. I'll run a camera down there. Won't be hard to fix if that's what you got."

"Could we have that problem?" Logan's voice was shakier than she'd like. She flicked the lampshade in a playful attempt at levity.

"Nah. Well, it's possible, I guess. We'll find out, won't we?"

Martin lifted his bag and his tools rattled. "I appreciate it. Yard smells like a farm. That's probably it."

"I'll cut you a deal. Might need help rerouting some wires in this old box one day."

Martin tugged open the door. "I'll leave you two to get on with it. Call me if you need anything. See you in the morning."

"Thanks, Martin." Once the door had closed behind him, Logan slipped into the sitting room. There were still boxes to unpack, and she wanted to find her nightstand before bed.

"You want to let me in on what's bothering you?" Grey folded his arms.

Logan wiped hair from her forehead. She wasn't hiding her inner turmoil as well as she thought. She wasn't even sure what the problem was herself. It was as if a hive of uncertain bees, each with their own angsty agenda, were engaged in a frantic attack on her psyche.

She stood and faced him. "Honestly? I don't. I don't want to get into it."

"I kind of wish you would. I don't want to spend our first few days here walking on eggshells. I want to have fun and make memories, not worry that you're mad at me and try to guess what's bugging you. Are you scared the house is going to fall down?"

"It's not the house." Logan pushed aside a box labeled Vodka, real contents unknown, and sat on the coffee table. "And, yes, I trust you. I wouldn't trust anyone else with a cracked whatever pipe."

"Good to know it's not me. Is it the house? You don't like it?"

She opened the box to find stuff of Grey's. Old yearbooks and memories tangled like necklaces in a jewelry box of adolescence.

"No, I like it. I do. It's going to be beautiful with the ivy ripped out and new plants. I forgot to tell you. I ran into Adelle at the market, and she convinced me to have a housewarming party. Something small with friends."

"That's a great idea. Jaleesa was asking if we were having anything."

Logan nodded, eyes fixed on the floor. "And that just piles on another thing we have to do. It's everything. I haven't seen the inspection report. I have no idea what needs fixed. I've been on my hands and knees cleaning this place for days with you, and I'm worried we can't afford it. We don't have joint finances. I have no idea how much money it's going to take to buy rugs and furniture and fill the oil tank. But I sure as hell know that I can't pull my weight and pay half of what this house is going to cost."

Grey wiped at the yellow soot on his shirt and shrugged. "You don't have to pay half of the bills. That's not how marriage works. We're not roommates."

"I know. I just feel like this is something that's happening *to* me, not something I'm a part of. Every time I clean something or unpack a box, I feel like I'm doing you a favor. It doesn't feel like it's mine."

And every time she unpacked a box and didn't find the house paperwork, she felt a little less secure.

She stood, brushing her palms dry on her jeans, and went to the window that looked out to the side yard. The grass was high and licked at the pines that edged the yard. Beyond were neighbors she couldn't see.

"This whole thing is yours," he said. "You're the one who knows what it should look like. You're the one who makes this feel like a home."

"Unpacking boxes is all I can do. I can't pay an electrician or get a new appliance if one breaks. And it's not that I'm poor. I'm not." Another bee broke from the swarm and left its sting. The sudden realization that she didn't have the same resources Grey had come rising to the surface. "You know, the way the whole electricity thing went down. That stings, too. I couldn't get Martin here that fast on my own town cred. I'll always be an outsider here."

Grey rubbed an eyebrow. Logan saw the confusion in his reflection. "You're not an outsider. You're the town bartender. Everybody knows you. Nobody here hates you, that's for sure."

"But I'm an outsider. I always will be." She turned from the window and pointed at an outlet. "This. If it weren't for you, I couldn't have gotten Martin here so fast. Or maybe at all. He just came running because he owed you a favor. You've got this whole barter economy here that's based on who you know and how long you've been here. I'm not saying it's wrong. Hell, it was like that in New York, too. It's just the way it is. People take care of their own. I'm not one of their own."

He shrugged, opened his mouth, and closed it again.

"The way Arvil sold you this house? It's just weird. If I wanted to buy this house from Arvil, there's no way he would have cut me the deal he gave you."

Grey's mouth twisted in a confused and defensive simper. "I do a lot of work for him. The house was kind of dirty, and it needs some work. If he tried to sell this thing as is to someone from out of town, you know how much harder the sale would be?"

"Of course, I do. It would still be sitting here empty because he'd never drop the price. But he did for you. There's something about it I just don't get. I can't figure out what it is."

"Why try? You just beat yourself up feeling bad about something you can't control."

Grey had a point. Maybe she wasn't giving Ramsbolt enough credit. They stood behind her when the tavern burned down. They supported her when the press came calling.

She unearthed her nightstand and sat on it. "My emotions have been all over the place lately. It's not like Martin would ignore me if I texted him. It's probably nothing. Besides, we're on the lucky end. This wasn't a financial setback. We have connections. We can be creative. It's Ramsbolt. Is what it is."

"Ramsbolt might be a lot of things. Old, grumpy sometimes. Set in its ways. But the place doesn't let anyone fail." Grey grabbed the box of his childhood memories. "I think we can get this stuff sorted before bed. If you make piles, I'll carry boxes. What do you say?"

"You got it. Can't wait to get this place straightened up."

But the nagging feeling that something was wrong had settled into her bones. She couldn't put her finger on it. But like anything else she couldn't quite place, if she ignored it, it would either go away or make itself known. That was how it worked when she lost her keys, anyway.

She opened a box and slammed the flaps shut.

"Grey! I found your winter work boots. They smell like sewage."

CHAPTER ELEVEN

Logan's internal clock was set to constant ringer. She woke for the hundredth time to find that day had broken, and Grey was propped up next to her, cup of coffee in his hands. Her arms ached from lifting boxes and bags, and her legs burned from hauling furniture up the stairs. Sitting up was a chore.

"Good morning." Grey put down his phone. He gestured to her side of the bed. "There's coffee on your nightstand."

It was an awkward reach, a few inches too low to grab from the bed without leaning precariously. She grabbed Grey's hand for leverage and leaned down to pick it up. He held it while she shuffled her pillows and propped herself against the headboard.

"How'd you sleep," he asked.

"I don't think I like the new bed. I slept in five-minute blocks. My brain was in overdrive. Does it smell like wet wood in here?"

"No. Smells like old wallpaper to me." He grasped the comforter for balance and put his cup down. "We must have slept in shifts. Every little noise woke me up."

"It wasn't the noises for me as much as the disorganization. I laid here looking at that peeling yellow wallpaper. Reminds me of that short story where the woman is confined to that room." Logan squinted. "I can't remember the author's name. Did you ever read that? Charlotte...somebody."

"Vaguely." Grey grunted, scrolling through his phone. "Wasn't there a bed bolted to the floor?"

"Yeah."

"Here." He tossed his phone on her lap and leaned for his coffee. "What do you think about these?"

"Nightstands?" She'd been up all night, worried about asbestos, foundation issues, toxic gasses, and energy costs. Grey was looking at nightstands.

"They're taller than the ones we have now. I thought it might be nice to roll over and not be looking at a lampshade."

Of course, the thing that kept him up at night was replacing all her stuff. She tossed the phone back on his lap. "Why not get a shorter bed. Or a taller lamp?"

He tilted his head and gazed at a distant spot; eyes fixed on nothing. "A floor lamp on a nightstand doesn't seem like an actual solution."

"I like the ones we have." She fumbled out of bed and stretched. Grey would have to jump and run when the phone rang like he always did. She couldn't blame him for enjoying the morning in bed, but she'd taken the day off to unpack and make the place feel lived in, and the sooner she got started, the more she'd get done. Lying in bed all day wasn't going to get the job done. And the sooner she got moving, the sooner her aching muscles would loosen up. At least everything was sorted and in the right rooms.

"I'd rather change the wallpaper than the nightstands. What do you think?" she asked.

Grey's attention was back on his phone. "I think whoever picked it died a long time ago."

Logan shoved her feet in her slippers. She couldn't help but snort. "Seems accurate. I'd rather prioritize the house over the furniture, though. If this is going to be our bedroom, I want to get rid of this paper and make it look like a place worth sleeping in. It looks like a scene from a horror movie." She hugged her elbows.

"It's not *that* bad, but I agree. It's a good time to replace some of our old stuff, too."

"Then I guess you don't agree." She grabbed her housecoat off a stack of boxes and threw it on, tying it tight around her waist.

Grey turned his palms to the ceiling and shrugged. "We can do both at the same time."

She stiffened against the sinking feeling she was losing herself in the shuffle and churning of stuff. "No. Before we get rid of the stuff that's already ours, I'd rather get rid of the stuff that makes this house feel like it belongs to someone else." Her voice hit a pleasing pitch. She hoped it conveyed her disinterest in getting rid of her stuff, settling the matter once and for all. "Who even lived here, anyway?"

"No idea. It wasn't Arvil, though. He said he never lived in the place. He bought it after the old resident died."

"Helen mentioned that. They said she was really weird."

Grey climbed out of bed and smoothed the comforter. "Let's

make a list and tackle it. It won't feel so overwhelming."

"Bedroom paint. Top of the list." She grabbed her cold coffee and made for the door, putting an end to the notion of replacing things that were perfectly good.

"I don't want to wait for winter to pull out that ivy. I'm sick of finding spiders on the porch. I'm putting on some old clothes and digging that stuff out this week. And I really want to do something about these." He pointed to his coffee cup that sat at knee height. "They're just…"

"What?" She spun to face him. She gave him a playful finger wag. "I don't want to fight this early in the morning, but you will have to claw those nightstands from my dead hands."

He put his hands up in surrender. "I get it. It's not a hill I want to die on. I was just thinking we could replace some of our old things with nicer stuff now that we're in our own place."

Logan thundered down the stairs, careful not to spill coffee on the floor. She paused at the bottom. "Can we just work on making it our own place first."

Grey veered around her and aimed for the kitchen. "I'll start pulling down wallpaper tonight."

She followed him down the stairs and into the kitchen, dumping her cold coffee into the sink. She refilled her cup from the pot and offered Grey another round, which he declined. "I think I want to paint it one of those trendy dusty shades of blue."

"That will look good with all that dark wood trim. I can pick up paint chips if you want. I have to swing by the hardware store anyway."

Hot coffee burned her tongue and hit the spot. "Can you pick up some painting supplies, too?"

Grey opened and closed cabinet doors. He pulled down a bowl and a box of cereal. "Yup. Then they'll be here when we're ready to paint. Milk?"

"No, thanks. Today calls for undiluted caffeine, I think. Straight into the veins. Lots to do around here."

He poured milk in his bowl, returned the jug to the fridge, and leaned back against the counter, chewing his way through Cap'n Crunch. "Want to go over to Penny's this week? She might have some furniture to fill up this place. I bet she has some nightstands."

Logan shot him a look that would silence an army. He returned it with a grin.

"I'm kidding," he said. "I don't know what it is about those nightstands, but if you want to fall out of bed looking for your morning coffee, more power to you."

"My nightstands *came* from Penny's Loft." She had no witty retort. Arguing with him would only prove him right. Of course, they were impractical. They were all she could afford at the time. The implication that they were insufficient was just shy of an attack. They weren't French antiques, but they'd looked good in her old apartment, and she'd carried them, one at a time, by herself, through the town. She invested in those nightstands, and Grey wasn't taking them away from her that easily.

She felt her face burning red as she gripped the edge of the counter.

Grey dropped his bowl in the sink. "I got to hit the shower and get to Carol's. Got a long day ahead of me."

"You and me both." She'd spend her day off unpacking boxes, breaking them down, and tearing them into strips so they'd fit in the recycling bin. And cleaning up after Grey, apparently.

"Can we add a dishwasher to the list," she called after him.

"You got it," he called back.

She downed her coffee and rinsed the last of it from her cup. The water dripped down the drain like a jackhammer drilling through the house's muted atmosphere. At their old place, the neighbor would be yelling at his hard-of-hearing wife about breakfast, and his wife would be yelling back from three feet away. It was trash day. Everyone would be dragging their cans down the sidewalk, and the dog two doors down would be begging the squirrels to play.

A tiny rip opened in her chest, and the hollow ache of yet another chapter closed against her will threatened to dampen her eyes. Moving into that old house with Grey had been like finding her long lost treasure at the bottom of a turbulent sea. The bar had been rebuilt after the fire. It was packed every night with people who valued her for her work. They'd been her happiest days. Simple days. Now she was isolated in a house with cold hard floors while she peeled off someone else's tattered wallpaper.

She washed Grey's bowl and her mug, drying them with an old dish towel, adding it to her mental list of things that were worth replacing. Throwing open a cabinet door to put them away, her old yellow plate with its chipped corner caught her eye from its place on the top shelf. She pulled it down from the cabinet and tilted it, letting light reflect off the surface.

She'd hated that plate when she bought it, but it was the cheapest thing in Penny's Loft. Every time she ate off it was like sitting down to someone else's meal. It had been someone else's choice for someone else's kitchen. In her hands, it had gone from sloppy seconds, chipped and worn, scuffed by other people's knives, to an old friend. They'd come so far together.

With any luck, she'd feel the same about these walls someday.

Flinging open the door to the basement, she padded down the stairs in her slippers. It was a creepy space, dark stone walls and damp air. Sticky webs dangling from bare wood joints. The house had no business having a basement, and she had no business being in it. She found her old Rimowa suitcase on a shelf as old as the house itself. Inside were the few memories she'd salvaged from her old life. A yearbook that should go upstairs out of the damp. An old purse she had no use for in Ramsbolt. She pushed them both aside and wrapped the plate in an old pair of jeans where it would be safe.

The suitcase back on the shelf and the house to herself, she trudged through silence thick as soup and into the dining room, where their tiny kitchen table occupied so little space it was as absurd to her as her nightstands must be to Grey.

Maybe Penny will have a suitable replacement.

She poured herself a glass of water and sat at the table with an old notebook of Grey's and a pen from the bank to start the list Grey had suggested. Painting the bedroom, the kitchen, and the bath. Getting the shop vacuum from his truck and clearing the basement of cobwebs. A shelf for the laundry room. New paint for downstairs. Every room needed an overhaul. They were expensive upgrades to a house she wasn't even sure they could afford.

She pushed the notebook away and slouched in the chair, arms folded across her middle in a defense against the economic reality. She couldn't afford to transform that shell of a house into a home. She wasn't independent enough to do it without Grey's help. He would only negotiate and barter his way through the list anyway, a fiscal process unavailable to her because she would always be an outsider.

Ripping the list out of her notebook, she turned to a clean page. What did she have to offer? She could make a great drink. She understood real estate. She was stubborn and outspoken, and none of those things could be used to buy paint.

The door flew open, and Grey rushed in, a gust of late summer air soaring in with the promise of autumn. Logan craned her neck to see him drop a five-gallon bucket of primer and a bag of supplies in the hall. He pulled off his cap and wrestled paint swatches from his pocket.

"Figured I'd drop these off before I run out to work." He dropped blue chips on the table, a monochrome rainbow of calming colors. "Whatcha got there? A résumé?"

"No." She covered the page with her hands and gave him a grin. "I don't even know what a résumé looks like. I'm trying to figure out what my skills are."

He stood behind her and looked over her shoulder.

She flipped the notebook over. "Don't look!"

"Why not? I think you have great skills. Come on. You think I'd make fun of you?"

She squinted. "Yes. I one hundred percent think you'd make fun of me."

"Fair enough." He pulled his hat down over his ears. "What's this for anyway? Quitting the bar?"

"Of course not." She leaned back in her seat and tapped her pen on the notepad. "I'm trying to come up with…I don't know what I have to offer. If I can figure out what I'm good at, I might be able to monetize it."

Grey squinted, as if her list of abilities were too small to see clearly. "What about that liquor store? Kyle is killing it with that cooking store of his. There are still some empty stores in town, and the rent is cheap."

"That was your idea. I'm not passionate about liquor."

He shrugged. "You could try something else. All you have to do is throw together some quick business plan and fill out an application. The town board would put it up for a vote pretty fast. I can't imagine anyone would vote against you."

"Especially not with you on the board." Just another thing in her life she would have on someone else's merit. She propped her chin in her hand and looked out the side window to the shrubs. Birds picked at the last of the summer blueberries. "I do like the idea of a store, though. Not sure what kind. My expertise wouldn't fill the hall closet."

She grabbed the pen, squeezing it harder than she needed to, and made little flowers in the margins. "I don't want to quit the bar, though. I like it there. I did think about making cocktail kits a while ago. Like, all the ingredients in a box with instructions. Everything but the liquor."

"You might be able to sell something like that in Kyle's store on consignment like Penny does with her furniture."

Logan waved Grey off. "It was just an idea. Too much work for not enough return, anyway. Forget I said anything. How does next weekend sound for a housewarming party?"

"Great," he said as he dove out the door.

"Great. Now I have to figure out how to pay for it."

CHAPTER TWELVE

Logan used her foot to push a case of wine down the bed of Grey's truck, and she smiled at the pleasing hollow metallic scrape. It reminded her of moving into Grey's old place and that time they bought a lawnmower from Sparky's engine shop and drove it home because Grey was too lazy to push it the whole way. Scraping stuff along the bed of the truck was the sound of projects, of fun times, and this time, it was the last case of beer she had to carry into the house for their party.

It was only because of her job that she could afford it. Able to order it all at cost through the tavern's accounts, she could return to the bar anything they didn't open.

She lowered the last box to the ground and slammed the tailgate. A flock of nuthatches took off from the shrubs, shouting out their staccato protests. Walking up the path to the porch, her jaw dropped. The house looked so much bigger with all the ivy gone. Black trash bags stuffed with ivy and leaves, and tall grasses were piled alongside the garage. The wood was worn with a little less paint where the ivy had clung, but it didn't look half as scary as it did before. It would look even better with a fresh coat of paint, but that was for another day.

Her phone's ring was almost lost in the clanging of bottles as she climbed the stairs. Cursing her full hands and tight schedule, she lowered the box to the porch and dug her phone from her back pocket.

It was her mother. On Skype again.

She rolled her eyes before she answered. "What's with all this Skyping?"

"France is boring." Her mother rested her chin in her hands. "I've been thinking about your plight and talking to money people."

Logan rested the phone on the box and let herself in the door. Out of view, she was safe to stick her tongue out at her mother. She had no intention of taking financial advice from a woman who fled the country to save what was left of her money and sanity after her husband went to jail for one of the biggest money laundering scandals in history.

Kicking off her shoes, she nodded at Grey who was setting their table with snacks and paper plates. She dropped the box on the stairs, grabbed the phone, and wandered into the sitting room, pulling her T-shirt up over her nose. The room looked great in a soft buttercream, but it still smelled like paint. She muscled open the window to air it out before people showed up.

"I have no desire to take money advice from anyone in France. No way."

"It's good advice. Why don't you let me set up an offshore account so you can be independent if anything goes wrong?"

Logan held up the phone and lowered the volume. She peeked around the corner. Grey must have gone back to the kitchen because he was nowhere in sight. "How dare you call me on Skype and say that out loud. Grey is in the house."

She slipped back out onto the porch. "And for the record, there is no way I will ever create a safety net in case something goes wrong."

Pulling the door shut, she hissed into the phone. "We've been through this, and I will never, ever take a penny from you. I have a question, though. What's another name for a butler's pantry?"

"A scullery? Why?"

"We have one, and I don't want to call it a butler's pantry. It feels icky." Logan brushed debris from the porch railing where ivy had once clung fast. "Anyway, I have to go. People are coming over."

In less than an hour, people would start to arrive, and the last thing she needed was a lecture about the dangers of having parties in rural landscapes from a mother who just learned about the internet.

"There is nothing icky about having a butler," her mother said. "To the contrary, my life has been plenty icky without one."

"Please don't talk about chickens. I have to go."

"I didn't call to talk about chickens. I called because I'm worried. When you two got married I told you to get a prenup, and you told me I was old fashioned. Now look at where you are."

"Mom." She hissed the word in her sternest voice, the one she had no control over, glad they didn't have close neighbors. The tone never failed to quiet her mother, so she welcomed it. "*Where I am.* Where I am is in a nice house with a butler's pantry that we worked hard for while you're in a chicken coop in the south of France without any of the money your husband grifted for you. And if you do have money, don't tell me, because I care less than the FBI does, and they're probably listening."

Logan's own words echoed off the wall of silence between them, bouncing back at her the way practical thoughts do in a storm of emotion. She winced against the chafe of embarrassment for the way she'd been acting, as if having a roof over her head was something to lament.

But her mother only saw through her own tinted glasses. "You have made a grave mistake, and I am just trying—"

"Don't you dare call me on Skype from exile and tell me I've made a big mistake. I'm not the one who shrugged my shoulders while my husband destroyed our family. I did not need a prenup then, and I do not need an escape hatch now. I am building my own family on a premise of trust."

Her mother grinned and fluttered her eyelashes. "Obstinate as always. But that's a terrible idea."

"Answering the phone was a terrible idea. I have a gorgeous old house to decorate before my real friends come over. I do not have time to entertain this terrible relationship advice."

"One day, you'll—"

"What? Hang up? I have to go. I'm not listening to this for one more second. Have a good night. I love you. I'll talk to you later."

Logan closed the app and shoved the phone in her pocket. She muttered to herself. "If I followed your advice, I'd be listening to a bunch of vapid women talk about each other while waiting for some ridiculous man to finish his round of golf."

Inside, Grey had found the box she left in the sitting room. She found him sorting bottles between the fridge and pantry counter.

"Your mother?" he asked.

"Yeah. She has it in her head that…" She didn't want to hurt Grey's feelings or make him think she was at all insecure about their relationship. It was a little white lie, but it wasn't far from the truth. "She's just concerned about the mortgage and the house."

Grey tossed an empty box into the game room. "I guess when you're used to having boatloads of money, you don't know how people with canoes get upstream."

Logan laughed. "Good point. Most of those people had to con their way into mortgages with foreign banks because they had more debt than brains. We're using our own money instead of stealing someone else's."

She stacked the empty boxes so they formed a leaning tower in the corner.

"Beer's in the fridge," he said. "Food is out. I'm going to run up and change."

Grey thundered up the stairs. She flung open the fridge door. Beers stood in rows, labels facing outward and lined up perfectly like little beer and wine soldiers. Everything was spotless. He'd even balled up empty plastic bags and thrown them in the cabinet under the sink. The cups and plates were out. Nothing to do but obsessively tidy things over and over until...

She jumped at the knock on the front door.

Sliding through the dining room in her socks, Logan skittered to a halt, tearing open the door to find Adelle with a plastic tray of plants and Kyle with heavy grocery bags in each hand.

"Marigolds." Adelle held out the tray. "The white things are called dusty miller. And there's a garden trowel in here in case you get the urge to plant them. I know it's not new, and it's not exactly a housewarming gift, but you can keep it. I have fifty."

"Or more." Kyle nodded.

"I've seen these white things before. They're in planters all over the place." Logan couldn't resist touching the soft leaves, like arugula covered in powdered sugar, before Adelle set them on the porch. "I hope I don't kill them. Thank you, they're pretty. Come on in. Welcome. Those bags look heavy. Can I take one?"

"Nah." Kyle adjusted his grip. "Happy to set them down, though."

Logan closed the door behind them and led the way to the kitchen.

"The plants will do well just about anywhere." Adelle trailed Kyle through the door. "I'd love to build a landscaping plan for you and help you plant some low-maintenance perennials. If you're interested."

"She's been sketching the place for days. It looks really good with all that ivy torn out." Kyle dropped the bags on the counter.

"Grey ripped it all out this week. He just finished it."

Kyle touched a cabinet door and bent to peer at the strip of lights. "This kitchen is gorgeous."

"Thanks. This is one of those things Arvil did. He did some work in the bathrooms, too. Trying to increase the value, I guess." Logan wrinkled her nose. "I think the color makes the kitchen kind of dark. I like the slate backsplash, but the cabinet handles make it look too modern to me. Maybe because the rest of the house is still outdated."

"I could definitely get comfortable cooking in here." Kyle raised a shoulder. He emptied the contents of the bag on the counter. "Here's the famous blueberry pie. I also have one in cherry. And this is for you and Grey."

"What's up, guys?" Grey slipped into the kitchen.

"Just in time." Kyle pulled a white paper box from a bag. "It's for both of you. For the kitchen. Great knives are important. You really only need a few, and these are my favorites."

Grey reached out and took the box. He lifted the lid. "I don't know a lot about knives, but these are cool."

Dark wood handles, almost black, with Damascus steel blades that swirled light and gray metals. They looked far too fancy for something in her kitchen. She ran a finger down one blade. "They are cool. Swirly."

"They're really nice." Grey closed the box. "You didn't have to do this."

Kyle shrugged and brushed it off. "No, really. There are some amazing knives on the market that will last for many years without sharpening, and they don't cost a fortune. If you ever need them sharpened, though, I have a guy. Just bring it by."

Grey set the box on the counter. "You'll have to show me how to use them the right way. I could cut my fingers off, clumsy as I am in the kitchen."

"I'd be happy to show you some knife skills."

The two men made chopping motions with their hands. Adelle grabbed Logan's wrist and dragged her into the library. They aimed for the window and looked out at the porch.

"I can't wait to show you my plans," Adelle said. "They're just ideas. If you don't like it, we can do something else. Or not at all. I have so many gorgeous things you can plant out here. My treat. I'll even come by and maintain them if you don't want to do it yourself. I was thinking hydrangea paniculata on both sides of the stairs. It grows these pretty cones of tight flowers in white or pink. Daylilies and yarrow. And some azaleas. What do you think?"

Logan chewed on her bottom lip. "Honestly, I have been self-absorbed lately. I don't deserve all this kindness."

Adelle turned to her. "What? Of course, you do. You've been moving."

"No. I've been losing my mind." She craned her neck to make sure Grey was still preoccupied with knives. "He wants to get rid of my stuff, and I'm getting really possessive about stupid, impractical things. My mother is back on her..." She flailed her hands. "You remember. She went through that whole *you need to protect yourself in case this relationship fails* thing. Anyway, I feel fragile and alone lately. I don't know how to thank you for helping make this place look nice. It means a lot to me."

"House hunting and moving are really stressful on relationships. It's probably totally natural what you're feeling. I'm willing to bet it'll get easier as you settle in. I mean, look at this house. It's gorgeous. You deserve some curb appeal. Why should you have to struggle with it when you have a friend who's happy to help?"

"I appreciate it. I do. It's nice of you, and I'm looking forward to digging around out there. Gardening isn't something I ever thought about before. It'll be fun."

"What are you going to do with the porch?"

Logan rubbed her eyes with the heels of her hands. "Paint it. I don't know what colors yet, but the whole outside needs paint."

Penny and Nate appeared from behind the arborvitae, strolling up the street hand in hand. Logan moved to the door, and Adelle followed.

"You must be terrified," Adelle said. "I would be. The mortgage on this place must be insane."

"That's the thing. It's not. I don't know why, but Arvil sold it to Grey for next to nothing."

Adelle folded her arms, eyebrows pinched. "That doesn't sound like Arvil."

"I know. It isn't sitting right with me. At all."

Logan flung the door open before they even knocked. At the curb, cars started to arrive. She hung a little chalkboard on the door. On it, she had written "Welcome. Come on in!"

Penny threw an arm around Logan's neck and pulled her into a hug. Orange curls tickled Logan's nose. She couldn't help but smile.

"I brought you something that I think you're going to love. I found them at an estate sale, and they have *you* written all over them."

Logan accepted the gift bag and poked around in the layers of tissue paper. "Coupe glasses! They're gorgeous."

"They're vintage. Nineteen twenties." Penny beamed.

"About the same age as the house. We'll have to make use of these at New Year's." Logan tucked the glass back into the bag where it would be safe, and she hugged Penny to say thanks. "I'm going to put these up so they don't get bumped. Come on. I'll give you the tour."

They moved into the library.

"We're going to tear out all this green wallpaper and repaint it a softer shade of green. We like the look of it with the dark wood." She paused in the dining room. "This room looks ridiculous with our little table in it, but we'll be by someday to get a new one. It definitely needs to feel warmer in here."

Nate held up a painting in a simple gold frame. It was their house on a sunny day. A pristine lawn bundled up against rose bushes, the house beyond in pink and cream. "This might help. I painted this house many times over the years, but this one was my favorite. I liked the lighting. I always imagined this house being blue, but I didn't have enough paint that day, so it ended up like this."

Voices filled the entrance. Grey's laughter carried through the house as he greeted Jaleesa, who arrived with her father, Warren. People piled in behind them, handing Grey food and bottles of wine, but Logan's eyes were fixed on Nate's painting of the house. Gentle swags of curtains dripped in the windows. He'd captured the warbled glass in the front door. A little orange cat slept beneath a bird bath, and a white mailbox sat at the end of the drive. It was a mood, a feeling she hadn't felt yet. It was the promise of an angle of light that hadn't set on the house since they'd moved in but would in the spring if they had enough faith. She clutched the painting in a hug.

"I love this so much, Nate."

"What's Arvil doing here?" Penny jabbed a thumb at the door and hissed in a whisper. "That's a surprise."

Logan gripped the painting, too precious to set down in the kitchen. "Grey must have invited him."

"Oh, I have news." Penny grabbed her by the wrist and pulled her into the kitchen. She waved everyone else to follow.

"Your cabinets are gorgeous!" Adelle gushed.

"Not now," Penny whispered, and they all leaned in. "Zeb came into the store this morning looking for Kyle. You guys were out somewhere."

"We went to the market." Adelle's eyes narrowed. "To get stuff to make the pies. What did he want?"

Penny peered around the kitchen door. "He didn't say. But he told me that he sold a chunk of land to Arvil. For cash. It's the chunk out by the creek with that old building on it."

"That was a mill." Nate's back straightened. "Why would he want that?"

"Zeb said Arvil's going to put a flea market in there."

"A flea market?" Nate wrinkled his nose.

Adelle slammed her hand on the counter and peered over her shoulder. "That son of a bitch."

"What?" The idea was slow to dawn on Logan. "Oh. People will rent space at the flea market and not downtown where you're trying to offload empty real estate."

Adelle had been fighting an uphill battle trying to offload empty real estate owned by the town. People were interested, but some were too scared to make the leap. Kyle had moved in. A newcomer named Stuart had established his newspaper there. And Shawn was working on starting a music store. It was a solid start, but she still had a way to go. And the longer the stores sat empty, the more taxes the town had to pay to the state.

"Why is he always trying to screw with somebody?" Adelle asked through gritted teeth. "I thought he was on my side."

Grey breezed into the kitchen, all smiles, and flung open the refrigerator door. He grabbed four beers from the top shelf. Magnets slid on the door when he slammed it shut, a traffic jam of owls and defunct pizza shops and cacti with googly eyes.

"What's going on?" Grey viewed them with mock suspicion.

Nate accepted a beer when Grey offered. He twisted off the cap and took a swig. "Surprised to see Arvil. That's all."

Grey nodded over his shoulder. "He sold us the house. Gave us a great deal on it, too."

"And used the cash to buy land from Zeb." Logan declined his beer offer. She would need something a lot stiffer. The pieces hadn't fallen together yet, and she wasn't even sure they were all on the table, but when she added in the uneasy feelings she'd had about the house and Arvil's generosity, she had enough evidence to start digging for his hidden agenda. She grabbed a bottle of bourbon from the counter and poured a splash in a plastic cup.

Everyone else declined, and she recorked the bottle.

Grey glanced between them. "I feel like I stepped into a mystery. I'm going to take these beers out to Kyle. You guys have fun."

"How would a flea market on the outskirts of town destroy Adelle's revitalization?" Penny leaned against the counter and adjusted her cat-eye glasses. Voices and laughter barreled in from the library as Grey passed bottles around.

Logan cleared her throat. "If rent is cheaper, it's competition. That's the obvious thing. It's easier to open a stall in a market than it is to rebuild a place downtown. You may not ever own the property, but how many people want that? The maintenance is hard on some of those older places."

Adelle snorted. "That's for sure. Kyle still struggles with that downstairs bathroom. More than that, if the flea market draws enough shoppers, the downtown stores could take a hit. The market. The newsstand."

"God only knows what Arvil's thinking," Nate said, sipping his beer.

"I'm going to find out." Logan set her cup on the counter. "Who wants some wine?"

CHAPTER THIRTEEN

The sun went down around the house. The bag boy from the market showed up with his girlfriend, an artist who made little pottery woodland creatures and had gifted Logan a set of fox and moose ornaments. Jaleesa gave Grey a set of jack stands she knew he needed because he was always borrowing hers. Marissa brought a cake iced with a rendering of the house's façade that made Logan gush and take too many pictures while people waited to eat it.

Logan knocked back drink after drink, getting better at saying thanks to those who offered them gifts before growing weary of her own scripted gratitude as the purple sunset faded to black. After the guests stopped streaming in, Grey unearthed an old radio and a set of speakers, and music filled the downstairs. People gathered in happy clusters, laughing and clutching drinks and plates. Logan bobbed and weaved between them as they spun around her, teacups twirling at her mad hatter party.

She'd managed to avoid Arvil for most of the night, planting her feet squarely in Adelle's camp. Though her deft maneuvers through the house had spared her the embarrassment of an inebriated outburst of opinion, she'd also not been able to thank him for the deal he must have cut Grey, which she intended to do, and interrogate him, which she knew would be a very bad idea.

The more she drank to convince herself it would be a good idea, the worse the idea seemed. After nearly running into him in the library, Kyle's drink in one hand and hers in the other, she ricocheted down the hall and pitched forward into the game room where Kyle and Nate played cards with a guy who might've been Warren if he came into focus and someone who was likely Heather from the church.

They sat in lawn chairs around a table made from stacks of cardboard boxes.

She slapped the heel of her hand against her forehead, searching for the names until one came to her, right or wrong.

"Kyle. No. Yes. Kyle."

He lifted his head from his cards.

"Drink." She held it out to him, and he chased her wavering outstretched hand to snag it.

"Thanks. Want to sit? It's poker."

Shaking her head was a bad idea. "No, thanks. I'm going to find some water."

Using the wall as an anchor in her bobbing sea of houseguests, she turned back to the hall and collided with Stuart exiting the bathroom beneath the stairs.

Snapping her fingers to bring his name to the surface, she gave up. "How *are* you?" she asked.

"Quite fine." He stuck out a hand, and she leaned back as her eyes aimed to focus. "I washed it."

She leaned in. "Want to know a secret? I'm wasted. Totally by mistake. Turns out seven-layer dip and Doritos are not a good enough dinner. You know who I am, right?"

Stuart laughed. He tugged on the sleeve of his green jacket and leaned in, too. "I definitely know who you are, and your secret is definitely safe with me. In case you're wondering why I'm in your house, I'm Sandy's guest."

Logan grabbed his shoulder. "I love her. How can you not love her? Did you know she hates reading real books? And her favorite drink isn't wine. She thinks it is, but she really likes tequila."

Stuart had a dimpled chin and a smile that put her at ease.

"I did know that. About the books. She hates to break the binding."

Logan shook her head and wrinkled her nose. "Weird. But she's a badass. She can also fix things. Very handy."

"She is the badassy-est. If you want to know a secret of mine, she's part of the reason I moved here."

Sobering, she leveled a sincere look on him, though he wouldn't stay in focus. "You guys are good together. I mean, I only see you at the bar, and we've never talked or anything, but you make her happy. And you have a nice newspaper. It's all…" She made a rectangle shape with her thumbs and pointer fingers. "It's the right shape for a newspaper."

"That's good to know. I was aiming for that. If I'm honest, it was hard to find my groove here. I know I offended some of your friends with my rectangle newspaper."

Logan put a hand to her mouth, her eyes wide. "Oh no. Who?"

Stuart aimed a thumb into the game room. "Kyle, for one. And Adelle. I don't like thinking about it."

"Right. I forgot about that. See?" She swatted at his arm. "People forget things. You don't have to live in the past. Take it from me. I spent my whole first year in Ramsbolt being difficult and trying to convince everyone that I'm a spoiled brat."

"I'm glad that Ramsbolt is forgiving."

"Me too. Lucky for me, this town is just as stubborn as I am."

He laughed and leaned against the wall, hands in his front pockets. "This may not be the best time to ask, because I'm not sure you'll remember this tomorrow, but I've been trying to find people in the community to write about. You have a neat story. Would you be interested in sitting down for an interview sometime?"

She tucked in her lower lip and put on the most sympathetic look her muscles would allow. "I'm not sure that's a great idea. I've been in the news a lot, and I try to avoid it."

"Oh! Not like that. I'm thinking about community profiles. Human interest stuff. What you like about bartending. That kind of thing."

A woman who smelled like a perfume counter breezed by and into the bathroom, and Logan nodded at her compliments, her senses addled by the aura. Kyle had been treated poorly by Stuart now that she thought of it. Adelle hadn't been his biggest fan either. But he seemed rather genuine, and she was fond of redemption. He'd never done her wrong.

"Anyway, I don't want to write anything salacious." He turned his attention from the perfume cloud and back to her. "I'm staying as far from the controversy as I can these days."

She raised her empty glass in a heartfelt toast. "Happy to. Not when I'm drunk. I'm speaking in typos today."

His eyes lifted with his smile. "It's a deal. I'll give you my card." He dug his wallet from his back pocket and procured a dog-eared business card, cream colored with his name in green ink. "If you can think of anyone else, I'd love to talk to as many people as I can."

The letters swam together on the card. "I can't think of anyone."

"You don't happen to know Meldrick, do you?"

Her eyes clenched, lips curled in a scowl, she shook her head, and the room went wobbly. "No."

"You're neighbors, so I figured I'd ask. He's quite the character. Thought he'd make a good interview."

"No. I don't like him." Her eyes rattled in her head, her brain sloshed in its own heady broth, as she protested. "Not after what he did to Adelle. If you want to write human-interest stories, there's that cat with one eye and one tooth that hangs out at Sparky's and stares at the traffic. That cat is a good cat."

Adelle turned the corner and came to a stop behind Stuart. Logan gave her a tiny wave.

Stuart rubbed his chin. "I've seen that cat. I agree. Very good cat. Totally forgot about the town manager thing." He turned to Adelle. "Hi. Long time, no see. We're not in line, but there's someone in there."

Adelle put up a hand. "No problem. Happy to wait. Did I hear you talking about that cat?"

"I love that cat." Logan reached for her and pulled her into a hug. "You're the best. Stuart is writing stories about people in town. Good stories. He asked if I know Meldrick, and I was like, ew. No. Write about that cat instead."

Untangling Logan from her hair, Adelle held her up straight and glanced, amused, at Stuart. "Oh, don't listen to anything she says tonight."

All smiles, Stuart nodded. "Definitely not. She's entitled to cut loose. This house is going to be a lot of work."

"You got that right." Logan pointed a finger at Stuart's chest for emphasis. "I might regret a lot of things in the morning. Why not one more? Meldrick is a dick. Giving that pot-stirrer a platform is a bad idea. Talk to that cat, though. He's got stories."

Adelle grabbed Logan around the waist. "I'm going to steer you toward some water and a chair."

More than happy to let someone else take her wheel, Logan wrapped an arm around Adelle's shoulder. "We should go on a vacation sometime. Just us girls. Oh, Stuart." She craned her neck back to see him as Adelle took a step down the hall. "If you're looking for a character, you should talk to Arvil."

CHAPTER FOURTEEN

Logan scraped the remains of seven-layer dip into the trash, her head a little fuzzy but otherwise none the worse for wear. The party had gone on past eleven, and for the sake of their neighbors, they'd pulled the plug, but they'd left the cleaning for the morning.

"I have regrets." She dropped the casserole dish on the counter, next to the rest of them.

Grey placed a beer bottle into the recycling can. "Head hurt?"

"No. Sick of doing dishes." She pulled on yellow rubber gloves and poured dish soap over the pile in the sink. A little rainbow bubble floated in front of her face, and she swatted it. "And drunk Logan agreed to do an interview with Stuart."

"With any luck, he's learned his lesson."

"I know I have. I will be extra careful."

Grey cinched the recycling bag and yanked it from the can. "Oh. Arvil said he's making a flea market."

"I know. Penny said. It sucks."

He shrugged and shook out a new bag. "Arvil looked for you all night. He offered you a discounted lease if you want space for a store. He needs to secure a few tenants to get started."

She blinked down at the pile of dishes. Silverware and serving spoons caked with dried cool whip and once-molten cheese. How much would it cost to throw it all out and start over?

"Why did Arvil think I'd want to start a store?" she asked.

"I don't know." He dropped the bag in front of the fridge. "Guess he heard you talking about it at the bar. He didn't say. But it gave me an idea."

"Does it involve throwing all of this away?"

Grey appeared beside her and peered down at the sink. He reeled back in mock disgust. "Better you than me."

She stuck her tongue out at him, ran water, and held her hand under it, waiting for it to get hot. "What's this idea?"

"It involves you setting up a storefront for your mixed drink kits. You don't have to clean that if you don't want to. I'll wash it if you want."

She grabbed the dish rag from the bottom of the pile, and it shifted and clattered when she pulled the rag free. "No, I'll do it. You took care of the trash."

"You know how to set up a sole proprietorship, right?" He leaned back against the counter.

"You'd want an LLC for that. More protection if someone slips and falls in a rented space." She dove and pulled all the silverware into a pile, soaking them in a dish of dried-on hot wing sauce.

"Smart. You wouldn't even need an employee. You could set your own hours."

"Hmm." She scraped at a clot of cheese with a butter knife.

"Can't you just imagine the sign? A great logo printed on cardboard boxes? You could even sell them online."

"I know you're excited, but this is just not my thing, okay?" She turned off the water and brushed hair from her forehead with the back of her hand, leaving a streak of bubbles. "I do not aspire to run a store in a flea market, and all of this needs to soak."

Shaking off the yellow gloves, she let them fall over the edge of the sink and turned her back on the kitchen, aiming for the front door and the tray of marigolds and dusty arugula that Adelle had given her the night before. Grey followed, trash bag stretched with clanging bottles banging into doorways on their way through the house.

She grabbed the tray, bounded down the stairs, and fell on her knees in the void where ivy had grown. Grey dropped the bag on the porch and leaned over the railing.

"Why not consider it? If the rent is cheap enough, it might work out. You'd have a second source of income. Weren't you just looking for a pet project?"

She skimmed the notecard Adelle tucked between the plants. *Dig a hole. Tease the roots. Pack soil around it. Water.*

She stabbed the trowel into the earth. It sank satisfied into the gritty soil. "Without the spirits, I'd need to sell my cheapest kits at thirty dollars to make a profit. That includes local jams and good quality bitters. If I had to rent a place, half my profit would go to rent. I would make less than minimum wage selling them."

"I didn't know you'd done all that math." Grey peered down at her.

"Yeah, for a space downtown." She sat back on her heels. "Do you honestly think I'd entertain a business idea without running the numbers?"

"Arvil said his rent is dirt cheap, though. Way less than downtown. 'Cause it's just stalls, not a whole facility."

She put a hand over her eyes to shield out the sun. "That does make it a little more appealing."

"It's not open all week, either. Anyway, you can talk to him about it if you want."

"God knows he'll be at the bar." She pulled a marigold from its plastic cup and dropped it in the ground.

Elbows on the railing and chin in his hands, Grey gave her a sultry smile. "You're gorgeous when you're dirty."

"Yeah?" She dug another hole. "You want to join me?"

He grabbed the bag of recycling by the handles and swung it over his shoulder. Bottles clanged. "You look like you're having fun. I don't want to stop you. Besides, I'm going to use all my muscles to take care of those dishes for you."

"Well, don't let me get in the way of that." She shimmied to her right, grabbed the trowel, and dug another hole, alternating golden marigolds and white floofs along the front of the house.

The bag landed in the can with a smash of breaking glass, and the nuthatches fled from the shrubs. Grey went back into the house, leaving Logan alone with her plants and her dirt. She could see the allure of gardening. It didn't require any thinking. Dig a hole, drop in a plant. Give it some water. No wonder Adelle was so calm all the time.

She slipped her trowel into the soil and dug another hole.

The plastic tub crinkled as she rolled it in her hand, squeezing to loosen the roots from the pot, like Adelle's notecard said. She gently teased the roots from the soil and let it fall into the hole, careful not to break any marigold stems. Packing dirt around the roots to make it happy and snug. When she was done, she'd water each one from a drinking glass, her hand over the top and fingers splayed. Plants didn't know their water wasn't from a watering can. But she made a mental note to buy one someday.

What would be the hazard in opening a stall in a flea market? If she couldn't run the register herself, she could always hire someone part time. It might even be fun to have a little shop of her own to decorate.

With half the tray of flowers planted on one side of the house, she stood and brushed the dirt from her knees and carried the remaining plants across the walk to the other side. She paused at the walkway, stretched a little taller, and took in a deep breath of earthy late-morning air still thick with dew. Evenly spaced and staggered, her little plants looked limp but happy. Adelle had warned her about that. She'd called it transplant shock and said they'd bounce back in a day. Logan had laughed. She knew the feeling well.

The old Logan Cole never would have put her knees on wet grass and caked her nails with dirt when that's what the landscapers were hired to do. But then again, if the landscapers weren't there, she probably wouldn't have minded. She might not have considered it self-care, though. She had to admit that it was fun planting the little yellow flowers and the fuzzy white leaves. She inspected Adelle's handwritten tag. *Dusty Millers.*

"You have a lot of work on your hands with this place." A man's voice boomed up from the street. Startled, she jumped, and pressed a dirty hand to her chest. She turned to find Meldrick at the curb. Setting the tray down, she gripped her trowel in one hand and brushed the other on her jeans.

Prior to last night, Meldrick's name had never crossed her lips.

Her interactions with the man had been limited to drinks he ordered at the bar and the pocket change he left her as tips. Knowing his history with Adelle, how he ruthlessly fought against her in his campaign to be town manager, slandering her to the neighbors and trying to sell them out to another town, she knew him enough not to trust him. That was why she'd warned Stuart away.

She didn't want to engage, but she knew his reputation well enough to know that cautious politeness was better than a snub. It might not make up for calling him a pot-stirrer, but if she was lucky, he didn't know about that.

She walked a few steps down the sloped front yard but not enough to split the difference.

"The house needs some work, but it has great bones," she said.

The corner of Meldrick's mouth lifted in a grin that was more like a snarl. "I know. I live right down the street here. The façade needs to be restored. Those windows are painted the wrong colors, you know."

She turned to glance at them. "The colors aren't that bad. But paint is on the list."

"They aren't historic colors. You should have been made aware." His head tilted; his posture leaned toward aggressive. "It's not listed as a historic property, but it should be. You are obligated to keep up with it and treat it with respect. For as long as you own it."

She twirled the trowel in her hand. "We don't have any intention of disrespecting the house we bought. I hope you don't have that impression."

"Everyone who lives here knows that this place has history. It's just sad to see it fall into the hands of an outsider."

It wasn't just the late summer sun that warmed her skin. Her blood boiled. Either he knew just where to hit her by calling her an outsider or it was a universally accepted truth that Logan Cole didn't belong and had no business owning a piece of Ramsbolt history. Perhaps both were true.

She lifted her chin against the accusation and the cool breeze that pushed across the lawn. "I can assure you that it's safer in our hands than it would be if it had fallen to someone who didn't care. Enjoy your walk."

Spinning on her heel, she returned to gardening, plopping down on the grass as her knees sunk in. She stabbed the bed with her trowel, shoveling soil to the side, flinging it against the porch. How dare he accuse them of mistreating their own property without any evidence or indication of their plans. Sure, they didn't have any plans. But they had no intention of creating a gaudy nightmare. Who did he think she was?

The sun was high overhead when her planting was done. Sweat dripped into her eyes despite the cool breeze. She pulled the plastic pots and trays into a pile. Grey pulled the front door shut behind him and stomped across the porch, work bag in his hand.

"I thought you were gone," he said.

"What time is it?" She placed the refuse from her planting by the door.

He looked at his phone. "One fifteen. Aren't you late for work?"

"Shit. Wait for me and give me a ride?" After a quick kiss, she rushed up the stairs, ran a brush through her hair, washed her face, and changed her clothes. Heart pounding, she leapt into the truck and yanked the door shut. Grey let her out at the tavern, where Helen's car sat pinging in the sun. She slinked into the bar, apologies piling one on the other into a mountain of heavy regret.

"You shouldn't have to be here because of me. I'm sorry. I was cleaning the house, and I lost track of time. Then I went outside, because Adelle gave me these plants, and I wanted to get them in the ground." She straightened her ponytail and slipped behind the bar. "I totally lost track of time. It won't happen again."

"You're an hour late." Helen leered and dropped the cash drawer in the register, annoyance sparking off her. "I got a call from the girls at the hotel that the tavern wasn't open. Someone coming through town was tugging on the door. Could have been a paying customer. I rushed over here to open the place, but they were long gone."

Logan tied her apron around her waist. "I feel bad. Meldrick came by and yelled at me."

"Losing track of time doesn't bring customers or money into the bar."

Her weight on her cane, a sigh escaped. Helen hauled herself to the door, and Logan's heart rate went down a notch. She wouldn't be making apologies all night.

"I know. I'm sorry." Logan pulled containers of prepped fruit from the cooler. "It won't happen again. I promise."

Helen gave her a dismissive wave as she stepped out the door. She'd been forgiven this time, but she heard the warning loud and clear: Logan might own a share of the business, but Helen was still in charge, and it shouldn't become a habit. She flipped on the music and let '90s grunge rock lull her while she finished her prep and her cleaning duties.

The bar remained a desolate landscape much of the night, save for Dan and Bern's brief appearance early in the evening. It gave Logan time to do a little research and think her way through the math. If she sold a few drink kits through Kyle's store, she could build up enough interest to sell an expanded line from the flea market. And if Arvil's rental terms were reasonable and short term, it was a low-risk investment that would, at the very least, give her something to do other than tend bar and stare at the walls.

Grey was welcome company when he plopped down at the bar shortly after eight. She grabbed an empty glass and waited for his nod.

"I have to tell you something. You want a beer?"

"Yes, please." He ripped off his hat, brushed his hand over his thick brown curls, and tossed down a pile of envelopes.

"What's all that?" Logan held onto the tap while the glass filled.

"Mail. Check this one out." He brushed the top one like a dealer shooting cards. She stopped it with her hand.

The green certified mail sticker made it look way more important than the handwritten address in tight all caps. There was no return address. She served Grey his beer, wiped her hands on her apron, and shook out the letter.

The same tight all caps levied a drawn-out complaint.

"Meldrick complained about our party last night with a certified letter? It hasn't even been a day. I just saw him. He didn't say a damn word about it."

"It only takes Riley a few hours to get through town." Grey leaned across the bar and took the letter from her hand. "I love this part, where he says the party was further proof that Adelle is incompetent because she attended the gathering. *Her presence bolsters my argument that the town needs a police force to keep the peace.*"

Logan pushed the letter across the bar to him and folded her arms. "I can't read this crap. What else did it say." Logan leaned against the bar. "I don't want to read it myself. It'll just piss me off."

"It includes a list of demands. This one's my favorite. Any future children we have must remain quiet. If we choose to get a pet, we must seek input from the neighbors first. And it says here *I am renewing my tabled plan to form an HOA for our street. Please be prepared to vote in my favor when notified of the upcoming town meeting.*"

"Future kids. We're not having kids. And now I want to breed outdoor rats and boa constrictors as free-range pets. Never had the urge until now, but I think I've found my life's passion."

Grey rolled his eyes. "I'm on the damn town board. What a piece of work. Oh. And he said he saw paint cans on our porch in *a shade of blue inappropriate for the house.* He demands a written explanation for the purpose of the paint."

"What's on the second page?"

"It's a photocopied list of signatures that he says are from the neighbors, supporting his demand for an HOA to *combat our unruly behavior*."

Logan held out a trash can. "You want to file that?"

Grey folded the pages and returned them to the envelope. "Something tells me this is worth holding onto."

"Should we send a response? Bern will be here soon, and if I ask nicely, I bet he'll spit on a napkin for me."

She didn't expect a laugh, but Grey didn't even offer a hint of a smile. "I don't have a good feeling about this at all."

"Me either. But I'm not sure what I can do about it. Can I change the topic for a second?" Logan plowed ahead when he nodded. "I'm thinking about asking Arvil how much he wants for that flea market spot. I might not trust him, but at least he's predictable."

CHAPTER FIFTEEN

Logan pulled Meldrick's letter from its envelope and passed it across Adelle's counter, over the stems and thorns. Adelle scrutinized it with the exasperated gaze of a teacher who saw the flaws in the math homework but lacked the tact to sugarcoat the critique.

"Why is he like this? He's always such a problem." Adelle flipped to the page of signatures.

"I was tempted not to show this to you. I didn't want it to hurt your feelings. But it seems like it might be worse to withhold the information." Logan plucked rose petals from the scattered refuse and stacked them by size. "I've been trying to figure out how to respond. Grey says we should do nothing, but I've seen my fair share of bullies over the years, and I really want to respond. I want to do it publicly. I want to send a message that puts an end to his bullshit once and for all."

"I don't know if that's a good idea. But Meldrick does keep pushing if he doesn't get a response." Adelle looked at the list of signatures.

"I don't want anything to get on you. Everyone knows we're friends. I just don't get why all of those neighbors who were so welcoming signed whatever the hell that is."

"I think this is old. I've seen this before." Adelle flattened it on the counter, palms flat at its sides. With a lab coat and a pair of goggles, she could be mistaken for a scientist reading microbes like tea leaves.

"I'm trying not to be overly emotional about this. I've been all out of whack lately. I don't trust my own judgement right now. Grey should be enjoying his time with his new house, not dealing with crap like this. I was worried the neighbors were conspiring against us. You don't think so?"

"No. I don't think so. I don't think these people know their signatures are being used in this way." Her words were slow and quiet. Something was brewing. It gave Logan hope that Adelle might come up with a magic button they could push to make Meldrick go away.

"That's good news," she said. "They'd be sad if they ever needed a plumber."

The door swung open behind Logan. She pulled the papers into a pile with the envelope and hid them under her hands.

"Shawn!" Adelle stuck out her hand and greeted the scruffy-haired young man.

"Nice party last night." He greeted Logan with a nod and handed a wad of wrinkled papers to Adelle. "I brought the application. I hope this is good. If I need to write more, let me know. I picked the smallest store on Main."

Adelle skimmed the papers he presented. "It looks complete. Tell you what, I'll look over it and send you an email. I think the town would love a music store. And the kids would love the lessons."

"I hope so. Thanks for setting me up with Kyle. He's a little scary."

Logan looked up. "Scary? Kyle?"

Shawn's eyes widened. "Have you ever talked money with him? Man, he's intense."

Adelle laughed. "He's definitely a fine print kind of guy. But if anyone understands the leap of faith, it's him. He's a good person to know if you need money advice."

Shawn shifted his weight, a parting question written on his face. "Um. You've heard about Arvil and the flea market, I guess?"

Logan dissected Adelle's reaction for any hint of flame or incense, but her friend rested her hands in her lap and tilted her head, her diplomacy gears engaged.

"I did hear about that, yes. I think it will be a great draw for the town."

Impressed with the smile she beamed at him and the speed at which she launched off her stool, Logan admired her friend's iron spine. Giving Shawn not a second longer to press the issue of the flea market and change his mind, Adelle walked him to the door. He shot a parting wave at Logan, who returned it, stifling a laugh.

"You didn't give him a chance. That was impressive."

"Thank you. I streamed a bunch of documentaries on the Queen of England hoping something would wear off."

"Maybe it did." But Logan's high regard for her friend's

willpower sank her own spirits like a lead weight. "I have more news. I'm such a bad friend. Arvil offered me a discount on space. Figured you should hear that from me. I mean, why not bring in all the bad news today?"

Adelle straightened up her counter, sweeping petals and stems into the trash. "I'm not surprised. A little sad, perhaps, but not surprised. I have to be logical about it. It's not competition. It's just a different option, right?"

"Grey is pushing me to take up a small space there and sell cocktail kits. I keep thinking about it."

Adelle pulled a square glass vase from a shelf and filled it with an inch of water. "You've been talking about these kits for a long time. They sound like a good idea."

"Don't bullshit me, Adelle. This sounds like the same diplomacy you gave to Shawn. I'm your friend. Be real with me."

Chopping through a stem with her knife, she threw the zinnia in the vase. "What do you want me to say? That I'm scared to death that the town will fade into nothingness? That if it does on my watch, I'll be ostracized forever? I can't afford to be upset about the flea market. I sure as hell can't stop it. But that's just my emotions. A flea market outside of town doesn't spell the end of Main Street. People won't walk there for groceries or go there for music lessons on Tuesday, and they sure won't go there for breakfast or wedding flowers. If I'm honest, it's absolutely the right decision for you. If the rent is dirt cheap, do it. You've been talking about this for a year."

"It hasn't been a year." Logan tugged on her earlobe, where a neglected piercing healed over and caused a bump. "Has it been a year?"

Adelle leveled with her. "Last year. Fourth of July. You made the drinks for us at the bonfire behind Penny's. You went on for an hour about sourcing ingredients. I haven't seen you that passionate about anything in a while. Are you looking for my permission? You don't need it."

"I guess I was excited. I didn't realize it was that long ago."

"Time flies." She let another zinnia stem fall into the vase. "I'm not sugar coating this. I really don't care about that flea market. Sure, I'm curious what's going on in Arvil's head because who wouldn't want to know, but I can't change it."

"It is weird, isn't it?" Logan glanced at the door, but no one was there. She kept her voice down anyway. "A flea market isn't exactly on-brand for Arvil. This is the guy who wanted to tear down the pub and build an office building."

Adelle shrugged and cleaned leaves from stems. "He's a shrewd investor. It could be that he finally realized a flea market is more our speed."

"I'm still not buying it. He was doing work to fix up the house and increase its value. That kitchen, the bathrooms. Yeah, it needs a lot of work, and it was sitting there taking up space, but he wanted more for it than he got. And a flea market?"

Adelle brushed hair from her eyes with the back of her hand. "Who knows why he does what he does. But if you did take space there, you could be my eyes and ears."

"Silver lining." Logan swept up crispy green leaves and brushed them into the trash. "Okay. I'm going to ask Arvil for more information. I'm not committing to anything yet."

"Good for you. Oh!" Adelle jumped. She sat up straight in her seat. "I almost forgot. That old HOA. A few years ago, Meldrick did try to form one. It was back when his son was town manager. It was only for the people in that quadrant of town. I never heard the details about it, but it caused a big stir and never got off the ground. It just fizzled."

"Do you think it will turn into something? I have seen the underbelly of the HOA world, and the last thing I want is to be on the bad side of one."

Adelle shook her head. "Nah. I'm glad you told me, just in case it turns into something, but I know Meldrick. He's more interested in causing drama and upsetting people than he is about actually doing anything. He's probably just trying to ruffle your feathers. Besides, no one on that list likes him. Jaleesa? Warren? Come on."

"Then why did they sign it? Rather, what did they think they were signing?"

"Who knows. Tell me about the drink kit. Are you still doing simple syrups?"

Logan shuffled on her stool. "I just made Earl Grey simple syrup. It's good and so easy. Dissolve a cup of sugar in a cup of water. Throw in three tea bags and let it sit for ten or eleven minutes. Perfection. I was thinking I could make up a recipe card and include the ingredients with some old-fashioned bitters."

Adelle swatted her with a pink zinnia. "See? Look how excited you are."

CHAPTER SIXTEEN

The house shed its old wallpaper skin in strips as Logan nudged it with a scraper. The paper was thick and dry. How Grey had tackled their massive bedroom without complaining about the arm pain she'd never know. Three walls of the big back room were done, the smaller middle room was untouched, and she was ready to collapse into a tub of ice, but she kept at it. The sooner the paper was gone, the sooner this room would be a nice sage green. And then she could fill it up with cocktail kit supplies.

She yanked her phone from her pocket at the hum of a phantom vibration. The last web page she'd visited was still open to a list of random drink terms. She'd been hoping one would spark her imagination for a company name. It was fun to dream. It needed to be snappy: a dash of snark and a lot of wit. She couldn't quite picture it yet, but she knew she'd come up with a cool logo once the name fell into place. Then the fun would really start, negotiating a decent price for custom boxes, designing labels for bottles and product bags, and calling wholesalers. She couldn't wait to get into the nitty gritty, doing some fast talking to get the best quality ingredients she could at the lowest prices. Her fingers itched to get started. But the notification wasn't real. Just her hopeful imagination, wishing Arvil would call her back.

She couldn't get him out of her mind. The man had exacting standards where money was concerned. Her limited research showed places going for thirty-five dollars a weekend. Knowing Arvil, his rent would tip the scale. But even if he charged two hundred dollars a month, he wouldn't be raking in enough money to sate his appetite. And for a man who wanted to build a state-of-the-art executive office building on the edge of town because the tavern wasn't generating enough income to feed his avarice, Logan was afraid to let her hope get too far ahead. Even if she could afford his rental rate, she might not want to risk signing up for whatever scheme he was cooking. Why would he sell this big house, a Ramsbolt landmark, for so little money?

Standing on the fourth rung of the ladder, holding on with one hand, she jammed the scraper under a stack of wallpaper until she created a flap she could pull.

She could push him to give up information, but in her experience Arvil would never be forthcoming without a fight. Picking one with him just to figure out his motivations wouldn't serve her well. No, the best course of action would be to ask no questions at all. Not even how much Grey paid for the house. She couldn't ask him a single thing until she knew what she was looking for. With too many questions and not enough leads, picking Arvil apart would be like digging at wallpaper. She had to start slow in one small corner and get the feel for the room first.

With another scrape, a curl of flowered paper fluttered to the floor. Then, her phone rang.

Triceps burning, she left the scraper on the ladder and sat on the floor, back against seven layers of paper, and answered Arvil's call.

"So, you want to know how much rent would be," he said. She could picture him lowering his tiny-framed glasses, peering down his nose at her like he did at the bar.

"Yeah. Grey said you were interested in offering up a discounted space. What kind of discount are you talking about?"

"Well, I have to say I'm thrilled." He cleared his throat. "I am willing to offer you fifty percent off."

"Fifty percent off of what?" If his idea of full priced rent were a grand a month, she'd never break even. Either way, she wanted it in writing. "And can you send me something by email, so we can have an agreement?"

"You and your written handshakes." She pulled the phone away from her ear as he chewed into the phone. "One fifty a month. For life. How's that float your boat?"

"Email me. I'll think about it." The price was right, but the reasoning wasn't settled. Not in her mind. She couldn't make him drink, but that didn't mean she couldn't lead him to the water. "What's up with this, anyway? You gave Grey a hell of a deal on this house, then you used the cash to buy a hunk of stone ruins while you have perfectly good, empty real estate downtown. I don't get it."

Arvil laughed into a cough. "As you get older, you'll find that profit takes on lots of different meanings."

"So, you suddenly became a saint, and you want to help Zeb? I'm not buying that, Arvil. I know you too well."

"Not well enough, apparently." He paused. Logan had no intention of filling the silence. She would let him sweat it out until he came clean. "Don't you have more questions to ask?"

A million. "I won't beg, Arvil. You'll tell me eventually."

"Oh, fine." He spit his words like an impudent toddler. "It's about sticking it to Meldrick. The way I see it, it's a win-win situation. Your best friend hates him. I hate him. You get discounted rent on a store. I get more income. Don't you feel better now that you have an answer you can sleep on?"

"Mmm. Slightly." Meldrick wasn't one of her biggest tippers, and he'd certainly bruised Adelle during the last town manager election, but she had no intention of being in the middle of a tug-of-war of the egos. Whatever Arvil had up his sleeve, he'd given her the reason she asked for, but she needed one more thing from him before she closed the case. "I don't want to get any of that on me, but I got to know. What's Meldrick got to do with the flea market?"

She'd been in one flea market in Virginia on her way to a concert, looking for a headband and a pair of cowboy boots. It had been a sober adventure. Every surface was sticky, covered in a dust grit concoction glued on with fryer grease, and it smelled like every food ever dipped in batter and frizzled in melted fat. It wasn't exactly on-brand for Arvil or Meldrick.

"What gives?" she asked.

"I may be greedy, but I got my reasons. And I still got a heart. Meldrick, though...that man is disruptive just for the sake of being disruptive, and I hate that. I figure a good deed for Grey will carry some weight when I need that land rezoned."

"There it is." Logan leaned her head back and knocked it against the wall a few times, quiet enough that Arvil wouldn't hear it. "I knew there was a reason. You need a favor."

"Not a favor. A vote. It's hardly a favor to ask someone to rezone a strip of old land on the outskirts of town that clearly would be better off repurposed."

Logan fanned the neck of her shirt. The house was heating up as the day wore on. "It's hard to argue with you today, Arvil."

"It's always hard to argue with me. I don't know why you do it so often. Anyway, once the place is rezoned, there'll be work for everyone. Plumbing. Carpentry. The retail spaces will need to be built out."

"Isn't it a conflict of interest to give me a discount on rent, though?"

"Not if I'm offering discounted rent to all my early tenants. And it's definitely not a conflict of interest if nobody knows about it."

Her sigh rebounded in the phone, rattling in her ears.

"I'll take care of it," Arvil said. "Just be your father's daughter and talk to Grey."

"Arvil, I know too much. I can't take a deal on rent in exchange for doing dirty work. I just can't."

"I offered it to Shawn, too. Don't think you're special. And I wanted to thank you."

"What for?"

"You and Adelle set me up with Stuart. I'm meeting him at

Marissa's for an interview tomorrow. With any luck, he'll buy me a muffin."

CHAPTER SEVENTEEN

"We haven't finished painting upstairs yet. The bedroom's mostly done, though." Logan led Adelle and Penny up the stairs. She swung around the newel post like a little girl and scampered down the hall, one hand under her rocks glass in case her whiskey spilled. She licked a drip that crept down the side. "Oops. Don't want that on the floor."

She dragged them down the hall, past the bath where Grey had just installed a shower head over the clawfoot tub and pointed into the middle bedroom. "This is the last room we'll do. It's just storage for cleaning supplies and crap right now."

"Those built-in shelves! The old glass in the doors is so pretty." Penny leaned in the doorway. "It looks like a museum."

"A museum of dust. I'm afraid to open those doors and break the glass. Check this out." They filed into the back room. Logan had left a square of wallpaper, preserving all the layers for posterity. She ran a hand over it. "This is the room where I pulled off all the wallpaper. Seven layers. It took me three days to get it all off."

"Is this the room you're painting green?" Penny peered out the window to the backyard below.

"Yeah. Like a mossy sagey green."

"Your yard is huge." Penny brushed aside a curtain shredded by the sun. "You could put a fire pit back here."

"Or a vegetable garden." Adelle clutched the open bottle of wine. "I can give you some seedlings if you want."

"I don't know if I'm ready for vegetables yet. That's a little advanced for me. We'll do something with it, eventually. Grey found a local kid to come over and mow the lawn for now." Logan waved them on. "Come on. You got to see the bedroom. I can't wait to show you the view."

She backed down the hall, and they followed. Waving a hand, she let them in first, but Adelle stopped in the doorway, glass of wine in one hand, bottle in the other. She gasped.

The room had come a long way in a short time. The peeling yellow wallpaper had been stripped away, the walls patched, and Grey had painted it a dusty robin egg blue with a white ceiling. Logan had polished the dark wood trim and wiped down the stone fireplace and its wood mantle. She'd painted the curved bench seat in the corner a bright white to match the ceiling. It needed curtains and cushions, but she was proud of her work.

Adelle's jaw dropped. "I love this. It must be like sleeping in the sky."

Penny nudged her out of the doorway. "Geez. Blocking my view of the best part." She went straight for the rounded corner and flopped down on the bench beneath the windows. "Heaven."

"I don't know what to do for curtains. White seems like it would show everything, and Grey is always leaving fingerprints everywhere. A print might be nice. For now, it's just these old blinds we lower at night." Logan sipped her drink and followed Adelle. They settled on the hard wood of the bench. "Hard to believe this is Ramsbolt, sometimes."

It was hard to believe it was her home at all.

Adelle rested her forehead against the glass and tapered her gaze, peering down the street. "This place is amazing. There's nothing else in Ramsbolt quite like it."

Logan swallowed a sip of her drink. "Thanks. It's been a lot of teamwork. Him in the evenings, me in the afternoons."

"What's next?" Penny tucked one foot beneath her.

"We have a list. It'll take a while. I wanted to get the walls painted so it felt like ours. I'm starting to fall in love with this place."

Adelle lifted her chin. "It smells happy. Like an old house. Any idea how old it is?"

Logan shook her head. "The paperwork says 1920s."

"Oh!" Penny jumped. "I keep meaning to ask you. What's going on with that Arvil thing?"

Logan set her drink down and leaned in. "He wants Grey's help getting the land rezoned for the flea market. Not in exchange for my cheap rent, he says." She rolled her eyes. "He swears it's not a bribe. Claims he offered Shawn the same deal."

"Sure, he did. Shawn's on the town board, too." Adelle narrowed her eyes, considering the impropriety. "It's not news he'd have to rezone the place. But why's he being shady about it?"

"It isn't any different from the way the rest of the world works, is it?" Penny asked. "The hospital was the same way when I worked there. People get used to being pushy and rude, treating everything like it's life or death. They just get used to acting that way."

"That's the truth." Logan had seen her fair share of grifters being sketchy even when they were doing the right thing to know that any kind of behavior could become a habit. Mob mentality. "It just sucks that Ramsbolt operates that way. It might not be any different than anywhere else, but what's right and what happens are two different things."

Adelle sighed into her glass and a little puff of condensation clouded her pinot grigio. "The rezoning request would probably go through without any intervention on his part. Don't think too hard on it. Think of it as an initiation into the Ramsbolt way of doing things. I saw it all the time when my dad ran the town. He had a hard time accepting it. It's just the way things are done."

"Besides," said Penny. "No one would ever say you shouldn't have a store in the flea market just because Grey voted to rezone that land. If we all recused ourselves from doing business with people we know, we'd never do anything at all."

"True." Adelle peered into her nearly empty glass. "Even so, get everything in writing. Rezoning a property isn't without complications, and you should cover your butt. Just in case. Especially with Meldrick around."

"I still don't get it." Logan grabbed the bottle off the floor and gave Adelle a refill. "Why would Arvil even buy a property that wasn't close to town, wasn't zoned properly, and doesn't even look like a good investment on paper. It's not his usual way of doing things."

"Where is it?" Penny wrinkled her brow. "I can't even picture it."

Adelle tilted her head back. "Go left at the tavern. It's about a mile out or so. Where the creek is. There's an old factory, part of a mill, set back in the trees. It's zoned for agriculture. To change it to retail, Arvil will have to make room for parking. He'll have to connect to sewer and water and electricity. The lines do go out that way, but he'll have to pay to connect to them. And if the town gets worried about the strain on resources just to build something new, considering everything else we have to maintain around here, they could try to block his effort."

Logan rested her elbows on her knees and her chin in one hand. "Maybe that's what's got him concerned."

"He's a squeaky wheel, though," said Adelle. "The louder he is about having to pay for it himself, the easier it might be for him to pull it off. No one will want to hear him complain. But you can't tell anyone I said that."

Penny twisted the invisible key to her pursed lips. "Fort Knox, over here."

"Me, too." Logan swirled her drink in her cup. "And Stuart's writing that article about him. That'll be out soon."

"Talk about giving a squeaky wheel a platform." Adelle spun the stem of her glass in her fingers. "That was a dumb idea I had, wasn't it?"

Logan shrugged. "Not as dumb as me telling the only journalist in town that Meldrick's a dick."

"I'm a little worried about that, too. He seemed sincere, though.

He's patched things up with Kyle since he slammed his store to the entire town. He apologized to me, too. And Sandy trusts him. If he's trying to do more human-interest stories and less salacious buzz, he probably won't lean into that Meldrick thing."

Logan smiled down at her empty glass. "I believe in redemption. I can't ask for it, then deny it for anyone else. I'm not going to dwell on that. I have enough going on with Arvil."

"Agreed," Adelle said. "It sure was funny, though. The look on Stuart's face was priceless."

Penny's concerned look volleyed between them. "What did I miss?"

Adelle gave Logan a sympathetic grin. "An extremely drunk Logan. You were playing poker."

"I hope that never gets back to Meldrick and gives him any fuel. Hey, did I tell you I made a prototype for my cocktail kits? They're down in the kitchen if you want to see."

"Let's go." Adelle leapt to her feet, and Penny followed suit. The stairs creaked, and they turned the corner, through the library, and into the dining room.

"I almost forgot to tell you," Penny said as they passed through the pantry. "Nate said he would design a logo for you, if you want."

"That would be great." Logan pulled a small cardboard box, the size of an old cigar box, from a cabinet and opened the lid. She pushed it down the counter.

"I don't know how you come up with these things." Penny sifted through the pieces—a small glass vial of bitters, a notecard with a recipe. She sniffed a little bag of herbs intended to infuse a simple syrup. "Lemon?"

"And lavender." Logan leaned against the counter.

Adelle flipped the notecard over. "This looks fun. I can't imagine coming up with that on my own."

"Yeah, well, I don't know how you do what you do. I couldn't deal with Meldrick the way you do."

Adelle tucked the card back in the box and shrugged. "It wasn't easy, but at some point, I just had to deal with him. Every day I either have to work with or against that guy. It's just part of Ramsbolt life, I guess. He wants to bring down anyone who gets ahead. Your best bet is to let him think he's done it. Then he'll go away. And don't do anything that will stir the pot."

Penny put the lid back on the box. "What did Grey think about that letter Meldrick sent?"

"He's still upset about it. He doesn't want to be seen bringing supplies into the house in case it riles Meldrick. He brings stuff in from the truck at night. I was even hesitant to go outside the other day and pull out those dead shrubs. I was enjoying gardening, too. I just don't want to do anything that'll add fuel to his threat of forming an HOA."

"That's a shame." Penny patted her arm. "You shouldn't have to feel like that."

"I know. It's silly."

Adelle set her empty glass in the sink. "I can help. I'll put together a landscaping plan he can't argue with."

Penny wrinkled her nose, mischief written on her face. "And then we can make a giant Coming Soon sign like they put up at new construction sites, and we'll stick it at the end of the driveway. That'll really piss him off."

<h1 style="text-align:center">CHAPTER EIGHTEEN</h1>

This wasn't Logan's usual pleasant walk to work. The mild summer had given way to an early taste of fall, and she pulled her sweater around her middle, shielding herself from the chilly blast that shot across the park. She should have taken Grey up on his offer of a ride to work, but she liked her stroll through town, and she only took him up on it when the weather was inclement. The walk helped her change gears from quiet time at home to loud evenings at the bar. This day was particularly brisk, however. Turns out she wasn't as immune to Maine's climate as she thought she was.

Crossing the bridge over the little creek, the houses fell back from the street. Lawns expanded, and cracked driveways stretched, reaching for houses that puffed steam and chimney smoke into the grey sky. The trees were swelling with their contrast, tinged with yellows and hints of orange. Winter was coming, and the whole town seemed to shiver under its weight.

As she passed Arvil's house, he emerged and climbed into his car. A million questions fluttered to mind. Why did he really want that old mill so badly? But she remembered Adelle's warning not to stir the pot. She really did want the space, and she was willing to be Adelle's eyes and ears as much as she could be.

"Hey, Arvil." She almost hoped he'd offer a ride, but she didn't want to be trapped in a car with him either. "How's the mill going?"

"You haven't responded to my email yet." He lifted his chin. "Are you taking the deal or no?"

"I am. I'll reply. Things have been crazy. How long do you think it will take to get it through rezoning and water and sewer?" She waved a hand in the air. "You know, all that."

"Not sure. Fast." He rubbed his red nose. "If I make Adelle angry, she'll quit, though. Then I'll have to deal with some other town manager. Like Meldrick. I'm ambitious, not stupid."

Logan held her reply until a passing car moved on, ticking engine and roaring exhaust slicing the thick air. "I'd never argue otherwise. I'm looking forward to it."

She'd been thinking about owning her own brand for days, dreaming about it in the shower. If she could build it up and turn it into something, she could sell it off to a bigger brand and invest her earnings into another project. She had an itch she could only describe as entrepreneurship, something her father had always encouraged, and her mother frowned upon as gauche. Wanting to get past the planning phase and stop making Grey taste funny syrups she made while he ate breakfast was a selfish thing. She was ready for a new adventure, ready to take a risk.

Arvil blew into his hands. "You can give her a nudge, you know. Wouldn't hurt."

Logan launched toward work. "I'll see what I can do. I don't hold that much sway."

"That interview went great yesterday. I'd say I owe you one, but..." He shrugged. "I wouldn't be me then, would I?"

"What did he ask you?" She didn't expect him to divulge, but sometimes he surprised her.

"Fluff questions for his Cosmo quiz. That rag has gone downhill if you ask me." He grunted and climbed into his car.

Logan shook her head and strolled on toward the bar. There was no use trying to read between the lines.

At the top of the hill, she crossed the parking lot and wiggled her key in the lock. The bar's door slipped open, much easier than the old door they lost in the fire. This one was a decent enough replica, with warbled yellow glass and black iron bars.

The chilly air brought in a different crowd. She spent the evening serving drinks to Arvil at one end where he read the paper in his usual shaded spot and serving beer to Nate and Kyle at the other. Nate sketched logos on bar napkins, passing them to Logan and refining his idea while Kyle looked over his shoulder.

When Meldrick stomped in, Kyle kicked the empty stool at his side further down the bar. Since he and Adelle had become seriously entwined, Kyle had wasted no words on the man who made her life a living hell. Logan, on the other hand, had to remain polite.

Meldrick settled onto a stool, sparing no glances for the rest of the patrons. Logan held onto the tap while she poured him a beer.

"What do you think about this one?" Nate slid a napkin down to the taps.

Logan stopped it with her free hand. She gave Meldrick his beer without flourish. He wasn't a big tipper anyway. "I love that. The circle around the logo looks more like a drink stain on a napkin."

"Fewer colors will make it cheaper to reproduce. And this will look good on a cardboard box. But I was thinking you could do a little more with the printed boxes and include grain and herbs in the design. Things that look like they came from a drink kit. And you definitely want your address and phone number on there."

"Is that what you were discussing with Arvil this afternoon?" Meldrick raised an eyebrow. "A new store?"

Logan's curiosity couldn't refuse a glance at Kyle. She got a kick out of the smirk he aimed at his beer.

"I suppose I was just having a chat with Arvil. He's a regular customer."

"He'll also be your landlord when you take a spot at the *flea market*." He drew out the syllables the way only someone wanting to villainize the ordinary can.

Suddenly, Logan cared far more about the flea market than she wanted to. She turned her back on him, grinding her teeth, and cleaned an already spotless tap to avoid the trap her emotions set for her.

"Why don't you just start a store downtown and support your best buddy?" Meldrick sipped his beer and licked foam from his upper lip. "Or is there some falling out? It seems strange you'd go against your own friend. Especially when so many people are complaining about you and that house."

Arvil shook the newspaper, the crinkling flutter slicing through the air, adding to the tension. The words were on the tip of Logan's tongue. All she had to do was open her mouth and a childish litany of phrases would have spilled out. *I'm rubber; you're glue.*

But Kyle swelled with a deep inhale, and Nate stemmed the coming tide with his own brand of snark.

"Figure you'd want to keep Logan on your good side, Meldrick," he said. "Considering you lost the campaign, and Adelle can make your life miserable at the drop of a hat."

Meldrick scoffed. "She doesn't have the guts."

"Why do you have it in for me, anyway?" She forced a smile she wasn't committed to. Her rag still clean after wiping down clean taps, she threw it in the sink for the satisfaction of it. "And Adelle. Out with it."

It was clear from Meldrick's posture that he had a retort at the ready, but the door flew open and Dan bumbled in, all six foot four of him, wide as a truck and solid muscle. Clad in plaid and his usually greasy denim, he changed the atmosphere of any room he walked into. It didn't matter that he was a teddy bear. Ramsbolt still parted the waters when he walked. He plopped down at the far side of the bar, midway between Meldrick and Arvil.

Logan shook out a paper bag and pulled a six-pack from the to-go fridge. Dan had his habits, and she was paid to oblige. She plopped the bag in front of him and accepted his cash, ignoring the scowl that Meldrick wouldn't drop.

"Thank ya." Dan yanked a bottle from the bag, popped the cap, and dropped the rest at his feet. The sizzle coming from Meldrick wasn't lost on him. "What's up your hole? I'm here to relax. In case you got other ideas."

Dan threw his head back and took a long swig of beer.

Meldrick looked him up and down, disapproved of what he saw, and leveled a look on Logan that made her skin crawl. Something about that man, the way he kept his motives hidden and lurked in the dark, turned her stomach. She rubbed at her wrist and turned to the office door. She wanted him gone. If she neglected to keep him happy, he might just go away.

As she turned her back, he cleared his throat and shuffled from his stool. She turned to face him, hands on her hips, ready for the worst.

Meldrick slapped cash on the bar, just three pennies more than the price of his tab, and before she could roll her eyes, he slammed an envelope down on the bar. "You're going to want to pay close attention to that."

Kyle twisted in his seat as Meldrick left, and he gave a finger to the door as it swung closed behind the man. "What an asshole," he said.

The envelope was plain, unmarked. It wasn't even sealed. She unfolded the flap and pulled out two pieces of thin copier paper. On top was a picture printed of her unloading beer from Grey's truck the morning of their housewarming party. It had a yellow date and time stamp in the bottom, as if she'd even refute it. The second page was a note.

Play nice. Or I'll tell Helen and the state liquor board that you used your role as a buyer for the tavern to buy liquor for personal consumption at wholesale prices. Which is against the law. Not that you'd know that, Ms. New York.

The coldest chill she'd felt all day washed over her. Helen could lose the tavern. The fines could crush them. She was going to pay the tavern back. She'd kept track of what she'd ordered and what she'd already returned. All of it sat in the back as inventory, already restocked in the pub's books. She knew how much to write the check for as soon as she got paid. But it wouldn't matter to Meldrick.

With a shaking hand, she tucked the pages back in the envelope. The ringing in her ears was slow to fade.

"Wonder what that was about? Logan. Logan?" Nate's voice cut the fog horns blaring in her head.

"Huh?" She spun to him, tucking the envelope in her back pocket.

"What was that? The envelope?"

She waved a hand as if it didn't matter. "Just stupid Meldrick stuff."

CHAPTER NINETEEN

The second Grey walked into the bar, Logan locked eyes with him and gave him a look and a nod that called him behind the bar and into the office. She wiped her hands and followed him in, closing the door behind them.

"This isn't a booty call, is it?" Grey balled his hat in his hands. "What happened?"

It was as if she'd swallowed a brick one bite at a time for as dry as her throat and dense as her stomach were.

"I didn't do what he says I did." She pulled the envelope from her pocket and pushed it into his chest.

"What are you talking about?"

"Read it."

"This is like some secret CIA shit." Hat in his back pocket, he skimmed the note and squinted at the picture.

"I had every intention of paying for it. Full retail price. Except the liquor, because we don't have a license for that, but I'm paying the store back by the pour. At retail price. And I'm paying for the beer, too. I just didn't get around to it yet, and things are tight at the moment."

He planted his feet, eyes wide, face reddening. "Shit. I thought you bought all that in Colby."

"Well, I didn't." Her face grew hot. It would kill her if Grey thought less of her for what she'd done. Putting the tavern at risk and hurting Helen was one thing. Putting Grey in the line of fire and making this worse with Meldrick was too much. In one small act, she'd put everything she loved at stake.

"I just ran out of time. This was easier. I'll put it right. I promise."

Grey ran a hand through his curly brown hair. His face tilted down; his expression was unreadable. She willed him to look up, to give her some reassurance that he wasn't angry. She yearned for anything, a tiny joke or a lash at Meldrick, that would loosen the knot in her chest and dislodge the lump in her throat.

"What the hell were you thinking? We just bought a house. We have a neighbor snooping around making life hell. You just told me how you're all upset that you can't make money doing anything but this, so you decide to throw it all away? What the hell is wrong with you?"

Her dry throat formed a lump, and hot tears pooled in her eyes. "I can fix it. I didn't think I was doing anything wrong."

"Can I just have five minutes without some major drama?" Grey threw the papers on the floor. "I'm trying to paint and fix radiators before the winter comes and make enough money to rebuild my savings account. I do not have the time or the energy to be dealing with this crap."

All the warmth went out of the room. Her vision blurred, and her hands shook. "I'm sorry. I didn't mean to make things worse. I just…"

"Stop doing risky shit. Please?" He picked up the papers. "I'll help you figure this out."

She wiped her eyes with the heels of her hands. "You don't have to do that. I can take care of it."

"No." Hands on his hips, papers balled in his fists, his expression was pure outrage. "I mean that I'll help you figure it out, so I know you're done making a mess of things."

Unfolding the paper on the desk and smoothing it out, he peered down at it, shoulders tensed and back rigid. Logan bit her lip, waiting for another explosion.

Grey held up the paper. "You can't see the brands on these boxes. It's too small. Do you remember what you ordered?"

"Of course, I do. I keep immaculate records. This isn't my fault. This is Meldrick's fault."

"Why is he like this?" Grey turned and sat on the desk, rubbing his temples.

"I don't know. Adelle said he just likes to cause trouble, and Arvil said the same thing about him. It's like he gets all his self-worth from knowing he can upset people."

Grey's face was growing red. He yanked his hat from his pocket and twisted it in his fists, his knuckles growing white.

"For some people, being a troll is its own reward. It's not about the result. He just gets off on the process." She crossed the space between them and put her hands in his. "Please don't be mad at me.

I'm sorry. I know I made a mistake, but it didn't seem like a very big deal at the time. I don't need you to solve this for me. I'm an adult."

"I really could use a drink right now." Grey squeezed her hand. His eyes softened.

"Still on the same team?"

"As long as I don't have to wait all day to get my drink." Grey pushed past her, out of the office, closing the door behind him.

"Yeah. I'll be right out." Logan picked up the papers and returned them to the envelope. She put them in her work bag where they'd be safe.

Alone in the office, the clock ticking on every drink at the bar, she didn't have time to lasso her emotions into one bundle and set them aside. The anger at Meldrick for taking surveillance photos of her, making her feel uncomfortable in her own yard, was just a spark. If she gave in to it, the inferno would eat her alive. And she would not let that man drive a wedge between her and Grey. She itched to pick up the phone, call Adelle, and savor the emotional rush of unleashing it all. But her patrons would leave if she didn't pull it together.

Grey barely looked at her all night. She sank into her work, keeping her hands busy pouring drinks, scouring surfaces, and dusting every bottle she could grab. The simple act of smiling at patrons and pretending nothing had happened lifted her spirits a little, as long as she didn't look too long at Grey, but at some point, Stuart had appeared next to Arvil with a wad of newspapers. She had no idea how long he'd been sitting there.

"Have I been neglecting you?" She put a napkin in front of him and gave him a regretful smile.

"No, no. Only been here a few minutes. I brought Arvil a copy of his interview." Stuart patted the stack of papers. "It won't be out until the morning, but I figured he'd be here. I'll have a Sam Adams, thanks."

She slipped a glass under the tap. Arvil's story wasn't the headline. He must not have given away any bombshells. Stuart had said he was writing human-interest pieces, but Arvil would have been stupid not to mention the flea market. If only she could read between those lines, she might find a clue as to why he sold that house for so little and why he wanted a flea market so badly.

Her eyes must have lingered too long on the paper, pining for whatever morsels he'd given away. When she put the beer in front of Stuart, he handed her a paper.

"Would you like one? It'll give you an idea of the kind of questions I ask. Sorry I interviewed Arvil first. He was available."

"Sure. Thanks." She wiped a hand on a rag and accepted the paper, doing her best to seem unaffected. "I'll give it a read. And I'll ring you tomorrow. Sorry I didn't get around to it yet."

Stuart shook his head. "No rush. Glad you're willing to sit down and chat."

She left the paper in the office, safe in her bag, until after the last customer left. It was just after two in the morning when she finally sat down to make heads or tails of what she owed Helen, but the article called to her, and she flipped through the pages, her tired feet propped on the desk.

Of course, Arvil mentioned the old mill and his plans, and he gushed for lines about how enamored he was with the landscape and the beauty just outside of town. Rolling her eyes, she refused to believe that Arvil had yearned to own a rural strip of creekside property. Anyone who'd been in his presence for five minutes would know that was a lie. He'd never called anyone *a dear old friend*, let alone Zeb, and it seemed implausible and oddly familiar when he said he was overjoyed to help save such a natural treasure as the old sprawling farm. They weren't her words exactly, but it had been her sarcastic claim when they spoke on the phone.

"*Spectacular views,* my ass. I doubt it."

Putting the paper back in her bag, she texted Grey that she'd be home late. As the faintest gray drove a wedge in the horizon, she finished accounting for every ounce of liquor and every drop of beer she had purchased through the tavern's accounts, leaving no possible way Meldrick could claim she'd stolen a thing. She wrote a note to Helen explaining what had happened and included a check that would bounce and drain her checking account, accruing overdraft fees that would leave her without cash for two more weeks. Even if Helen waited until Friday to cash it, when she got paid, she still wouldn't have enough to cover it, but it was the only thing she could do to put it right, to take the power from Meldrick's hands, before everything went from bad to worse.

The note in her bag and her bag on her shoulder, she locked up the tavern and crossed the lot. Birds picked stray scraps from the dumpster at the hotel across the street. The squeaky wheels of the maid's cart bounced off the buildings, making her cringe. The long hours and emotional exhaustion took the steam out of her legs and her patience. It was just another walk home, she told herself. No longer than any other day. But it felt a thousand miles longer.

The sound of Grey's distant truck made her slow, and her heart warmed. She paused beneath a birch tree as he crossed the creek and slowed to meet her.

"Seems I found me a damsel in distress." He leaned toward the open passenger window.

She climbed in. "Ordinarily I'd scoff at that, but my legs are tired, and I could use a nap. If I let you think I'm a damsel, will you take me home?"

"It'd be my pleasure." Grey made a four-point turn in the road and ferried them back toward the house. "I'm sorry I was grumpy."

"You had a right to be. I paid Helen and sorted out all the accounting. I'm square with the bar. Or I will be when I give this check to Helen. I'll go see her later today." She hugged her work bag to her chest. She wouldn't tell him she was broke. His pity and his money were off limits. This mess was all her fault, and the pieces were hers to clean up. "I never meant to cause any trouble. I'm really sorry this got on you."

"Hasn't gotten on me at all." He steered around the park.

"Not yet anyway. It's all my fault."

Grey put a hand on her knee as he pulled onto their street. "Meldrick's the one causing trouble. Not you."

"Can I borrow the truck later?"

"Sure." He nudged her with his elbow. "Just don't go knocking off any liquor stores." .

CHAPTER TWENTY

Logan knew the lobby of her father's office like she knew her own home. The double glass doors moved silent on approach, and she cringed at her school uniform in her reflection, slowing her walk to pace their aperture. She threw a wave at Hayden who occupied the receptionist's space, and she let her bag fall to the floor as the doors closed behind her. A stack of mail sat on the corner of the front desk, junk her father would collect on his way to the office. He'd skim them as he walked, magazines and sales garbage, and leave them in office trash cans as he made his way across his empire before dragging his leather chair to whatever spot he fancied to get the best view of New York. If the mail was there, he wasn't in yet.

"Where's Dad?" She flipped through the pile. Nothing exciting.

"Lawyers." Hayden untangled her headset from her hair and fiddled with the earpiece. "Should be back soon. You need a ride? I can call you a car."

Logan worked the perimeter. The row of conference rooms was dark. The trophy shelf was spotless. Not a speck of dust on anything, though it was more crowded than before. Plaques and trophies lined up in perfect rows. Her father's partner loved those back-patting self-aggrandizing awards you buy your way into. Dust collectors. She nudged a glass obelisk etched *Developer of the Year* and got a strange satisfaction from the disarray.

"Nah. No, thanks. Elizabeth is meeting me here. Shopping. What's that smell?" Acrid and bitter, the office smelled like a hot mix of construction adhesives and cheap furniture. She wrinkled her nose and peered down a hall. "Are they renovating?"

Hayden spun in her chair to follow Logan's gaze. "Yeah. Again."

"Seriously. If you get cancer from all these fumes, you should sue."

Earpiece nested back in her ear, Hayden leaned forward in her chair. The look on her face said she was dying to share some news without it spreading. As keeper of the keys, Hayden knew what was behind most of the doors.

"They are way overpaying for that project. They ran Josh ragged getting bids on everything, and you know how they always go for the lowest bidder then demand more work for less pay, but this was—"

Logan put up a hand. Her father's business bored her to tears, and office drama was the least of her concerns. "No offense, but I don't want to know. I can create my own anxiety. Besides, I'm not much of an office carpet enthusiast."

Hayden turned back to her computer, wiggling the mouse to rouse the screen from its sleep. She scrolled through a calendar. "Your dad should be back soon unless he stops somewhere on the way. You want to wait in his office? It doesn't stink back there."

Logan was two steps down the hall already.

"Thanks," she called out over her shoulder.

Following her father's well-worn path through the office, she moved faster than he did. He loved to make *his people* squirm. He got a kick out of it when they loosened their ties and straightened their desks, turning off their monitors. Logan hated the way they looked at her, sometimes like a kid and sometimes like their boss. But she waved at William on the way by, his giant old calculator still at the edge of his desk. Accounting felt safe when she was a kid. Numbers never lied like fairy tales did. And William would give her a chocolate bar and let her sit at his desk and color while he clicked and clacked and paper spooled from the calculator, and they'd sing along with the radio until her dad came to whisk her away.

William's tie was tight as always, his thinning hair smoothed across his dome. And he gave her the same gap-toothed grin as always as she bounded down the hall, but something in it looked empty this time.

She turned the corner, the ticking of typing and rattling of printers fading. The executive end of the office was still. Like Hayden predicted, the smell of carpet adhesives was absent.

"He's got your name on the door now."

Logan spun to find her dad's partner leaning in his office doorway, apple core in his hand. juice fell from his wrist and landed on the rug.

"Really?"

He pointed with his apple, and a drip of juice fell from his wrist and landed on the rug.

A little brass name plate, just like her father's, was affixed to the wall beside a closed door. He hadn't mentioned it.

"A little early, isn't it?" She scowled.

"Foundation. That's what he said to me anyway."

"Yeah. But I don't graduate until June." And it was only October. Her sights were set on Coachella in April and the four years she'd have to put in at college. "What about Yale?"

She turned, but he was gone, back to his desk.

His apple core thudded into a trashcan. "It'll still be here after Yale," he said.

She nudged the door open with her hip. It was heavy and windowless, giving her tons of privacy. Inside was bright white. Cream colored carpet tucked under white wood trim—real wood, not rubber like the front offices. A big solid desk and a brown leather chair were the only furniture in the room. She could picture the walls covered with art, and a little shelf of plaques she actually earned.

The door clicked to a soft close behind her. If it were anything like her father's door, it would slam with a deafening bang if she flung it hard enough, but it felt like a place she shouldn't be. Like snooping for Christmas presents in November. She tiptoed to the window and peered down at the street.

New York looked like a different world from the sixteenth floor. People running around with shopping bags, streaming out of buildings and hopping into cabs. The choreography was fluid and perfect the way movie scenes were, but there was no soundtrack. No horns, no music streaming from stores, no one yelling. The distance from the ground below was isolating. And a cold block of steel formed in her chest with the realization that her freedom would be short lived. She'd be looking down on that street longingly for the rest of her life if she didn't love what she was doing.

She sat on the corner of the desk, her school skirt skimming her knees, and the city unfurled before her. Old tenement buildings, butcher shops, jewelry stores, and fancy apartments. As ecosystems went, New York had too much and not enough of everything. It was either opulent and over-made or desperately in need. She chewed the inside of her lip, wondering where her place would be when the door was closed on her college days and the slog of adulthood nine to five began. Somewhere along the way, she'd work with her father to steer the foundation, to write out a mission statement and fulfill it. She'd pick charities that would further her goals and work with them to raise funds among her father's rich friends. They needed a tax write-off. Her father needed the networking. But the city needed more than she could compute.

It was a good future to have, much more solid than anything Elizabeth or Julie had to look forward to. They all fretted about Ivy League applications, but Logan had a road map to follow. And it would do some good in the world, change some lives for the better.

The door flung open behind her, and Elizabeth's head rounded the door. "You ready?"

Logan held onto the leather chair and hopped from the desk. "Yeah."

Elizabeth strolled across the room and gripped the window ledge. "Your name's on the door. Fancy. And look at this view."

"Yeah, well." Logan grabbed her backpack. "No big deal."

"What do you mean, no big deal? Real people don't get this, Lo. I don't know what I'm going to do for a living, but my name won't be on a door, and what I wear to Coachella will probably be the only decision I get to make after graduation. The people look so small from up here."

"It's all a part of the way my dad does business."

"I thought you were going to run a charity." Elizabeth pushed away from the window.

Logan led her into the hall, closing the door behind them. "A foundation. It's just a line of back scratching, that's all. He hires a concrete company to pour a foundation. They make a profit. They give money to our foundation to use as a tax write-off, which ensures they stay in dad's good graces, so he'll pass more work their way. The foundation gives money to organizations that need buildings, and they hire us to do the work."

Logan sped up the pace as they passed a cluster of people in the break room digging into a cake. Someone's birthday or an anniversary. Balloons were tied to the back of a chair.

"Thing is, it's not about doing a good job," Logan said. "It's not about hiring a small business or supporting the economy or any of those noble economic things we learn about. This is about a network of trust. You're either in it, or you're not. You think you'll be out of choices? I'm just a cog in a machine I don't even want to be in. I just hope any good I'll get to do is actually good."

She waved at Hayden as they marched out the door.

"Must be nice to have a network, though. And that office. I could die happy in a room like that."

Logan took a deep breath of city air as soon as the sun hit her face. "If that's your idea of a happy place, you really need to see more rooms."

CHAPTER TWENTY-ONE

Logan hated driving with the window down, but the crisp air was worth being lashed with stray strands of hair. She squinted in the sun, vowing to buy a pair of sunglasses when her income matched her aspirations. A small traffic jam of two cars in the roundabout gave her pause to smell the trees.

Grey's truck was the only vehicle she'd ever driven, and sometimes she'd glance down at smaller cars and wonder what it would be like to zip around that circle in something nimbler than a boat on wheels.

Over the creek, between the rows of matching houses, she came to a stop at the red light, the rumbling engine and grumbling exhaust echoing off the brick tavern that was closed for the morning and wouldn't open until she unlocked the door in the afternoon. She breathed deep, filling her lungs with the air that only rose from the town in those days of transition. It seemed to make the whole of Ramsbolt slow down a little, walk a little slower and take their time, but it always stirred an urgency in Logan to squirrel away comforts for the long winter ahead, to soak up outdoor pursuits before they were too cold to bear. But it didn't feel constrictive or at all like the decay the yellowing leaves promised. That crisp air was freedom and newness, the promise of better things coming.

She held the blinker stalk down with her hand, primed to turn left when the light turned green. If she let it go, it would snap back up, just another thing on Grey's list of repairs to make when life calmed down. But life never seemed to calm down.

The light turned red, and she slipped out of town.

The trees closed in on the street as it contracted, growing slender, and the shoulder disappeared. Two lanes became one, and the dividing line faded between them. The shoulders diminished into gravel ruts that sloped toward the ditches where snow would thaw and rains would flow. Mere miles from Main Street but a lifetime away, her hands went clammy with the familiar prickling chill that compelled her to turn back whenever she strayed too far from town. Bear and moose and rutting deer weren't the sum of the fears instilled in her by tavern chatter. Worse were the tales she dismissed as urban legends of reclusive rural mad men who lurked at the ends of dirt roads.

A guardrail appeared at a gap in the trees, the only sign that the street crossed a creek at all. She slowed as it came into view, following Arvil's directions, and turned right down the little dirt road. It opened to a clearing, the short end of a long stone building peering out from the tall grasses that licked at the foundation and a giant water wheel rotting at the water's edge. The truck shimmied as it crept across the low grass, lumbering over rocks.

It smelled different out here, like the earth, the trees, and the air were all the same thing, wet rocks, and moss in every molecule. As nature went, it was serene, and it sounded nice, but as retail locations went, it was a little remote. It almost seemed a shame to ruin it all by putting in a parking lot.

She breathed deep and squinted through the windshield, steering through shaded puddles. "What could Arvil possibly see in this place? Or Grey? What a mess."

The further she bumbled from the road, the more the whole thing made sense. It would take a lot of pipes and faucets to fix this place and make it viable. Grey would benefit from the work. If Arvil accepted less than the house was worth in exchange for a deal on the plumbing, her house was less a home and more like a bargaining chip. The handshake deal came into view as the truck lurched around a copse of pines.

Her phone rang in her pocket. She steered through the clearing and let the truck slow to a stop behind the stand of trees, grateful she had a signal this far from town. Listing to the side, she snagged her phone as she cut the engine. It was Helen.

"I got your note on the door, dear. You should have knocked." Helen's voice was stern, disappointment dripping down the line.

Logan rubbed at a worn spot on the steering wheel, bracing for a sign that she'd let Helen down for the second time in recent days. "I didn't want to wake you."

"I very much would have liked to discuss this with you."

She swallowed hard against the lump in her throat and closed her eyes, letting the sun warm her face through the windshield. A fly buzzed through the open window, landing somewhere on the dash. "I'm sorry, again. I wasn't thinking." She didn't mention Meldrick's threats, and she vowed never to regret their omission.

"This is not how things are done. You can't just make personal purchases like that on the account without talking to me."

"I know. I was busy doing purchasing that day, and I threw the order together. It won't ever happen again. I'm sorry."

The silence from Helen's end of the line was painful. Her palms sweated as she fumbled for the words to repair the damage. Helen was like a grandmother to her.

"I imposed on your kindness. How do I make it up to you?" Logan winced.

Helen's sigh rattled the line. "I'll cash the check today, like you asked. And I'll see you next week. I know you have a lot going on with the house. I just hope things even out soon."

"They will. They have. I'm sorry." It would leave her with next to nothing in her account when Helen cashed the check, but it would be worth it to have it behind her.

"On a nicer note, what do you have going on today? Working on the house?"

"Just errands." She couldn't lie, not to Helen, but she couldn't tell the truth either. Sneaking around Arvil's property would only call for an explanation, and she didn't have one to give.

"No rest for the weary." Helen must have been making breakfast. A microwaved beeped and a plate scraped a counter. "I will see you next week, then, dear."

The call ended, and Logan hopped from the truck, lighter for the relief. She pushed the door shut with her hip to avoid a slam from being heard by the wrong ears, however distant they seemed.

The old mill was long, solid as the rocks it was made from, with windows from a more recent era nested into openings meant for something more rustic. If the building weren't two stories on the inside, it could have been considering its height. The roof was obscured by leaves, moss, and pine needles, and without seeing it from both sides, it was anyone's guess how stable it was. And the whole thing was streaked with vines and hardly the picturesque setting Arvil gushed over in the newspaper.

She rounded the corner and eyed up the entrance, fading red paint flaking and damp. Ghosts of old latches peppered the double door, paint lines and unpatched holes where bolts once adhered weak security measures. A truck could fit through them if they opened at all. Pressing the latch and giving a tug, the door let go and inched open, and hot, wet air made its mad escape. The path leading to the door was low enough that the door left no fresh marks when she opened it, a sign both good and bad. No one would know she had been inside, but no one else had left traces either.

The hair stood up on the back of her neck, and she slipped into a pool of air so thick her long-sleeved T-shirt grew heavier. She wiped her clammy palms on her denim shorts, wishing she'd worn pants.

The darkness smelled of old cars and rocks, and light from the windows fell on shredded leather belts that hung in tatters from the ceiling. Levers dangled from the roof, large hands reaching down to shake with the past. She remembered a childhood field trip to some historic mill, a man in oilcloth overalls using levers to move the belts around. They looped around pulleys and grasped machines that were reduced to piles of wood and rust on the ground.

From what she knew of the mill's past, it had been used to make fabric of some sort. She could make out the shape of lathes and large bobbins made of wood. There were old frames that spun threads and giant crates of old spools, and the old soundtrack of some history class education film played back in her head, clicking and clacking.

It was hard to imagine the space cleaned up, divided into stalls, and smelling like fried food. And it was hard to imagine it would be done in her lifetime. She'd seen her fair share of colossal renovations, however, and she knew that money and persuasion could move mountains. If only she could have grabbed the Logan of the past by the shoulders and warned her that one day she'd look forward to opening a stall in a flea market, she'd have been kinder to the office her father tried to give her. Or would she?

A long table rested along the wall, stretching beneath a bank of fogged and mildewed windows. She tested it, shaking it, and finding it sturdy, she ran a hand across the surface. Dusty but not dirty, it was safe for sitting. Placing her palms on the worn surface, she hopped up, crossed her ankles, and took it in. All of it. The balmy air and motes of dust. The sounds that only lived on in the imagination. It must have taken a hundred people to run a place like this. What had happened to them all?

"What the hell does Arvil want with a place like this?"

There was a sadness to the still air that thickened with the awareness that those who work there probably lost it all when whatever industry propped it up came tumbling down. What happened to them, and where did they go? She'd like to imagine the men in oilcloth coveralls and the women working at the machines had plenty of warning, that they built new lives, even better lives, and never scraped to make ends meet. The air seemed less muggy when she imagined a boss who gave them fair warning. It's more than her father ever did.

The table creaked as she shifted her weight.

If she'd known back then what her father was up to, would she have squirreled away money to prepare like her mother did, or would she have stood her moral ground? Did she even have the same moral ground back then? Of course, when the FBI came calling it all seemed temporary. It hadn't even seemed real when she got off the bus at the edge of Ramsbolt. For months it had felt like a waiting game.

"Who cares?" Her voice echoed in the large hall. "You wouldn't want to go back there anyway."

She swung her feet and grains of dust scattered in the light.

She didn't want to go back, but it did feel like unfinished business lurked in the past. As if she hadn't properly closed the doors and boarded the windows. A giant piece of who she was never really formed properly, because the lessons she was supposed to learn from the life she was living back then just stopped in the middle of class.

The unmistakable sound of car tires cut the silence, treading the earth. They came to a stop at the door. The driver cut the engine, and she leapt from the table. Stuart, no doubt, coming by to take pictures for an article. From where the car stopped, whoever was driving couldn't have seen Grey's truck parked behind the stand of trees.

She brushed grime from her shorts and wiped her palms together, skirting the remains of a rusty heap of machinery and aiming for the door to greet him. Excuses flashed like fireflies. If Grey had a shady handshake deal with Arvil, Stuart was bound to find it. Maybe he already had. Her being there, wandering around, wouldn't make anything easier.

Scanning the shadows, her muscles twitching, she was caught between making herself known, justifying herself, and hiding. Turning toward the door, she passed a cracked window. It wasn't Stuart. It was Meldrick, circling the building.

He couldn't be up to anything good, and nothing good would come from him finding her there. She paced the dusty concrete floor and shook the tension from her hands, ducking behind a half wall of wood crates full of old spools. A rusted machine two feet taller than her made a shadowy corner, and she huddled there, making use of the darkness.

His footsteps crunched on gravel, a sound that gnawed at her insides. What would she say if he discovered her there, crouching behind old crates? He'd never believe that Arvil sent her or that her intentions were good. He considered her honesty suspect. Her curiosity wouldn't earn her favors. He would figure it out, that Arvil and Grey had formed an alliance. Her whole world would come crashing down.

No, she'd tell him the truth, that she was just curious what the old place looked like. Rehearsing the words, it became a mantra. *Just curious. Gorgeous old building. Just looking around.*

His steps passed the door and retraced their path. She slipped against the wall, careful not to make a sound, ducking beneath a window. Four paces. Five. He was getting farther away. Grit on the floor stung her palms as she braced herself, giving into the urge to know where he was. A few windows down, he aimed his phone at the building.

He's taking pictures. What for?

Crunch. Crunch. Pause.

She ducked beneath the window again, her back to the wall, eyes wide. Her heart thundered, and she strained to hear past the throbbing in her ears.

Crunch. Crunch.

A rush of sweat streaked down her back, itching her spine. She rubbed the back of her neck, leaving a cool streak of filth that served as a fragile release, an anchor to the moment as the darkness of lightheaded swoon washed over her. She clamped a hand over her mouth to silence her breathing, not daring to stand or make a sound.

A car door slammed, and the engine started with a roar. She winced when the transmission engaged and only let out the breath she held when the wheels gnawed at the gravel and the car got quiet, further, and then it was gone. Nothing but birds, the trickle of the creek, and the pounding of her heart.

She wrapped a hand around her throat, swallowing hard to relieve her dry mouth. This stupid dispute she'd found herself in made no sense at all. She didn't even know what she was hiding from, but she couldn't leave just yet. Not until Meldrick had a good head start.

Counting her breaths, she steadied her heart, but anger swept in with the tide.

She cursed Ramsbolt, with its stupid rules and way of life and its small-town ways. It might be home, but she didn't have to like it. Maybe in a few years, Grey would get tired of the hassles and routine, and he'd be willing to start a new life somewhere else without these stupid games, but with another breath, the tide went out again. How could he put her in this position, knowing what she went through? She trusted him.

There were Meldricks and Arvils everywhere, and she never thought Grey could be one of them.

No, she was being emotional.

Wiping her face, sweat mixed with the grit on her hands.

"I hate this place." She spit her words. "I just want to go live in a condo somewhere by a beach and never talk to another human again. Why is everything always so shady?"

She rubbed her cheek on her shoulder and pulled her phone from her pocket. Hands shaking in anger, her fingers itched to dial Grey and scold him for choosing some gluttonous handshake with Arvil when he knew how she felt about stupid business drama.

"No, don't say anything you'll regret. Just get out of here and go hang out with Adelle or Penny." She shook the tension from her hands. "They'll think this is hilarious."

But it shook out the old familiar feeling that something better could be out there, that there was somewhere she belonged, someplace calm without subtext and drama and schemes you had to see through to survive.

A gust of crisp air pushed through the open doors, rustling fodder, and stirring the trees. It brought with it a squall of reason. Everything had been off lately. It wouldn't be like Grey to turn on a dime like that. He would talk to her about it, wouldn't he? She couldn't call and accuse him of some vast conspiracy with Arvil. But she did have to talk to him.

The first step was to get up off that grimy concrete.

She pulled up one knee and tried to stand, but her foot slipped on the powdery floor. She reached out for a rusty bar that jutted out from the decayed machine at her side, searching for purchase, and with a deafening clamor, the pile crumbled, wood clattering against ringing steel as the pieces slammed to the floor around her.

Raising her arms to cover her head, she drew in her legs too late. The steel frame of an alien machine, oxidized to a cinnamon brown, pinned her left ankle in a narrow void between fallen wood and the cold concrete floor. She screamed out in pain and pulled on her leg with both hands, but her ankle was trapped in the unforgiving vice. Shoving on the pile of rubble, it wouldn't budge. With a second push, its weight shifted. Creaking metal and rubbing planks teetered overhead.

"Oh no. No, no, no, no."

Begging wouldn't quell the onslaught.

Loose lengths of wood, old shelves, and boards tumbled down on her. She raised her arms in defense as tubes rained down—the last spray of munitions in a ruthless assault. A thick plank of dense wood cracked into the back of her head and pain seared. Another crashed into her shoulder. The room went dark, fireworks exploding in the night. Clenching her jaw and bracing against the pain, she covered her head with her hands. Sucking in air between her clenched teeth, she couldn't see but could hear the unsettled mass of metal and wood groaning and clattering as it tumbled down. Hair tangled in her fingers, she squeezed her head tight, hunching, bracing for impact.

Metal tubes rained down. One the diameter of her index finger punctured her left leg. She heard the scream as if someone else were calling out for relief as hot pain bolted up her thigh. A spray of blood erupted from the wound and pooled on the floor, mixing with the dirty and ancient wood shavings. She clamped a hand around the pipe. Pulling it would be a bad idea. Her ankle pinned and leg pierced with no way out, her breath quickening and out of control, she steadied the metal with one hand and searched her front pocket for her phone. But it was gone, out of reach, cast aside in the chaos. It was feet away, perhaps too far, but she had to try. Screaming out in pain, hot blood gushing between her fingers, she shimmied and reached, her fingers inching across the floor. The pool of blood grew beneath her.

"God damn it. Grey. Oh my God." She gasped and choked on each word. "Please. Please. I can't reach it."

There was no way to rest. Nothing to lean on. She begged and pleaded, but the phone wouldn't oblige. She cursed the day she turned off voice recognition. Why did she have to hate technology so much?

The pool of blood grew bigger, hotter, wetter beneath her, staining her shorts.

Nothing was close enough or light enough to use as a lever to help her reach the phone. Her hand sifted over the rubble of wood and rust, but nothing budged.

With a gasp, she filled her chest with air, and she let it out with a lunge. If she could reach her phone, it would all be okay.

Hot, sharp pain shot up her leg and into her hip. It coursed a vein up her side to heart and into her head where it spiraled and swirled, and without any warning, the lights went out.

CHAPTER TWENTY-TWO

The world came back in splotches of white, twisting in a nauseating spiral, and Grey's voice cut the ringing in Logan's ears. He was calling someone a wuss. Her mouth watered, stomach contents knocking on the door, and she clenched her eyes tight. She wasn't drunk, but she had the spins.

Wiggling her toes, she tried to free herself from the scratchy, starchy sheet, but her ankle was sore, wrapped tight in a bandage. It would take more effort than she could muster. Had she fallen down the stairs? Focusing all her might on her left knee, her effort to bend it was thwarted by the numbness and a hint of distant pain. Her knee belonged to someone else. Maybe that person at the foot of the bed.

She opened her right eye enough to let in some light. Red curls took shape against white wall.

"Penny." Her throat was sore and dry.

Grey leaned over her, close, and her eyes lost focus. "Hey, you. Welcome back."

"Where'd I go? Thirsty."

Penny got closer, and Logan's eyes fought to focus. "Not yet. We'll get you water in a second." To Grey, she said, "I rang for the nurse."

She clamped her eyes shut again. Feet shuffled into the room, rubber soles on a smooth floor. Someone slipped her finger into a plastic clamp.

"Spinning. Am I drunk? What happened?"

"You decided to eat some rust. All that time I spend around pipes," Grey said. "And you're the one who gets impaled by one."

"Lucky me." The old mill. She reached down, the bandage on her thigh thick and soft.

Grey slipped into a chair at her side. "You have stitches."

"I can't feel it. How many?"

Her eyes landed on Penny, of whom there were two. As the shapes merged, she could make out the glasses on her friend's face. "Fifteen. It didn't go all the way through, but it tore some muscle fascia."

"Lot of blood." Her arms were too weak to push herself up.

The nurse pulled a machine closer and pressed buttons. "Not enough to need a transfusion. You'll be okay after you heal up and the meds wear off."

"Where am I? Can I sit up?"

"You're in Colby." The nurse abandoned the machine long enough to hand Grey the bed controls. He pressed a button, and she slowly raised.

"We need one of these at home." She reached for the controls, but he swatted her away.

"We really don't."

The nurse and Penny exchanged quiet chatter at the foot of the bed. Logan couldn't make out all the words, but she gathered she'd had a tetanus shot. The nurse left the room with a promise to return with water.

"When can I get up and walk?"

Penny pinched and snapped at the hair tie on her wrist. "As soon as your body tells you to. Not right now, though. You've had a local."

Grey wound his fingers in hers, and she squeezed his hand back as well as she could.

"What were you doing out there, anyway?" he asked.

"Arvil's interview. I just wanted to see the place. I was wondering what my shop could look like."

"Was it worth it for you? Because it scared the crap out of me."

"Grey." Penny shuffled. "She needs to relax."

"No shit she needs to relax. She's been acting insane for weeks. She could have got herself killed, and I'm supposed to act like this is a miracle?"

"Stop, guys." The world still hadn't come back into focus. "How did you find me?"

Grey cleared his throat. "When you didn't show up for work, Dan texted Helen. She said she'd just talked to you, but Dan told her he saw your truck head toward the old mill a few hours before."

"Then Helen called me." Penny shuffled her weight at the end of the bed. "Her gut said something was wrong. She didn't want Grey to panic, and she knew I was around because the shop is closed on Tuesdays. So, I drove out to the mill and found your truck. You were lying under a pile of crap with your leg pinned and…" She waved a hand at Logan's thigh. "Your leg, pinned. I called Grey and told him to meet me here. Then I called the ambulance. You had a little surgical procedure to pull it out of your leg. Do you remember calling me Mom?"

"No. That's kind of funny, though." Logan ran her left hand across her forehead, and the back of her hand pinched where the saline needle was stuck. Anesthesia, sutures, a hospital bed, a tetanus shot. Panic rose within her, giving her the strength to push up in bed. She tried to swing one leg off the side, but the monitors were hooked to wires stuck to her everywhere and that stupid needle in her hand hurt like hell. "This is going to cost so much. Does Arvil know?"

Grey raised his shoulders, brow pinched. "I doubt it. Why would he know?"

Penny folded her arms and lowered her chin, a serious expression set on her face. "I can assure you that Arvil is not going to go climbing around in there."

To Logan, she looked every bit the confident doctor she'd studied to be, but how could she know that? "Why not? The last thing we need is for him to sue us for trespassing or ruining his property or some dumb thing."

Penny shook her head. "Nope. He already asked me to go in there and pull out anything valuable, because it's too dusty and gross for his liking. As if I'd know. He's not going in there."

"She's right." Grey smoothed the rough blanket over Logan's arm. "He'll pay someone to demo that interior before he'll go in there."

But Logan's fears weren't quelled. Life was hard enough already with Meldrick causing problems and all their work on the house. If her being at the mill created more problems for Grey, she would never forgive herself. "Stuart was there, though. Taking pictures."

"Did he see you?" Penny shoved her hands in her pockets. "Was it before or after you became a voodoo doll?"

"I don't remember. Everything is fuzzy. Can I go home now?"

She grabbed Grey's arm, and he pushed her back. "One thing at a time. You are not going home until they tell you."

Gathering his shirt in her fist, she tried to pull him close but only managed to stretch the fabric a bit. "I can't afford this. I need to go. You didn't tell them who I am, did you?"

He wrinkled his nose and smiled down at her. "You're adorable when you're drugged up. Penny and I have everything under control. Your job is not to make our job difficult."

She gave up under the weight of his hand on her shoulder and sank back into the hospital bed. The mattress wasn't as soft as the one at home. She didn't want to take it with her after all.

The nurse came back with a cup of water and placed it in Logan's shaky hand. "You got it? I don't want to let go until you're sure."

"I got it." Logan pounded it like a beer and held the empty cup to the light. "Can I have more?"

The nurse pressed buttons on the machine and motioned to the sink. "Your knight in shining armor can refill it from that sink over there."

Grey took the cup from her hand, and she stared at her fingers. "What did you give me?"

"Morphine," the nurse said. "Do you have any pain?"

"No. I want to go home."

She spun the monitor back to the wall, out of the way. "As soon as the doctor signs off on it. We'll set you up with some prescriptions. You can pick them up at the pharmacy downstairs on your way out."

Penny thanked the nurse and followed her out of the room, engrossed in some talk about vascular things and stuff that made Logan's stomach lurch. Grey stood and rounded the bed.

"Where are you going?" she asked. "Don't leave."

Grey reached into his front pocket. "Give me your hand. The left one."

Her fingers were swollen from the saline. Grey fought her wedding finger back onto her hand. "I took this off when you went in for a cat scan."

"How much does a cat scan cost?"

"Stop worrying about it."

The morphine must have been making her eyes runny. She wiped hot tears away with the back of her hand.

"Do you remember exactly what happened?" Grey returned to the other side of the bed, back to the chair.

"No. Flashes of things. Stuff falling." She couldn't remember her leg being hurt, and it would be just fine with her if she never did. But she did remember the promise she made to herself to stop feeling like Ramsbolt was a temporary waypoint on a trip to somewhere better.

"Grey?"

"Yeah?"

"I wanted to tell you something, but I forgot. I'd marry you all over again."

"I'd marry you again, too. Can you please stop looking for drama, now?"

"Yeah. I promise."

CHAPTER TWENTY-THREE

Logan clutched her stomach, the coarse grit of wedding dress lace sticking to her sweating palm.

"I've been here for three years, and this is my first time inside this church. Except for rehearsal. That seems weird." She tugged a tissue from the box and wiped her hand. Better not to smear sweat on Adelle's dress. She felt bad enough borrowing it as it was. "Is it hot in here, or is it just me?"

Penny stuck another bobby pin in Logan's hair, securing her brown waves in a low chignon. "Not just you. It's as hot as Hades."

The whole day was uncomfortable: the room was too hot, the metal chair was hard, the lighting was terrible. Her reflection in the mirror was dark and ruddy. Like she'd just run a mile. The stupid corset she ordered online was half a size too small, leaving her painfully aware of her ribs and lumbar spine. Everything leading up to that moment had been a series of leaps from faith to faith, and as she blinked at herself in the mirror, she wasn't sure whether all of them had been bad choices or if only one or two had spoiled the lot. She wouldn't regret marrying Grey, but none of it was what she imagined for herself. Not that she'd fantasized about her wedding day, but she'd pictured something bigger. One of those European rental castles or an island in the Maldives. She didn't need or want to elaborate, really. Their relationship was more important than the wedding. But something about her drugstore makeup scattered on an old folding table in an upstairs room at the Ramsbolt Methodist Church made her feel further from home than she'd felt in a long time.

She tapped her foot to let off some steam.

"Sit still, Lo." Penny yanked the lid off a tube of lipstick and held it out. "You're shaking the table. Here."

Logan leaned forward and applied it, blinking at herself in the mirror propped against the wall. The corners were spattered with the torn remains of stickers.

"Do I look red to you? It's the lighting, isn't it?"

From behind, Adelle winced at Logan's reflection in the mirror. "Definitely the lighting."

Penny clicked the lid back on the lipstick and glanced at the time on her phone. "Six minutes. I know you were about to ask. Are you freaking out?"

"Yes, I'm freaking out. Look at me. I'm in a wedding dress." She leapt from her chair, and it scraped the concrete floor. "I'm in a children's room in a tiny church, putting on lipstick I bought at a dollar store. I can't even see what I look like under this 1970s light bulb. My parents aren't here. I'm marrying a plumber. And I love all of this, but sometimes I feel like I'm in the wrong place, and I really just want to go home."

She smoothed her dress. It wasn't even a wedding dress. It was a white spaghetti strap sundress with a lace overlay that Adelle found in a thrift store a decade ago and never wore because Ramsbolt was so damn small that she never had anywhere to go while wearing it. It was borrowed. Everything about the day felt like it belonged to someone else.

Adelle crossed the room and spun Logan to face the ground-level window.

"Listen to me." She squeezed Logan's hands. "He's not just a plumber. He's Grey. He's your soulmate. If all that stuff never happened, and your dad hadn't gone to jail, you wouldn't have ended up here. You wouldn't know us or Grey."

"I know. I don't mean to sound ungrateful that the universe put me here. This is where I'm meant to be, and I wouldn't want it any other way. It's just that some days…" She pushed the chair under the table and pulled her makeup into a pile. Penny stopped her by snagging eyeshadow palettes.

"You don't have to worry about this stuff," Penny said. "It's your day. Let me take care of this for you."

Logan let her arms fall to her sides. "I have to do something."

"It's only a few minutes." Adelle spun her around. "You look great. Your mascara isn't even clumpy. He's going to lose his mind when you walk down the aisle."

"But I'm walking down the aisle alone." Her breath hitched, and she blinked up the dim bulb in case any tears started to well. "I don't want to talk about it."

Penny set the lipstick aside. She closed the lid of Logan's pink

Caboodle and snapped it shut. "You don't have to—"

"I know. The more I talk about it—"

"That's not what I mean." Penny dug a bottle of champagne and three plastic glasses from a tote bag. She yanked out the cork and poured.

"She means walk alone." Adelle nudged Logan with her elbow. "Someone can walk with you."

"Who?"

Penny handed her a bubbling glass. "Arvil?"

"Funny." Logan sipped. "I haven't eaten anything since that banana at breakfast. Too much of this and you'll be dragging me down the aisle."

"I think she's getting it." Adelle held out her drink to Penny, and they clinked plastic flutes.

"You're trying to get me drunk?"

Adelle checked her hair in the mirror, tucking a brown curl behind her ear. "No. We're trying to say you're not alone."

"I always feel alone." She plucked her flowers off the table, blue hydrangea and white roses with little sprigs of Queen Anne's Lace all tied together with a glossy green ribbon. They were Adelle's doing. The evening they spent looking at pictures of flowers on the internet was one of Logan's favorite parts of wedding planning.

"I have friends here, yeah. I love you guys. And there's Grey, of course. But I feel alone. You all have this shared history."

"Not me. I don't." Penny killed the last of her drink and dropped the plastic glass in her tote bag.

"But at least you get this place. You know how to get to Colby.

You guys can spend hours in Target looking at things. I don't know my way around this world like you guys do. Did you know there's a Starbucks in there? I just learned that, like, a week ago. And it's not just Ramsbolt being small. This is a whole lifestyle I didn't grow up in. Getting married just feels like a giant commitment to this thing that isn't me. I know I'm not going back to that life, and I don't really want to. This is just a giant door closing between two worlds. I can't ever go back. No matter what happens, that door is closed forever."

Adelle looked at her phone. "Two minutes." She kicked the chair out from under the table and pushed Logan into it. "Look at me. If there's some massive miracle and you suddenly become the richest woman in the country again, you can take us with you. But even if you don't, you already chose. You chose us when you stepped off that bus. You chose us when you gave up your anonymity to save the bar. You chose us when you decided Helen deserved better. You chose us when you thought Arvil was doing the town a disservice, and you had to wrestle that bar from his hands. You choose us every single day. And all of us chose you a long time ago."

"I know." Nobody knew better than Logan how much she wanted to belong. Yes, Ramsbolt was a backward little town sometimes, pushing away new things that could make their lives better and easier. They would stand around and complain about the broken clock and giant potholes that never got fixed, and it drove her nuts until she realized that all those little flaws weren't cracks. They were glue that held the town together. And she wanted to be a part of it. Ramsbolt never pushed her away.

Tears threatened to well behind her lashes, and with seconds to spare, she couldn't let them fall. She stood and smoothed her skirt, checked her makeup in the mirror, and grabbed her flowers. "You're right. It's just cold feet."

Penny grabbed a tissue. "Just in case," she said, wrapping it around her flowers and hiding it in her hand. "Logan, most people who get cold feet want to flee the country. You? You have cold feet, and your gut is telling you to dig in. I know your old life was amazing. Mine was, too. I think what you're feeling is totally natural. Your parents aren't here. Your childhood friends aren't here. I'm no substitute, but I'm here. Adelle, too."

Logan grabbed her, flowers be damned, and pulled her into a hug. "I know. I love you for it."

Adelle's phone chirped. "It's Heather. She says the chapel is packed. They're ready up there."

"What do you mean the chapel's packed? We only invited fifty people."

"It's Ramsbolt." Penny swished the champagne bottle. Empty. She added it to her tote bag with the rest of the empty cups. "Weddings are open to everyone. The town likes you. They want to see you and Grey get married."

"Weird." She slipped into her white strappy sandals. "I guess this is it. Do we just leave everything up here?"

"No," Adelle said. "You have to carry this tote bag and your pink Caboodle full of makeup down the aisle with you."

Penny pointed up. "And that light bulb. You have to take that, too."

"Something burgled, something blue." Logan followed Adelle

into the hall. Penny closed the door behind them.

They traced the narrow hall to the stairs. Logan descended like a champ in her heels, but Penny and Adelle lagged.

Logan paused at the bottom to wait for them. "I think one of the things that gets me is these unwritten small-town rules. There's this social rank based on how long you've been here and who you know."

Penny laughed. "As if you didn't have unwritten rules in your old world."

"Sure, we did. But I was a kid. I didn't need to pay rent, and all those rules worked out in my favor."

"I've been here forever," Adelle said as she reached the bottom. "The barter economy is great, but it doesn't always pay the bills."

They walked side by side to the chapel door. Heather opened it an inch to peek inside, and she turned back to them with a smile, hand resting on the door pull. "It's packed in there, but nothing to worry about. Just like you asked, there's no Logan side or Grey side. It's one big happy Ramsbolt crowd. Almost looks like Easter service in there. Helen and Arvil are right up front, just like you asked."

"Thanks. Grey's okay?" Logan did her red-carpet check, glancing down at her shoes and the sides of her dress to make sure she hadn't ripped anything or picked up a stain.

"Grey is great. Bottle of nerves, that one. Nate had to remind him to stand still a few times. He might faint when he sees you, but he's doing fine."

Penny stepped in front of her, checked her flowers and her hair. "Are you ready? You're going to knock him dead. You look amazing."

"Thanks," Logan said. "I'm almost ready."

She handed her flowers to Heather, who gave her a quizzical look, then reached behind her and grabbed Penny with her right hand and Adelle with her left, pulling them forward.

"Walk with me." It was a statement, not a question. A demand from some voice deep within her that didn't want to face the town alone. Adelle's deep roots would help her tap her own, and Penny's loud and defiant cementing of herself in Ramsbolt would lend her some credibility. Logan had faced flashbulbs and walls of cell phones at red-carpet events and after drunken club stumbles, but none of that had been half as brittle as the eggshells that lined the path through that chapel.

Adelle squeezed her arm. "You got it. Happy to."

"Making our own rules," Penny said, looping her arm through Logan's. "I like it."

Logan reached out for her flowers. "Thanks, Heather. I'm ready."

CHAPTER TWENTY-FOUR

Logan stopped Grey's truck at the curb outside Stuart's newspaper office. Eight days after surgery and suturing, she was finally venturing further than the mailbox, grateful it was only her left leg, and the truck didn't require use of it. The wound swelled in her jeans, and the stitches itched. She pressed the parking brake with her good foot, slung the bag with her drink kit prototype over her shoulder, grabbed her crutches, and crossed the sidewalk.

Stuart's office was almost as new as his newspaper. Halfway between Nate's Toy Store and Sparky's Small Engine Shop, it filled an old storefront. Newspaper copies tied with string sat in the deep window ledge, yellowing in the sun. Inside, bookshelves in every style and color lined the walls. There must have been a thousand books on the shelves in every size and color. And boxes were stacked in small islands here and there.

Stuart sat at an old metal desk in the corner, beneath the stained drop ceiling. Except for his laptop and a coffee cup, the desk was bare.

"Sorry for the mess." He stood to shake her hand and pull out a chair. "This became an extension of my home. I just store crap here that doesn't fit in the cabin. Please, sit. Do you want something to prop your leg on?"

"No, thanks. I'm good. Glad to be out of the house. I brought you a sample of the drink kits I'm rolling out soon." Sliding the chair out to make room for her leg, which preferred to be straight, she rested the crutches on the floor beside her. "Nice digs."

"I do ninety percent of my work on a computer. I don't have much to fit in here. I'd like to have real chairs to sit in someday. For now, it's these old chairs from Penny's and stuff strewn everywhere." He sifted through the box contents, holding up the recipe card and looking at both sides.

"Thought these chairs looked familiar." She craned her neck to look around. "I expected you to have some big Gutenberg press in here."

Stuart shrugged. "It's all digital files. I don't print anything here. I upload it to a place, and they drop them off the next morning. This is cool. You make the simple syrup, and all the ingredients are in here to make the drink. You're selling these?"

"I will soon." She adjusted in the seat. All the sitting and lying down had irritated her lower back. "They'll be available in Kyle's store to start. You can keep that and make the drink if you want."

Stuart put the contents back. "I'll put it in the article."

"That would be great. Thanks. Are you moving in here or are you going to keep the cabin?"

He rubbed his chin, eyes sparkling. "I really like the cabin. I know that surprises a lot of people, but the cemetery is quiet, and I like the rustic feel of the place. I figure I'll rent out the upstairs either as a small office or an apartment."

"That makes sense." She fidgeted with the truck keys. "What kinds of questions do you have for me?"

Stuart jumped and pulled a notebook and pen from his desk drawer. He flipped through pages. "I have a few questions jotted down, but I find that conversation tends to draw out much more interesting topics. Here." He folded the pages back and laced his hands above the bullet points. She tried to read them upside down, but his handwriting wasn't forthcoming. "Is anything off limits?"

She shifted her weight and propped herself up in the chair. After the fluff piece he wrote straight from Arvil's mouth, she figured Stuart to be malleable. Whether or not he was honest remained to be seen. He'd earned forgiveness from Kyle and Adelle, but that didn't mean she had to let her guard down.

"I don't want to talk about New York. Or anything that came before Ramsbolt."

"Totally off the record." He leaned forward. "To be honest, I was a bit awestruck. First time I went into the bar and saw you, it was like being in the room with news royalty."

Trying hard not to roll her eyes, she fiddled with the hem of her T-shirt instead. She wouldn't be goaded. "Oh, I don't know about that."

"A lot of people would love to interview you. And here I am talking about anything but the elephant in the room." His smile was disarming, but he'd clearly missed the point.

"There's so much more to me than where I grew up or what my family did." Her jaw set and shoulders stiffened, she stared past him at a spot on the wall. "I'm sure you have one question in your notebook that isn't about my father."

"I'm bad at compliments sometimes." Head down, he straightened the notebook on his desk. "I'm not trying to persuade you. I'm a news junkie, and I followed the court case and saw your pictures in the papers. You heard more than your share of vulgar comments, I'm sure, but I read the news with more empathy. I had no idea you even lived in Ramsbolt until I moved here. Sorry if that sounded bad."

She forced her hands to relax on the arms of the chair. "You missed all the kerfuffle after the fire then. The press crawled around here for a day after the competition. Mostly it was hungry bloggers."

He nodded. "I saw. I didn't put the pieces together, though. Not until I went into the bar for the first time."

"You know how I ended up here, then. How about you?"

"A girl. Two girls. Long story." His sad smile said he wanted to talk about his past just as much as she wanted to talk about hers. "Anyway, how did you end up working at a bar?"

"That's a great place to start." She rolled the tension from her shoulders. "It was the first place I came to. I got off the bus, walked into the lobby, and ran right into Riley."

Pen poised over his notebook; Stuart paused. "Is this on the record?"

"Sure." She warmed at the memory of that day, getting off that bus at the edge of the country and walking back to that sad intersection. It had felt hollow at the time, like a scene someone else acted out. She figured she'd make it a month, two at the most, then the court would toss out the charges, and her life would go back to normal. "That bar saved me as much as I saved it."

"You're talking about the fire? I wanted to ask about that night. Not in a hard-hitting *what really happened* way. But what it was like. You were there that night, right?"

"That night plays out over and over again in my head." The spark when she turned off the light. Grey screaming for her to run. Standing across the street and feeling the fire on her face. "It was cool outside, but for as hot as that fire burned, you'd have thought it was the middle of July."

She shivered out of the memory. "I will say that's where Ramsbolt differed from any other community I've ever been a part of. A lot of things weren't insured, and it took a ton of work to get the bar back into shape, but everyone here pulled Helen and I through. You really find out who your friends are at a time like that."

"Understandable. For background, not for the article but for me, Helen was in a tight spot when she lost the bar, right?"

"Yeah. Things were tight for both of us. They'd been getting better, financially speaking, but she would have lost that bar. Arvil… Are we on the record?"

"If you want to be."

"Okay. This is common knowledge around here, anyway. At the time the bar burned down, Helen was behind on rent. The economy here had tanked over the years, and anyone who's ever met Helen will tell you her desire to give to others is stronger than her desire to line her pocket. Arvil wanted to tear the place down and build offices there. Deep down, I suspect he knew all along it was a bad idea. When the competition came along, I had nothing to lose."

"About the competition? I know you don't want to talk about your life before Ramsbolt. Feel free to ignore this if it's too close to all that, but your worlds collided a little that day, didn't they? Your old life and Ramsbolt had a bit of a pileup."

Shaking her head and smiling to herself, she couldn't believe how far she'd come. "I was naive about keeping my old life to myself back then. At first, I thought I'd wait out the storm here for a while. By the time I won that competition, all I really wanted was to belong."

"You seem like a natural fit."

"Appearances can be deceiving. The competition didn't just save the bar. It saved me, too. Without Helen taking a chance on me to begin with, then the bar bouncing back after the fire, I'd have had nowhere to turn. I had no idea where I would go. I probably would have left town. But I'd have just kept running forever. It wasn't until I almost lost Ramsbolt that I realized running wasn't solving anything, and I just wanted permission to stay. No one else gives you permission, though, do they?"

Something she'd said must have struck a chord, because Stuart was smiling at her like he knew what she meant. "Sometimes they do."

"Yeah. They do. I didn't need Ramsbolt to tell me whether I could stay here, but they chose to treat me like I belong. They really did. And sometimes I'm so damn blind that I don't see it."

If it weren't for Grey and if she needed a new roof, would Martin show up? Of course, he would. Or Dan would. He'd drag Bern along kicking and screaming. Maybe she had a more solid footing in town than she thought. Just because she didn't need support every day didn't mean it wasn't there.

Stuart clicked his pen shut and placed it on the notebook.

"Can I ask how you injured your leg? Everyone at the bar misses you something awful. Just between us, Helen's drinks are good, but they're just not as good as you make them."

She couldn't help but grin. "That's nice of you to say. It's nice to be missed, but I don't want that on the record." It wasn't just that she was crawling around on someone else's property or that she had Meldrick to worry about. She didn't want to be seen as a snoop.

He put his hands up. "Oh, sorry. Off the record. I was just curious. None of my business and definitely not for print."

"Thanks. No. It wasn't a big deal. Just stumbled into trouble while wandering around in nature. I saw you that day. You were taking pics out at Zeb's farm." Zeb's farm. Arvil's mill. Same thing. "Were you working on a story down there?"

She hoped he'd say yes and spill the beans on whatever scheme linked that mill to Arvil's flea market and the house Grey bought. But the way he pursed his lips and squinted his eyes at the bad lighting said any links he might have were broken.

"No," he said. "I haven't been out that way...ever." He raised one shoulder.

"Oh. I thought you were there taking pictures of Arvil's new property." Either he was lying, or her memory was faulty.

He shook his head. "Once it's open, for sure. Pictures wouldn't print very well in black and white. I asked Arvil if I could head out there, but he said it's not much to look at. Just a tangle of knotted weeds. Have you seen it?"

"Me? No. I haven't seen it." She was a terrible liar, but she took a stab at it. She looked at the time on her phone. "Well, I have to get this truck back to Grey. It's almost time for my next dose of anti-inflammatories."

"Sounds like fun. When do you go back to work?"

"Two days. Stop by. I'm looking forward to getting back behind the bar."

"I bet. I'll swing by."

With the blood rushing to her leg, it had swelled against her jeans, pressing the stitches against their bandage. She leaned on her crutches more than she had that morning and wished Stuart well as she left his office. It took a few tries to get settled in the truck seat, but her mind was fixed on her fuzzy memory. Had she really seen Stuart at the mill that day? Things were foggy, but that part was so vivid. She started the engine and headed for home.

CHAPTER TWENTY-FIVE

Ten days could have been ten years for all the distance they'd put between Logan and the bar. The skin was tight over her stitches, tugging as she took short strides, dusting off bottles and arranging things the way she liked them. She didn't enjoy putting all her weight on that leg, but she'd refused physical therapy on the grounds that Grey was paying the bills, and the papers they sent home with her said that moving was better than lying around. The crutches were safe in the office if she needed them, but she was determined to get through a night of work without them. Things had to get back to normal. The sooner the better. In the meantime, she was sweating like crazy, strands of hair were plastered to her forehead, and her leg itched like the worst case of hives ever.

She wiped hair from her eyes with the back of her hand and clutched the edge of the sink.

"You okay out there?" Helen yelled out from the office in a tone that said she wouldn't believe Logan no matter how she answered.

Helen had her own way behind the bar, and though Logan could tell she'd taken great strides to keep things tidy, a lot of work lay ahead to get organized for the night. Fortunately, it was town hall night, giving her time to clean up and get organized without spending too much time on her feet.

"I'm good. Just taking it easy before the crowd comes in."

"You picked a good night to come back." Helen shuffled papers in the office, clearing the desk of clutter. "It'll be quiet until the town hall is over."

"All hell will break loose after that, but the rush never lasts long." Logan moved the orange bitters to the left of the Angostura. "I'm really sorry about all of this mess lately. I feel like I've been letting you down. Between the house and..." She caught herself before mentioning Meldrick. Things had been quiet on that front since she got home from the hospital, and if nothing were to come from his threat to expose her for buying alcohol through the bar, then she wasn't going to make Helen worry.

"I think your tenth apology was enough, but I appreciate the sentiment." Helen fanned herself with a catalog and glanced around the office. "I do believe I've put things back in some kind of order."

"It's almost six. You don't want to be late." Logan shuffled bottles in the cooler. It was fully stocked, but the light beers were on the wrong side of the IPAs. "Any idea how long it will last?"

Helen breezed past her as fast as her cane would allow. "There are only two votes tonight, but they're toughies."

"Grey didn't mention anything." Goosebumps ran up her arms. She'd promised to stop looking for drama, but that didn't mean it wasn't out there looking for her. "Is it Arvil's rezoning thing?"

"That, and one for Meldrick. He wants to form an HOA."

Logan slammed the cooler door closed. "Nobody said anything about that to me. Adelle was at my house yesterday. Why didn't she say anything?"

Helen gaped at her, shock at the outburst shadowing over her face. "Well, I don't know, dear. Maybe she didn't think you'd be interested."

"Not interested? It's town business that affects my life. Did you know that Meldrick wants to put my house under an HOA? He wants to be in charge of my whole street. Are you kidding me? Why wouldn't anyone think I'd be interested."

Helen cast a glance at the door. "There was an email. Didn't Grey get the email? He's on the town board. I guess Adelle figured he'd tell you."

"Grey doesn't read email." Logan rolled her eyes at the ceiling. "He doesn't even know what the email icon on his phone looks like." Even if he had gotten an email, he wouldn't have told her anyway.

"Everyone knows Meldrick's a scoundrel. This will all pan out for the best. You'll see. No one ever listens to him." Helen offered her a sympathetic look that Logan couldn't accept.

"Nothing pans out for the best unless someone does something to prevent it." Logan slapped her palm on the bar. "Dammit. Now I'm stuck here, and I can't vote."

"You can vote. Just email Adelle now." Helen inched to the door. "I promise you that everyone will vote in the best interest of the town. In all the years I've known that man, no one has ever trusted him."

She was right. Logan ran the heel of her hand across her forehead.

"I'm just twitchy, I guess. Stupid pain makes me grumpy. I'm surprised no one told me about it, that's all. Adelle was just at the house. I can't believe she didn't tell me."

"I'm sure she just didn't want to worry you while you're recovering. You need to use all your energy to heal up that leg."

"Thanks. I'll email Adelle. Can you tell her when you get there, in case she isn't looking? I want to make sure my vote counts."

"I will. And I'll rush back as soon as the meeting ends to give you a hand." Helen leaned forward, a sly twinkle in her eye. "And to give you the dirt."

"Thanks. What happens next with the flea market?"

Helen raised a shoulder. "Assuming it gets enough votes, the paperwork goes to the state. Then it takes as long as it takes to get it filed. Less than ninety days, I'd guess. As long as there's no opposition."

"Any hint of—"

The door flew open next to Helen, who stumbled out of its way, hand to her chest and her eyes wide. Arvil rushed in before it closed, cheeks and nose a healthy red.

"You damn near gave me a heart attack, Arvil. What could be that important. Rushing in like that. You could kill a person."

Arvil put up a hand like a traffic cop. "Stop. I'm here for Logan."

"Me? What'd I do?" Logan took weight off her leg, leaning against the cooler.

"You have to come to the meeting. You can't be here in an empty bar. You have to stand up on my behalf and say you want the mill rezoned. Are you ready to go? Coat? Jacket? Is that what you're wearing?"

Helen burst into a fit of laughter. "Never thought I'd hear Arvil ask Logan what she's wearing." She slapped him on the back and slipped out the door, shaking her head. "I'll see you there, Arvil."

"I never go to meetings." Logan blinked at him, incredulous. "Why would you think I would go to a town meeting?" The conflict of interest would put Grey in harm's way. Arvil had to know that. And to say something publicly, in front of Meldrick, would be the quickest way to ruin her whole life. She'd just spent the last ten days sitting quietly, not making a stir, so Grey would stop giving her side-eye and wondering when she'd cause another massive snarl in his domestic tranquility.

Arvil gaped back at her, eyes wide and frantic. "I need as many people as possible to stand up and say they'll open stores at the market. I need to prove that rezoning will benefit the town, and I can't do that without some support."

"I have to work, Arvil." Her voice rose an octave. "I can't go all the way to the library like this."

"That's why I came. To drive you there. I need you to stand up for me."

"I can't. No." She turned her back on him, on the whole ordeal.

"You can sit down then. Just get in the car." He waved a hand to the door and froze.

"I can't put Grey in that position. I won't do it. The conflict of interest is far too big. I'm sorry, but I won't be dragged into things like that. I just can't do it."

Arvil crossed the room and placed his hands on the bar as if he thought he could reason with her. "You don't understand."

"Oh, I do. You paid money for the property, and you need it rezoned before it will turn a profit. I'm kind of looking forward to it myself. But I will not go to that meeting and shill for you."

Arvil's face reddened, his eyes narrowed. "Meldrick will have plenty of support. That HOA isn't the only thing on his agenda. You know half the town will believe him when he says the market will siphon business from downtown."

She folded her arms, no intention of budging. She could be just as stubborn as he could, but he had less time to play the game. "You want a drink, or do you have a meeting to get to?"

"Are you making me beg? I need you. Alright? Does that make you feel better?"

They locked eyes, yet another stalemate in their never-ending tug-of-war. He might make her crazy, and he wasn't always a straight shooter, but he never lied about his selfish motivations, and as real estate magnates went, he wasn't the worst. He needed her, and she would support him if Grey's position and her friendship with Adelle weren't factors. Maybe there was a way to help him without stepping too far out of bounds.

"Every time I turn around, you're trying to rope me into something," she said. "Just stand there. Give me three minutes."

Helen had left the laptop on in the office, the faint glow of the screensaver casting colors on the wall. She woke it from its slumber and typed a quick note of support. Though conflicts of interest prevented her from voicing strong support, her history with Arvil proved him to be a man of his word.

The town will benefit from a diversity of retail, from opportunities for even the smallest of businesses, and though his actions may be self-promoting, he has given meaningfully back to the town, and never to my knowledge acted against its best interest.

Arvil may be unconventional, but his intentions are for the good of the economy.

She stopped herself from claiming he had a history of maintaining the properties he owned. Anyone who remembered the tavern fire years before could be forgiven for assuming his negligence contributed.

I believe he will follow through on his promise that the market will make a positive, meaningful contribution to life in Ramsbolt.

She hit print and found an envelope in a drawer while the printer spit out the paper. She sealed it away and wrote Adelle's name on the front.

Waking her phone from its slumber, she sent a quick email to Adelle, voting yes for Arvil's rezoning and no to anything Meldrick asked for.

Using the desk as leverage she left the office and went back to the bar, where Arvil waited with increased impatience.

"What's this?" he asked as she pushed it into his hand.

"I can't leave the bar. I need to be here when people show up. But give this letter to Adelle and tell her to read it out loud. It's the best I can do. And tell her to check her email."

CHAPTER TWENTY-SIX

Stuart was among the last to show up at the bar after the town meeting. He shuffled onto a stool between Grey and Sandy and laid a newspaper on the bar. Together, the three were Logan's town hall barometers. Grey was always among the first to leave the meeting and his arrival at the bar meant the influx was imminent. Sandy locked the doors when it was over, and she signaled the lull. Stuart lingered on the sidewalk, interviewing people from town to gauge reactions. When he showed up, Logan could breathe a little easier. From there, it was refills, cashing out tabs, and cleaning the bar.

Logan had scanned every face throughout the night, searching for anyone who would spill the beans. After any other town meeting, half the people in the bar would be ranting and raving about excess squirrels in the park and the other half would be whining about the diameter of the trees, but now that there were things on the ballot that impacted her life, no one wanted to talk. Grey was the last person she'd ask. He already thought she didn't trust him and had asked her to stop sticking her nose in drama. She didn't want to risk an argument while she was trying to work. And there was no way she could beg Sandy for the minutiae while he was sitting right there. Grey's body language gave nothing away, and he had to know it was driving her crazy. At least it was taking her mind off her leg which felt three times its usual size and throbbed so bad she was sure her jeans would burst.

Stuart waved her over and slid the paper her way. "I brought this for you. Copy of the interview." He yelled over the din. "Comes out tomorrow."

There was no way she'd have time to read it no matter how much her hands itched to flip through the pages and inspect every word. "Thanks. I'll skim it after work."

Sandy leaned across the bar. "I read it. It's great." She aimed a thumb at Stuart who beamed at her side. "He interviewed Helen, too. It's all about how you were the town hero after the fire."

One small flame in her inferno of anxiety died down. At least she didn't have to worry about being dragged in the town paper. "That's nice. Did you like the drink kit I gave you?"

Stuart nodded. "I did. It was fun. Sandy and I made drinks and watched hockey. I talked about it in the article."

She gave him the broadest smile she could muster with the energy she had left, yelling over the chatter of a full bar. "That's kind. I'm glad you liked it. What can I get for you?"

"Gin and tonic, please. Thank you," he said.

Logan filled a highboy glass and garnished it with a lime wedge just as Helen slipped through the parting crowd and crept behind the bar.

"How'd the meeting go? I'm dying to ask." Logan handed Helen a bottle of white and motioned to Penny and Nate. "Mind doing refills?"

"Of course." Helen grabbed the bottle. "The town voted for the market. Arvil is a happy camper."

"It's been so busy I hadn't noticed, but he's not here. I wonder why."

"He was asking Adelle a thousand questions. Driving her crazy."

"Should have known. What about the HOA?"

Sandy leaned toward her. "Oh my God. You should have seen it. Everybody voted against it. He was really mad."

Helen patted her arm. "No one wants a world where Meldrick is in charge of anything."

"Yeah, well. Did he have any evidence of support? Like a list of signatures?" He would have been dumb to present that list, knowing the people who signed it were in the room, and that it had been collected under different pretenses, but nothing would surprise her anymore.

Sandy shook her head and scowled. "Nah. He just got up and rattled off a list of reasons why it would be a great idea. Stuff like unified paint schemes."

Logan tugged her ponytail tighter. "Did he mention anything specific?" Like her house, her plants, or the paint they purchased and set on their own porch for half an hour?

Helen reached past her for an empty beer glass. "He didn't name any specific offenses. He just said that HOAs happen because people want rules and order, but the only disruptive thing going on is

Meldrick."

Logan wasn't buying that it was swatted down that easily. Meldrick was much more strategic than that. Something else was up his sleeve, she just didn't know what. It sent chills up her arms that she brushed away.

She took a silent order from Shawn, who'd ordered nothing but Blue Moon since his twenty-first birthday. "Wouldn't be the first time he caused a panic just so he could fix it."

Adelle pinballed her way to the bar and snagged a stool next to Shawn. She shimmied it closer to the bar as she sat and waved down the line of people to Grey, Penny, and Nate. "It was over in a flash," she said, as if she had read Logan's mind. "No surprises."

Shawn thanked Logan for the beer. "I keep thinking a spot in the farmer's market might be a better place for me than downtown. Except Adelle has a point about the apartment."

"I'll swat you with Arvil's newspaper if you break that lease." Adelle wrinkled her nose at him and scowled, reaching for the paper that sat unread on the bar. "You already filled out the paperwork, and you can't live in the flea market for free. Your mother will kill you, too."

Shawn raised both hands. "Fine. I hear you."

Adelle switched gears, turning her attention to Logan. As the crowd got louder, she yelled above the din. "How are the drink kits coming along?"

"I'm antsy to get started. I have two kits ready to put in Kyle's store. I just need a few more suppliers, and I'll have everything ready for when the flea market opens. It's starting to get exciting."

"You're the anonymous letter." Meldrick loomed over Shawn, his jaw set against some slight that didn't exist. Logan was sure she would hear about it.

She threw her hands on her hips and leaned to the right, taking weight off her left leg. "What can I get for you, Meldrick? Other than an answer you're not entitled to."

"Everyone knows it was you. You're the only one here who likes Arvil enough to go to bat for him. I guess it's easy to feel sympathy for a greedy crook when you've been one your whole life."

Adelle nearly spit out her drink, resting it gently back on the bar, her wide eyes landing on Grey, who pushed his stool out. He'd stick up for her, but the last thing she needed was commotion at her bar. She shot her husband a look that put him back in his seat and squared up to fight her own battle. Even if she weren't sure what it was about, the least she could do was entertain Adelle.

"Yeah, I wrote the letter," she said. "My business plan doesn't call for a big retail space. The lower rent is a good financial decision. And unlike you, I'm happy to support growth in the town. What's your plan? Annoy the shit out of everybody? Waste time to stay relevant?"

Her simmering blood boiled when Meldrick turned to Grey.

"I've been thinking about making an appointment with the liquor board," he said. "Make sure things are on the up and up around here."

It would be easy to lean across the bar and slap the nonchalant look off the man's grinning face. Instead she wrapped a bar rag around her fist. She never should have lashed out at him, forgetting for a moment the leverage he had over her when it came to the bar.

The photograph he had of her with the liquor boxes, as Grey had pointed out, might not be clear enough to prove her demise, but the original might, and there was an evidence trail long enough to cause trouble for Helen.

Grey didn't budge, but he knocked back his drink, and when he slid his empty glass Logan's way and said, "Hit me," she knew it wasn't just another drink he was asking for.

Helen, however, must have picked up on the cue because she handed Meldrick a beer. "Seems I poured an extra here, Mel. Why not have one on the house. I'd hate to be wasteful. If you do run down to the liquor board, you tell the women in the office I said hi. Been a while since I ran into 'em. I'd love it if they'd swing by for a day. We can catch up on old times."

Meldrick's face said he was fuming, but he thanked Helen for the drink and turned away to annoy someone else in the crowd. She rolled her eyes, but Grey didn't look half as willing to let it go. She poured an ounce of whiskey in a rocks glass, neat, and put it in front of him.

"That guy is such a dick." Grey sipped his second whiskey. "Thanks. I needed this."

"I'm nothing if not an attentive bartender."

"Don't let him get to you. It's exactly what he wants." Sandy's voice could barely be heard over the crowd. "I hate the way he treats people. Thank God he doesn't read. That kind of behavior is just not suitable for the library."

"Not suitable for the bar, either." Logan grabbed a rag to wipe down the dribble she left from Grey's drink.

Grey mumbled, but all she could make out was something about "the pictures he took."

"The pictures he took." She repeated it to herself, under her breath. It meant something, but she couldn't place it, like leaning over a bridge and peering into a rippling stream and trying to make out a fish among the rocks. Then it surfaced, rushing into focus, and she reeled. The returning memory of Meldrick taking pictures at the mill hit her so hard she gripped the edge of the cooler.

"Do you need to sit? Grab my arm." Helen stood at her side, but Logan wouldn't lean on a woman half as strong.

"No. I'm okay."

"You don't look good." Grey leaned across the bar and put his hand against her head. "You don't feel clammy. You okay?"

She looked up into his eyes and lied. "Yeah, I'm fine. My leg, that's all. Just a little swollen."

CHAPTER TWENTY-SEVEN

Pieces of memories rushed in all at once, like photographs thrown on a table. There was a familiarity to them, like a movie she'd seen a decade ago, but the still frames weren't quite enough to fill in the dialog. She shook her head to bring it into focus. Meldrick hadn't spoken to her at the mill. That much she knew. But she'd seen him through a spider-web cracked window, walking around. Taking pictures.

He wasn't responsible for her leg, at least she was pretty sure. The sequence of events was out of order, but she was certain she was alone when it all came crashing down on her. She'd been mad at Grey; she just couldn't remember why.

Grey was still ranting about Meldrick, his voice cutting through the hum of the full tavern. Sandy was saying soft, low things, trying to calm him down. Logan clutched the edge of the open cooler, her face low to the cold air as she pretended to count bottles, letting the memory piece itself back together. She couldn't tell Grey that she'd seen Meldrick that day. He'd only fly off the deep end and cause a scene. And she couldn't tell Adelle or Penny while Grey was in earshot.

The crisp snap of an open newspaper scattered her crystalizing memories, and her attention fell on Arvil, who shot his trademark look at her, a signal he wanted a drink. She grabbed a bottle of vermouth and made him a Manhattan, whether he wanted one or not. Using the bar to steady herself, she kept some of the weight off her throbbing leg and set it in front of him without ceremony.

"I didn't order this." The corner of his mouth twisted with a scowl. "And where the hell have you been? Why are you walking stupid?"

"Shush. Listen. I have to tell you something." She tightened the caps on bottles of bitters, staying as far into the shadowed corner as she could. "I broke into the mill."

Arvil probed his eye tooth with his tongue. "What the hell were you doing out there?"

"I just wanted to see the site. Anyway, Meldrick showed up while I was there. He was taking pictures. That's how I hurt my leg. I was hiding from him. I don't think he knows I was there."

He ducked behind the newspaper. "That scamp."

"Scamp? What year is this?" She curled her lip. "The door was unlocked. I just wanted to see it, that's all. What do you think he was doing out there? Why was he taking pictures?"

"I don't know." He yanked the stirrer from his drink and shoved it into his mouth. "But I'm glad you hurt yourself so I could find out."

She pushed away from the bar and balanced her weight on her

good leg. "Thanks. You're all heart."

He wagged the stirrer at her. "Good work. Smart move on your part, digging around. That's what good investors do. Never let someone hold you back from seeing your own future."

She rolled her eyes at him. "I'm not an investor. And I'm having second thoughts about this, to be honest."

"Why?" He turned the page of his newspaper and laid it on the bar, tracing lines with his finger as if he cared what it said. "Didn't like what you saw?"

What was she supposed to say? That Meldrick was ruthless, that he could lie about her and ruin her in that tiny town forever?

"Meldrick's been threatening me and Grey. It's not above him to do mean, sneaky things and lie just to ruin people. I'm afraid he's going to frame me for something just to get his rocks off."

Arvil tilted his head and peered at her through squinched eyes. "What did you do to him? What does he want?"

"I didn't do anything. He's not asking for anything either." She folded her arms and returned his leer. "Not like you do. He's just giving me lists of things I can't do, like have kids or pets or paint my own house."

"You should definitely not have kids. This doesn't seem like an unreasonable demand to me."

"Arvil. I'm being serious."

"Me, too." He shook the paper. "He just wants to intimidate you so he can control you, that's all."

"No, something bigger is going on."

"Who cares what he wants? You'll know when he asks for it."

She raised her eyebrows. It wasn't like Arvil to be cavalier about someone snooping in his business. "You have no idea why he'd be stomping around your mill taking pictures? I really doubt he was there because of me. He didn't even know I was opening a store there until a few minutes ago, when he realized I wrote the letter Adelle read at the meeting. It's not like it was in your interview with Stuart."

"No. You might be wrong." Tilting his head back, he seemed to search the ceiling. His words formed slowly. "It's possible he could have heard about your store from somewhere else. Or even that he knew before today that you were involved with the mill."

"What do you mean *involved with the mill*? I'm not involved. I'm a tenant leasing space. Period." She wiped a glass with a clean bar rag, finding calm in the repetitive motion.

"Well, I'm just saying that he could have put the pieces together, that I sold the house to Grey and used the money to buy the mill."

Logan's jaw set. Sure, Meldrick may have put all those things together in the blender of his imagination and puréed them, arriving at the conclusion that she was intimately involved with Arvil's project. "But that doesn't explain the threats and the pictures."

"It's just evidence. Did he say anything else? You said threats." He waved his hand as if he were trying to speed her up. "Out with it."

Arvil was only an inch more trustworthy than Meldrick. There was no telling what he would do with the information once she divulged it, but she had to give him something. "He wants to start an HOA."

"I know that." He shook his head. "I was at the damn meeting. He wants the power to intimidate you into doing what? Painting your house a color he likes? What does he want?"

"I don't know, Arvil." She raised her voice, and Grey glanced her way. She leaned in and whispered through gritted teeth. "That's what I've been trying to figure out."

He shook his paper at her. "Seems weird then, doesn't it?"

She hadn't allowed herself to think the worst. Putting it into words would only make it seem possible but holding it in was only making it feel dangerously real. "I'm afraid that whatever he has up his sleeve, he's going to make Grey lose the house."

She needed someone to tell her that it wasn't possible. Even if that person were Arvil, who only swapped one section of the newspaper with another and blinked back at her over the sports section.

"That's why I'm having second thoughts."

Arvil's aged and lined hand reached around the paper and clutched the Manhattan. He made a sour face and set it down on the bar next to his napkin. "I will make your life more miserable than Meldrick ever could if you make me drink one of those again. Or if you back out of our agreement. You got that?"

Jaw set, eyes blazing, her dour expression took up the last of her energy. Her leg was begging for relief. She had just enough mental muscle left to see through his veneer.

"Stop running me in circles. Meldrick knows I'm involved with the mill because you've been running around telling people that I'm involved. Haven't you? You've been using me as leverage to get other people on board for the flea market. And you're still looking for tenants, and you don't want me to leave. Otherwise, you'd be happy to let go of my discount lease in favor of someone who'll pay full price. You want me to be square with you, but you're only giving me half the story."

With a glance down the bar, he let the paper fall and leaned toward her, matter of fact. "I got a national pretzel chain coming in. I got a national candy chain opening a store. Penny wants to put furniture in there. I got a hotdog guy coming in from Colby. There's going to be a fruit stand, a butcher. A shoe company. I tell people that Logan Cole is behind this thing, and they're ready to jump on board."

"I can't believe you're using my name to build this thing. No wait. I can." Her father would have a fit. The only child of one of the biggest real estate developers in the country backing a flea market? In the years since he went to prison, she'd excelled at putting him out of her mind, but the thought of his reaction, in her state of utter exhaustion, made her laugh. It swelled inside her, pushing against her reason. She covered her mouth with the back of her hand and shook with laughter.

"What's so funny? I'm not using you. Like I need your help." His face twisted with derision. "I told the pretzel people I had a retailer already. They asked who, and they were impressed. They didn't even ask for proof." He shrugged.

"And you went with it."

He sighed, pushed his drink at her, and swapped the sports section for the news she'd interrupted. "Stop freaking out, work on your product, and leave the rest to me. You have nothing to lose."

"Yeah, I do. My house."

"You got the deed. Meldrick can't change that. Just calm down and make me something to drink that isn't this." He nudged the glass, and she dumped it in the sink.

She might not be happy, and she may not have answers, but she got the reassurance she wanted, however hollow it might be.

"Fine. You owe me," she said.

Arvil didn't argue.

CHAPTER TWENTY-EIGHT

"Nate, this looks amazing!" Logan nudged the laptop and leaned across the toy store counter to see the logo better. "This will look good on the boxes."

"Thanks. Glad you like it." He leaned back on his stool, and Logan turned to take in the art that plastered the back wall. Teddy bears shot missiles at flying saucers, dinosaurs swatted at cartoon-faced cars, and a model train ran on a track suspended from the ceiling. Every time it passed, robots shot laser beams from their eyes at the train.

Gone were the tall shelves once stocked with toys in colorful boxes and the dusty figurines that once stood in rows. Nate had spent the last few months tearing the store down to bare walls, building new shelves from colorful blocks. He'd made a wonderland.

Penny swung in the door, a cookie in one hand, coffee in the other. "What's up, Logan?"

"Checking out the logo. This mural is cool. This is what you've been doing for weeks?"

"Yeah, it needed a refresh." Hands hooked behind his head, Nate beamed. "Glad you like it."

Logan dug into the messenger bag she carried on days she didn't have to work, and she pulled out a cardboard box smaller than a nine-by-thirteen baking dish. She handed it to Penny. "Check it out. A prototype."

Penny flipped the lid back. Inside was a small glass jar holding tea bags, a small sachet of lavender, and a tiny bottle of bitters. Two silicone molds to make round ice cubes protected the glass jar, and all of it was nested in wood-shaving packing material. On top sat a notecard with a recipe.

"Each kit will have a few options. You can order it with drinking glasses or whatever. This is a prototype for Kyle, something small to sell through his store. I'm thinking about asking Stuart if I can pay the newspaper to lay out and print some little recipe booklets for me."

Nate grabbed a piece of paper off his printer, pulled the pencil from behind his ear, and started sketching. "I was thinking about the booth. You said it was small. Without dimensions, this is just an idea, but what if it had shelves along the sides like this? If you could get some whiskey barrels, you could use them as displays."

She leaned over the drawing as he sketched barrels down the center of the store with vague hints of display racks on top. "That's kind of what I pictured. I don't know how I'd pull it off yet, but I was thinking if the shelves were wood, I could char them somehow."

Penny beamed and nudged Nate's arm. "Don't you have a wood-burning kit that you use to make picture frames?"

"I do. You're welcome to use it. It's really easy."

"That would be great. Thank you! Then I could just seal them and—"

The door flung open.

"Arvil." Nate leaned back again and tucked in his chin, amusement expanding from his smile to his eyes. "Need some toys?"

Arvil ran a handkerchief over his brow, a broad grin on his face. Logan took a step back and leaned against the counter, giving into the amusement. The man never smiled. He grinned or sneered, but he never smiled like that. Whatever mischief he was up to, it was sure to be entertaining.

"I always need toys, Nate," he said. "We just have very different ideas of fun. I'm here for Logan. Been looking for her everywhere."

Logan waved her open palm in circular motion in front of his face. "What's this? What's with this happy thing?"

"I finally figured out what Meldrick's problem is."

Penny leaned back against the sales counter, coffee mug in her hands. "Drama. I'm here for it."

Nate gave her a puzzled look, but Arvil shushed her before she could fill him in.

"When did Meldrick first get mad at you and Grey?"

Logan exchanged looks with Penny. "I guess it was when I was planting those flowers Adelle gave me. But it must have been before that, because he complained about paint cans on our porch and that was the first week we lived there."

Penny nodded. "Seems like it was right when you bought the house."

"That's what I figured." Arvil paced an aisle between shelves of jigsaw puzzles and board games. "I'm a real estate guy, right? I bought that house years ago. Old Lady Lynette was about to keel over in that place, and she sold it to me for cash. I rented it back to her until she died. Like a reverse mortgage thing."

Nate rolled his eyes, unhooked his hands from behind his head, and leaned forward, the stool clattering as it returned to four feet. "You have to be careful with talk like that, or people will think you're altruistic."

"Very funny, toy boy. Anyway, I never went further back in the property records than what the state had on file, because I really don't care that much. I was going to hold on to the house until we had an upswing. That house is huge. It should have turned a profit." Arvil picked up a game of Monopoly and shook it. Little plastic houses and metal tokens rattled. "Thing is, the taxes made it a losing proposition, and I sold it to get cash in hand to buy the mill from Zeb instead."

"Meldrick was snooping around the mill taking pictures. Does he think the properties are linked? What's it got to do with him and why would he take it out on me?"

"Slow down, grasshopper." Arvil put the box back on the shelf. "When you told me that Meldrick had old signatures he collected to start an HOA, I figured Mack and Lewis would be the people to talk to. If anyone knows why that blowhard would want something, it would be those two. And it would be easy to get it out of them because they're easy to persuade. You just have to agree with all their kvetching for a minute, and they'll tell you anything you want to know."

Nate tapped his pencil on his drawing of Logan's store. "I'm lost.

What were you trying to figure out?"

Logan cleared her throat. "Meldrick tried to form an HOA a few years ago in that quadrant of town where our house is."

"It was all because Jaleesa wanted to put an apartment above her car repair place to make some cash. Meldrick got wind of it and started collecting signatures to support her. But it has nothing to do with Jaleesa. It was all about..." He jabbed his finger at Logan. "Your house."

Penny set her empty mug on the counter. "What does collecting signatures have to do with the house, though?"

"Apartments," Logan said. Her pulse quickened. "If he could convince enough people that Ramsbolt's rules were restrictive, and they formed an HOA, they could allow Jaleesa's apartment and also let him split that old house into apartments, putting money in his pocket. Damn, you're good."

Arvil threw his hands in the air. "Bingo. Of course I am. Mack and Lewis said Meldrick was in the newsstand one day, asking Warren all kinds of questions about how much he makes off those apartments he rents out. A few months later he was back, whining that he couldn't divide a residential house into apartments. Warren said Jaleesa had run into the same problem trying to make some cash on the side by putting an apartment in the loft. Had something to do with zoning in that quadrant of town."

"What's an HOA going to do for zoning?" Logan furrowed her brow. "Wouldn't the town rules come first? Why not just change the town rules?"

Nate laughed. "He'd never get the whole town on his side. Not that guy."

"That's it exactly." Arvil gave Nate a thumbs up. "He couldn't get the whole town on his side, but if he could start an HOA and prove that his case was for the greater good, the HOA could convince more people than he could."

"What a convoluted mess." Logan shook her head.

"Just the way he likes it," Arvil said. "He marched over to Jaleesa's after talking to Warren, and he offered to start a petition to start an HOA. She went along with it. Why wouldn't she?"

"But wasn't Meldrick's son the town manager then?" Logan looked to Nate for confirmation.

Nate and Arvil conferred, placing broken streetlights and small-town landmarks in the Ramsbolt timeline.

"No. This would have been when Adelle's dad was still town manager," Nate said.

Arvil nodded in agreement. "Meldrick had no expectation of support. Not from Adelle's dad, that's for sure. But the town loves Jaleesa."

"Of course, they do," said Penny. "She keeps the cars running so we can get the hell out of here. And she's super nice."

"Everybody signed that petition to help her out. And Meldrick must have figured that once the zoning work was out of the way, he could buy the house from Old Lady Lynette, and start raking in the cash."

Logan's palms began to sweat. If what Arvil was saying were true, then Meldrick wasn't just making a disruption. He was trying to take their home by force.

"But you swooped in," Penny said. "You bought the house instead."

Arvil folded his arms. "None of it turned out like I'd expected, and it's all your fault."

"Me?" Logan plucked at the bandage covering her stitches through her jeans. The constant itching was a distraction.

"Yes, you. At the time I bought that house, I figured the tavern would be gone. I'd have an office building in its place, and the house would be rented by office workers. I'd someday make a killing off flipping it to an investor. It just didn't pan out that way. Meddling kid."

She shrugged. "I'm not sorry. But that doesn't explain why Meldrick hates us. He's not any closer to getting the place rezoned or getting the house. If he's this persistent, he must have a hell of a plan to take it away from us."

The glass counter creaked as Penny shifted her weight. "Damn, Logan. This sucks."

Nate stopped sketching hoops on barrels and dropped his pencil to the counter. "I do remember Meldrick flipping his lid when you bought that house. He was throwing one of his temper tantrums before a town meeting. *It was supposed to be mine. I didn't even get a chance to bid on it.*" He flailed his arms in the air in mock panic.

Unthinkable scenarios unfurled in her imagination, unknown lengths that Meldrick might go to out of spite. She pictured ridiculous lawsuits and tax assessments. Poor Grey. He could lose his dream house before he even got to really live in it. And there was no way of knowing Meldrick's plan of attack. A few weeks ago, she couldn't have cared less what Meldrick Lacey wanted to do with his life, but now holding onto that house felt like a matter of life or death. And maybe it was just paranoia, but she wasn't yet convinced that Arvil hadn't been involved somehow.

Outside, dark clouds pushed up the street. A light flickered to life and made a pool on the sidewalk. The first blast of wind made a cyclone at the door, gathering up bits of leaves and the chaff of grasses, and the ghost of a forgotten anger stirred in Logan. Arvil could only be trusted to take care of Arvil, and she kicked herself for ever forgetting it.

"What are you looking at me like that for?" Arvil's lips curled in a snarl.

"I don't know. Sorry." She shook the sour from her stomach off her face and lied. "I wasn't thinking anything at all."

Whether it was true or not that Grey colluded with Arvil in some scheme to profit off that land, there was no way it had been Grey's idea.

"I don't know what's going on. But I sure as hell am going to find out," she said.

CHAPTER TWENTY-NINE

Logan kneeled on a floor mat she borrowed out of Grey's truck, hands in the garden, eyes shielded by the big floppy hat he gave her as a gift. She might not know anything about gardening, but she knew she hated the way her hands sweated in gloves. Stitches itching beneath their bandage, she prodded her thigh with her elbow.

With the trowel Adelle gave her, she dug a hole twice as wide as the tub her hydrangea came in but not yet deep enough. Digging more earth from the hole, she wondered if the woman Arvil called Old Lady Lynette was the last one to shovel that soil. Her trowel scraped on something metal. Brushing away the dirt, she unearthed a little toy car, gray with hints of eroded green paint. She set it on the porch, another story from the house to hold on to, and bailed another lump of dirt from the hole.

The more she dug, the more her mind wandered in the dark abyss of indulgent paranoia. Hands caked with dirt, her mind filled with grainy images of Grey meeting with Arvil in dark basements downtown, plotting the pipes that would lead to the old mill. She imagined their whispers in dark corners, calculating how much money would line his pocket, Grey coming to terms with Arvil on a deal that would sell him the house, then Arvil would get the land, then securing the votes they'd need to build the market. She never did find the paperwork from Grey buying the house. She imagined him snuggled in a hoodie in the woods, burning them in a pit a mile from town to keep her from unraveling their scheme.

But they were lofty plans better suited to old films than the truth. The image of Grey hiding in the basement, speaking in code on his phone to Arvil, saying she didn't suspect a thing seemed cartoonish, uncharacteristic of Grey. And the more she indulged, the happier she was to be wearing a big floppy hat to hide her shame. Silly girl. There had never been a reason to mistrust him.

The Grey she knew wasn't that calculating. The simpler story played out better in daylight and felt much more like the truth. Grey simply wanted a house, and the papers got lost in the shuffle. There was no doubt some scheme existed, but its gears weren't churning because Grey set them in motion. It was Arvil's doing. Meldrick was just noise. Or a consequence she hadn't yet unraveled. How could he be so cruel? He had a perfectly good home of his own, and he only wanted theirs out of greed. He raved about life in a small town, swearing it was the best way to live because it forced people to show respect for each other, but that respect only ran one way in his world.

If she had it to do all over again, she might have warned Grey that buying the house would put them on his bad side. She'd weathered more than her share of stormy men long before she arrived in Ramsbolt, and she'd sworn that Arvil was the last.

Scraping soil from the edges of a rock the size of her fist, she couldn't help but wonder if it was worth the hassle, the rock or the house. If Meldrick wanted it so bad, he could have it.

She didn't really mean that, though. She loved the house and what it had become. Even more, she loved their plans for it. Not that they were all that grand, but she couldn't wait to cozy up in front of a fireplace and watch the plants come up in the spring.

They had to face this together. No more ruminating about schemes. Grey was right. She hadn't trusted him. He could feel the ties between them growing brittle before she could even wrap her brain around it, and she owed him explanations, apologies, and change.

Sitting back on her heels, she brushed dirt from her palms, and searched her pockets for her phone.

A car pulled up the driveway, a steady engine she didn't recognize. She kept her head down, expecting it to stop and turn around, another lost soul too close to the Canadian border, but it crept slow up to the drive and the engine shut off. She steadied her hat on her head as she stood, ready to face Meldrick and whatever advancement he hoped to make in his power struggle over her home. Ill prepared and covered in dirt, she adjusted her shorts, but it wasn't Meldrick.

A lady older than her mother climbed out from the driver's side of a nondescript SUV in pearly white.

"We don't really need any…" Makeup? Tupperware?

"I love the landscaping you've done," she said, hand on her own hat as a breeze swept across the lawn.

Logan looked down at her progress. The marigolds were mostly dead, but Adelle had said their season was done. The white arugula she couldn't name was still alive somehow. And then there was a hole in the ground with a rock stuck in it.

"Thanks. We pulled out a bunch of ivy." Logan shrugged. The clouds had parted when she looked back at the woman, and she squinted in the setting sun. "I'm already registered to vote or whatever, and I don't want to join a church or buy any kitchen stuff, so…"

"I'm not selling anything. Though I am a fan of Jesus. I've just been waiting for the house to change out of that evil man's hands."

Logan didn't bother to stifle her laugh. "Well, Arvil's an acquired taste."

"You can say that again. I tried to see him once. He ran me off his property and barked at me like a dog."

Logan raised an eyebrow.

"No, really. Like a dog. Woof woof and all that." Her car door swung shut behind her but didn't click to a close.

"Sounds right."

"Anyway." She turned, flung open the door, and butt in the air, dug through her car, emerging with a cardboard tube longer than Logan's arm. "These are yours now."

The hem of her shorts rubbed her bandage as she walked, and her stitches itched for attention. She took the tube from the farthest distance she could. "What is it?"

"It's the architectural plans for the house. There's a landscaping plan in there, too, that my great-grandmother Emma paid for."

"But the house was built in the twenties." Judging by the woman's age, the house would have to be much older than that, or her great-grandmother had lived a very long life.

"Eighteen forty something. It's on the plans."

Logan's eyes bulged. She wanted to pry the end from the tube and spread the papers out on the lawn. "The state had the date wrong. That explains a lot."

The plaster and lathe, the lack of closets. The giant fireplaces.

"The landscaping plan never happened. Emma lost her son in Gettysburg, and she was never the same again after that. The second that boy walked out the door, she'd started sewing tents for the Union. She convinced her dad, my great-great-grandfather Arthur, to convert their mill and make worsted wool uniforms and tents for the army."

"Wait." Logan's hands were sweating so much she was sure she'd sweat through the tube and turn it to pulp. "A mill?"

"Just outside town. Emma sank her whole soul into making uniforms and tents after John died."

Logan's throat went dry. She couldn't talk. She wanted to ask if the mill was the same as the one on Zeb's farm, but she couldn't get the words to form in her mouth.

"Zeb's farm." It was all she could spit out.

"That's where the mill is. I suppose it's in ruins now, if there's any trace of it at all."

Logan wanted to tell her that it was still there. Belts and machines and the descendants of whatever it used to produce. She wanted to tell her that evil barking Arvil owned it all now, that it was about to become a flea market, but she couldn't make the words happen.

"Anyway, the plans are all yellowed now. You'll probably want to preserve them somehow. If you'd like, we can spread them out on the hood of the car here, and I can show you some things."

Her body moved forward without her consent, not that she'd have argued. She held out the tube, and the woman unfurled yellowed pages, time-gnawed with bent corners. There were layers of papers and in the center, a smaller more homely sketch with clouds for trees and triangle shrubs. In browned ink, a list of plants ran down the margin.

Logan spun the page, aligning the drawing with the street. "The property was massive. There was so much more of it back then."

"Most certainly." The woman held down a curled corner. "The main intersection is here. There was no roundabout back then, but if this plan is right, this was the only house on this side of town. The boom in Ramsbolt didn't happen until after the Civil War. This was one of the first houses here."

Logan unstuck her tongue from the roof of her mouth. "An Asian garden, it says. Behind the house. Does that say *manicured lawn*."

The woman tilted her head to study the writing. "I believe it does."

Logan stepped back from the plans. "Have you ever heard the name Meldrick Lacey?"

The woman licked her lips and pursed them. Eyes fixed on the weedy driveway; the discomfort came off the woman like heat from tarmac. Logan's heart raced.

"Did I say something wrong?" she asked.

"No." The woman pushed the rolled papers back in the tube and pushed them into Logan's hand. She flung open the car door. Logan wanted to grab her arm, beg her not to go, but the woman ripped the hat from her head and tossed it in the car. She ran a hand over her head. "My hair is a mess. Forgive me, but that wind is brutal today."

"You know Meldrick?" She clutched the tube of drawings to her chest, wanting for answers and unafraid to push for them one at a time.

"A few years ago, we...the distant cousins...we started getting phone calls from Meldrick. He wanted to see if anyone had any claim to this house. He asked for pictures and documents, and I remembered these plans. I figured they belonged more with the house than with him. Ours was a sprawling family. Emma was one of a dozen kids, and my mother's siblings were plentiful, too. I don't know Meldrick from Adam, but one of my aunts did marry a man named Lacey. My father was very young when his father's textile operations folded, and the family lost a lot of money. Most lived humbly after the collapse of the mill, and the rural economy being what it was saw most of the family flee. But not the Laceys. They were always bigger than their britches and felt they owned everything. Even what isn't theirs."

"Do you have any idea why Meldrick might still want the house?"

The woman's eyes traced the tower, and by the time they reached the roofline, her body had let out a sigh of awe. "Look at it. It's got better bones than anything else around here. It's probably worth a fortune. You would know that."

Logan had suspected, but Grey had brushed it off. Arvil knew it was worth more than its value, but he couldn't have known all this.

"Well, I should be letting you get back to your garden. Would you do an old woman a favor and promise to keep the plans with the house?"

"Absolutely. Thank you for sharing them with us."

The woman climbed into her car, flipped down her visor and reapplied her hat.

"Ma'am. May I ask? What's your name?"

She started the engine. "Hannah. Hannah Barnett."

"Thanks, Ms. Barnett."

Logan held the tube in her arms until the car was out of sight, then rushed them inside, breathless, and carried them upstairs to the little neglected middle bedroom that would someday be their den. She spread them out on the floor, grabbed her laptop from the top of the filing cabinet, and paced while it came to life. She had to trace the ties that connected the house to the mill and unlace the story.

"Ancestry." She plopped down on the floor with the computer and made an account on a genealogy website. "Hannah Barnett."

She found the woman on someone else's family tree, traced her back in time and forward again to Meldrick. Their connection was legit, but Meldrick's claim to her home was not.

Tapping her knee on the floor, her stitches screaming to be scratched, she opened a document and typed in the names. Emma. John. Arthur.

"He thinks he's entitled to this house." She looked at their names in the family tree. "This man wants to make an HOA, set the rules, make the whole town crazy until he's the only one in it. He couldn't get control of the town because of Adelle, so he wants to take it by birthright? Is that it? No way."

The familiar rise of a threatened ego thrashed within her. Her hands grew hot and her temper flared. She hated the feeling and shook out her hands, but the demon that fueled her father's ambition was stirred by Meldrick's imposition, and she wanted it squashed.

She added Arvil's name to the list. How did he not know what that property was worth? There's no way he didn't know. If Maine had online property records, she'd be able to prove that he knew how old the house was and what it was worth. It took three tries to find the address on the county's website, but when she did, it said Arvil still owned it. The website was behind. No wonder Meldrick thought she owned it.

The website also said the house was built in 1845. That wasn't what Grey had said at all.

"Dammit. Arvil knew." Pulling her phone from her pocket and brushing the dirt from the face, she texted Grey who was elbow-deep in someone else's problems.

What year was this house built again?

He replied. *1940 something?*

She rolled her eyes. *Did you read any of the house docs?*

There were so many pgs? What's this about?

She laid her phone down and popped open three real estate websites. There were five comparable properties available in Maine. Three or four bedrooms, two or three baths. One was on a private island, going for 6.7 million dollars. She pinned the tab. The pictures would be fun to drool over later. The other four properties were closer in size to theirs. Two million dollars. One million, three hundred thousand dollars. They were all in better condition without the peeling wallpaper. Narrowing her search to unrestored properties, the asking prices were cut in half.

Their house was easily worth seven hundred thousand. There was no way Grey paid that much.

She grabbed her phone. *What did you pay for this house?*

You know. It's in the docs I gave you.

"Oh my God, Grey. You never gave me the documents." She yelled at the phone. "I looked everywhere. I ripped open boxes. You hid them from me."

Composing herself before she said the wrong thing, she ran a hand over her face, gritty with dirt.

Where are docs? You never gave them to me.

Thought I did. In the den cabinet on right. Set them aside for you so they didn't get lost.

All that time she'd spent looking for them, worried he was hiding them from her, and they were right in front of her all along, sitting on a shelf.

"I really should trust him more."

Leaving her laptop and the house plans on the floor, she went to the right cabinet, and there they were. A stack of documents half an inch thick. An orange sticky note attached to the front had her name on it. All that time.

She pried the door open carefully, praying the glass wouldn't crack or shatter on the floor, and collected the papers. Sitting with them on the floor, she flipped straight to the numbers.

"Two hundred and ten thousand dollars. That's less than a quarter of its closest comparable value. There's no damn way. This makes no sense."

She found the mill on a parcel map and looked up the number on the county's website. That sale hadn't been reported yet either, but she was willing to bet Arvil purchased the mill for the same price Grey paid for the house. He'd admitted as much, but she wanted to see it in writing.

Slamming the lid to her laptop closed, she rubbed at her stitches and rested her chin on her hands.

"What does this mean? If Arvil was telling the truth about the straight up swap, using the money from selling our house to buy the mill, then for the first time in his life he wasn't all about the cash. He could have made a profit on this house. What could he want more than money?"

Her phone buzzed. It was Grey, but she couldn't lay it all out for him in text messages. She hadn't even sorted it out herself yet.

Some guy just showed up, he texted. *IRS guy with 2 forms of ID. Mortgage fraud investigation.*

Logan dropped the phone. She clutched her stomach and twisted her wedding ring around her finger. Her skin went cold, a shiver running down her arms, but her insides spiked to a thousand degrees. Rocking in her seat, she remembered the advice her father's lawyer gave her before her dad was sentenced. Every camera would be poised on the family, her expression dissected for any hint of guilt. Concentrate on looking calm and eventually you'll feel it.

She closed her eyes gently, no clenching or tight muscles, and taking in the slowest breath she could, she let it out in a long, measured exhale. In through the nose, out through the mouth. Force the anxiety down, into her feet, into the floor.

When her heart no longer throbbed in her neck, she picked up her phone again. She would not be undone by the IRS. Not again. And not for a sham instigated by Meldrick.

A sense of calm scrubbed her clean. A sham was all it was.

Don't panic. Don't say anything, she replied.

Didn't. Just took papers. He left. Can I call?

Logan dialed Grey. He picked up right away.

"I'm in the truck outside the church. I haven't read it all, but it says something about Fraud for Housing." His voice was panicked. "We need a lawyer."

"Stop. Listen to me for a second."

"The paper says Financial Income Fraud. I didn't do anything wrong."

"Stop. Meldrick called the IRS and reported us for possibly inflating our incomes because he doesn't know how little we paid for the house. The sale records haven't even been recorded. Meldrick probably thinks the same thing I did, that there's no way we could have afforded this house on our income. If Arvil had sold this house to us for what it's worth, of course it would be fishy."

"I don't understand what you're saying." His voice was strained but quiet.

"Just finish the job and bring the papers home later. I don't think we have anything to worry about. I'm sure we don't."

The call ended; she closed the laptop. Pretty pictures of private island estates would have to wait. Down the stairs, one at a time, she threaded the house and plopped at the dining room table. Elbows on the hard wood, spinning her ring around her finger, she gazed out the window and saw nothing at all. The red-breasted nuthatches had left the shrubs for the fall, flapping off to wherever they weathered their storms. The shrubs were changing, dropping their leaves, dragging their energy down to their roots to prepare for the winter.

There was no way of knowing how far Meldrick would drag them, but he was wrong to assume that she'd use the same schemes as her father to launder money anywhere, let alone Ramsbolt. And he would be wrong to think her husband and friends would be compliant. A simple review of their taxes and income would turn up nothing and make Meldrick a fool.

But that was only one piece of the puzzle. Why did Arvil undervalue the house? Had Grey been manipulated into doing something nefarious? If Meldrick had been willing to buy the house for a much larger sum, no old grudge or general disdain would be enough to keep Arvil from earning a buck.

She'd always played it straight with him. Sure, she'd stood up for Helen and the tavern, perhaps to his detriment, but he knew she was right, and an office building had no place in Ramsbolt. He made much more profit saving the tavern than he would have if he'd taken that ill-placed leap of faith. If this were revenge, Arvil was better at the long con than she'd given him credit for. It was far more likely that he saw Grey as an opportunity. Arvil knew Grey wanted that house so bad he could taste it, and he took advantage of her husband, and she was not going to stand for it.

White hot rage swelled within her.

For all the times she swore she would never find herself in greedy company again, she ended up caught between two men every bit as carnivorous as her father anyway.

And all she wanted to do was dig a hole in the ground and plant a shrub.

CHAPTER THIRTY

Logan pounded her fist on Arvil's door. The whirlwind of confusion and frustration tossed her emotions, scattering them in a thousand shattered pieces on his porch. She wasn't sure which Logan to give him when he answered. Should she be the angry Logan, demanding to know why he undervalued their house against his nature? Maybe she should be a sad Logan who had endured enough financial trials in her life and didn't need to lose everything again? But playing to his sympathies wouldn't work on a man who lacked empathy. She already tried being the sly Logan who'd scrutinized every little thing. All she had to show for it was a giant cloud of paranoia.

Wind burned, her lips were chapped from the crisp, brisk walk. Her cheeks were raw, but her insides blistered and raged.

No more waiting. No more looking for clues in the dust. With more hunches than hints, she'd sloshed around in the mire for far too long, worried about Meldrick's intentions and waiting for his next move, second-guessing Arvil's involvement. Those two were in cahoots, and she would demand to know why.

"What's taking you so long?" She pounded on the door a second time with cold knuckles. The house wasn't that big.

It all wound inside her chest, a tight little ball of fury and confusion. She would beat that door down to see it unravel.

Arvil undervalued that house on purpose and dragged Grey into some scheme. She didn't know how or why, but if she hadn't been wrapped up in her own problems, worried about how much she contributed to their relationship, she could have stopped it. If she hadn't been focused on whether she belonged, she wouldn't have pushed Grey so far away. She would have seen what was happening, figured it out, made it stop. Hopefully, whatever wheels Arvil had turning, she wasn't too late.

She banged on the door with the heel of her hand. There were answers inside, and nothing was keeping them from her.

"I know you're home, you conniving bastard." She yelled at the front window, trying to see through the holes in his curtains. "Your car's still hot. I have questions. Answer me."

The door flung open. Red faced and glowering, Arvil opened his mouth, but she pushed him aside. Leaving her work bag on his porch, she stomped into his dingy living room. It smelled of salty TV dinners and sweaty slippers. A bag of groceries sat on his kitchen floor, half unpacked.

She spun to face him. "You know that story about the scorpion and the frog. The scorpion asks the frog to carry him across the river, and the frog says no. You'll just sting me. The scorpion convinces the frog that he'd never do that because they'd both drown, but when they get halfway across the river, and he stings the frog anyway, he says he had no choice. That it's just his nature. You know that story? You're a scorpion, Arvil. But I am not a frog."

His delight at her fury was palpable. "I'm a scorpion. I never said any different. Everyone's a frog to me. I don't know what you're talking about, but if you trusted me, it's your own darn fault."

Logan gripped the back of a recliner, some drab brown chair with a crusty afghan pooled on the seat. Why that man had so many seats when he was averse to companionship was beyond her. "Doesn't mean you get to keep treating people like crap. Not while I'm around."

He put his hands up like a six-year-old cowboy caught by the neighborhood robber. "Ohhh. Whatcha gonna do there, scary girl?"

He slammed the door shut and darkness fell on the living room. Arvil fell onto his loveseat, and it groaned under his weight.

"I don't even know what I'm being accused of," he said. "Doesn't matter, though."

"Did you manipulate Grey into buying that house?"

"Manipulate him?" Arvil pulled a lever on the side and his half of the loveseat flung itself into a reclined position. "He begged for it."

"The whole town knew Grey wanted that house."

Arvil looped his hands behind his head. "Then how could I possibly have manipulated him? I knew he wanted the house. You think I'm the only guy in town who knows nothing about this town?"

She gripped the chair, his words chafing through her reason. She couldn't spit her anger out fast enough, and the words didn't carry enough rancor. "I know you're conspiring with Meldrick to take me down. I just want to know why you're..." Rubbing her hand across her forehead, she gave herself pause to reconsider. Blaming him for seeking revenge for some old wound healed over years before would only rip them open and make it harder to get at the hurt. On the other hand, she needed a bloodletting, not a Band-Aid.

"What? What do you want to know? Did you come here to ask me questions or did you come here to tell me who I am? Because I don't have time for both. *Twin Peaks* will be on in ten minutes, and I don't know who killed Laura Palmer yet. It's confusing as hell, but I'd much rather watch that nonsense than yours. At least it's going somewhere."

She took a breath so deep it added sparks to her fire, blurring her vision. Clenching a fist, nails digging into her palm, she let it settle inside her and fizzle. If she didn't calm down and ask the right questions, she'd never get the answers she needed. Why was he conspiring with Meldrick? What was in it for him?

The blaze ate its own embers, dying back. The flames of her rage withered.

Her voice steady, she found the words. "You know what that house was worth, don't you?"

"Of course, I do. I already told you I couldn't get what it was worth on paper. Not in this town."

"But you didn't even put it on the market. You renovated the kitchen and the bathroom. If you really thought you weren't going to make a profit, why go to that extreme?"

Arvil swatted at the air. "Time is money. I did the work then changed my mind. Rather than let it go to waste, I chose to sell it. Grey wanted to buy it. That's how real estate works."

She folded her arms, eyes narrowed. "I'm not buying it. There's more going on here. Why would you intentionally undervalue the house. No one as greedy as you takes less money on purpose."

"Now you're asking the right questions." He wiggled his feet, a slow grin radiating. "I'm not conspiring with Meldrick to bring you down. I'm conspiring with myself to take down Meldrick."

"And Grey's your unwitting accomplice." She shook her head, and her ponytail came loose. The elastic band snapped around her wrist with a satisfying pinch. "That doesn't make any sense. Why are you in competition with Meldrick? You don't even want the same things. You're all..." She waved a hand. "Real estate guy, and he's just a chaos monster."

"Meldrick isn't my competition. He's the town's enemy. He's blinded by his own self-interest. Every time he loses a battle, he gets just a little more reckless. It's fun to watch." Arvil leveled a look at her unlike any he'd shot her way before. Unclouded by concealed intent, he almost looked honest.

"You're telling me that you, Mr. Greed Incarnate, sold that house to Grey for a fraction of its value just to get on Meldrick's nerves? And you're saying Meldrick is the reckless one? That doesn't make any sense." Hair lashed at her shoulders as she shook her head. "No way. There's more to this. If you didn't have something up your sleeve, you wouldn't have hidden it from Stuart. You used my words in your interview. There's no way you bought that mill because of its beautiful, picturesque setting. Anyone who's been in this town four five minutes knows you better than that. Why lie? Why not tell Stuart the truth? Or me?"

He shrugged, half his mouth twisted in a grin. "Why shouldn't I use your words? They were better than anything I could have come up with."

She threw her head back and sighed. "We're just going around in circles. Look, I know you have some scheme going on, and I really don't care why you wanted that dumb building. I care that it somehow put me and Grey on Meldrick's bad side, and I think it's pretty crappy you're not being transparent with me."

Arvil gripped the arm of the loveseat and heaved himself forward. The seat snapped upright. "You asked me why I took less for your house instead of marketing it and trying to make more profit. Come on, real estate heiress. You know what happens to a real estate market when a high value sale happens."

"Yeah, pricing goes up." Her chest tingled as it started to make sense.

"You want a conspiracy? Manipulation? Here it is. I'm conspiring with myself to manipulate the town's real estate values to keep that urchin in his place. If I sold that house for way more than anything else in this town, it would drive up…"

She spoke over him. "It would drive up the real estate values and price us out of our own market."

"Now you've got it. Men like Meldrick would be crawling all over this place in loafers without socks. Before you know it, there'd be golf balls everywhere, we'd have artisan bread coming out of our wazoos, and the town would be covered in boats like gentrified glitter."

Her nostrils flared as she stifled a short laugh. He might be gruff and taciturn, but he was honest when she pushed him. And she had to give him credit for being consistent. The man selfish, not stupid. He wouldn't cut off his nose to spite his face. But she wasn't ready to let him off the hook that easily.

"And you expect me to believe that you went from wanting a fancy office building on the edge of town to settling for a flea market on the outskirts because it's better for your wallet?"

He wiggled his feet. "Frankly, yes. That's all there is to it. I want more income, and I don't want to have to do anything to get it."

"Nope. You're not the greediest man I've ever met, but you're close to it."

They locked eyes, a staring contest neither was programmed to lose. She'd worn him down before, though, so it wasn't a surprise when cracks appeared and his gaze dropped, landing somewhere on the floor. The sadness in it was a surprise, though, the way his cheeks sagged, and his eyes softened. He looked older, somehow.

"Arvil, I'm…" She stopped short of apologizing, unsure what she was supposed to be sorry for.

"I don't want this town to change. Okay?" His voice was soft, low. "The price I paid for lowering the value on that house is the cost of admission for keeping Ramsbolt the same."

"But you're always going on about the potholes and the broken stuff." What could he possibly want to keep the same?

"Bigger fish, kid." He rolled his eyes. "They'll swallow me whole. I can't put a price tag on the good thing I have going here."

The fear glinting in his eyes was as familiar as her own toes. She'd seen the same look in the bathroom mirror a thousand times. It wasn't money he was afraid of, it was belonging. The price tag was superglued to his place in Ramsbolt, to the people who accepted him for being a stodgy curmudgeon without demanding apology or requiring explanation. Outsiders would only challenge him, just like Logan had. If they came with money, it would only be worse. If the town changed, he might never belong again.

She didn't need to press him. He was already down enough. But she did need to let off some steam.

"Fine. But your little stunt to keep property values in check has opened the door to an investigation into our purchase of that house, and I'd like to know what you plan to do about it."

He perked up at the word *investigation*. "The bank?"

"The IRS."

"What do you want me to do about it?"

"How about a notarized letter stating your intentions when you undervalued that property?"

Satisfaction waned from his face, and he glared at the ceiling with stern consideration. He shrugged and pulled the handle of his chair. Feet flying, the chair slamming back to a recline. "Nah. There's nothing in it for me. Besides, you paid what you paid, and you got a house. It'll all work out as it should."

CHAPTER THIRTY-ONE

Logan dimmed the lights over the bar and scooped up Arvil's tips. She could tell by the weight of the coins and the number of bills that he'd tipped her more than usual. Twenty percent to the penny, compared to his usual fifteen. Maybe there was empathy in him after all.

"Refill?" Penny and Adelle were the last remaining guests after a slow night, nursing their half-full drinks by the taps. Logan suspected they were keeping her company, watching her with the kind of stiff-backed cautious curiosity that made her want to kick them out and send them home. But neither of them had pushed her to open up, and she didn't want to encourage them. She was itching to get home and apologize to Grey.

They both declined a last round, huddling instead over Penny's phone and laughing at cats on the internet.

Stuffing Arvil's tips in her jar, Logan cringed a little. She'd only earned the extra cash by storming his house, blaming him for conspiring with Meldrick to do God knows what. And she still wasn't any closer to understanding why Meldrick was being irrational and cruel. Grey had been out of reach all night, probably freaking out somewhere about the possibility of losing the house and the IRS tearing through his financial history. With every text he didn't respond to, the pit in her stomach got deeper and darker. She couldn't tell him how stupid she'd been, how wrong it was that she hadn't trusted him. Worse, she couldn't give him reassurance that it would all be fine. Why would he believe her? The fact that he knew her at all was a testament to the power of the government to prosecute financial crimes.

She pressed a button on the register and yanked out the cash drawer with a shaking hand. She hadn't eaten all night. Instead she'd chewed on every word Arvil had said. He knew that town's economic heartbeat better than anyone, and he had a point that keeping real estate values in check would preserve the way of life. It would also keep deeper outside pockets from taking the reins. She could see his point, too, about wanting more income. If the house were costing him money sitting unoccupied, he might as well turn it into an income-generating asset that wouldn't compete with downtown properties. Everything he'd said made sense. But none of it polished Meldrick's tarnish.

She carried the drawer of cash to the office, ripped the bills from the tray and counted them out. She'd been on a reconciliation spree, and for months her drawer had matched the tape at the end of the night. She put another hash mark in the margin of the calendar, where she'd been keeping score.

"We're finished out here." Adelle's voice resounded from the bar.

"Want us to put our glasses in the sink?"

Logan zipped the day's profit in a bag and locked it in the safe with the fresh drawer. At least with the quiet night she could close a little faster.

"I got 'em." She put the glasses in the dishwasher and started the cycle. It whirred and water rushed.

"Are you sure you don't want to talk about whatever this cloud is?" Penny leaned forward and pushed her glasses up her nose.

"Nah. Just a lot on my mind." She would keep their troubles a secret as long as she could. If it drove Meldrick mad not knowing, all the better.

"Okay. I'll pick you up at nine?" Penny grabbed her jacket from the bar.

Adelle threw her purse strap over her shoulder. "Time to get the stitches out?"

"Finally. Thanks for the ride. Looking forward to it." She'd be able to wear jeans without a bandage guarding the scar. The muscle twinged and burned, a reminder that healing was harder than the injury. "Lunch after? My treat. Penny and I can grab something in Colby and bring it over."

"Sounds good. That'll be fun." Adelle pushed in her stool. "Want us to wait and walk with you?"

"No, you guys go on ahead. I still have some cleaning and restocking to do. Prep for tomorrow." She gestured to the coolers, already restocked, but they didn't need to know that. If she opted for their company, she'd only pour her heart out, embroiling Adelle in whatever would come of Meldrick's attempt to have them charged with fraud. There was nothing they could do but gasp and stammer their support anyway. It was better she got home to Grey, to apologize and press the reset button, to read the letter for herself, and start to plan their defense as a team.

Adelle and Penny smiled and waved. They slipped out the door and into the autumn air that soon would turn cold and take the breath from Logan's lungs.

When she heard the outside door slam behind her friends, she did one last scan of the bar. The coolers were stocked, fruit prepped. The counters and bar had been cleaned and sanitized. She itched to run. The thought of Grey sitting alone in that house, digging through paperwork like his life depended on it broke her heart. She felt responsible somehow, like the bad luck followed her. That feeling was familiar and not easy to shake. It wouldn't go away until she figured out why Meldrick would have it out for Grey, one of the nicest people in town and someone he'd have to call upon one day in an emergency. The simplest conclusion was that Meldrick had it out for her. She just didn't know why.

She gathered her jacket and work bag from the office and closed and locked the door.

Sometimes she wished they'd never bought that house, and she had half a mind to rush home and tell Grey to sell it. Take the money and run. But if they sold it for even a penny profit, they could get into trouble for flipping it, and the only defense would be to prove they never knew the value of it to begin with. But how do you prove that?

Meldrick's taunting could go on forever if she didn't find the root of the problem and living under the weight of it was lonely.

"I never thought I'd miss having lawyers hang around."

She grabbed the last bag of trash from the can, closed and locked the bar for the night, then heaved the bag into the dumpster on her way home.

The walk was more like a sprint, her duffle bag slamming into her hip with every stride. Pausing at the bottom of the driveway, she caught her breath before climbing the hill.

The porch light was on, drawing moths that circled like spastic satellites. She dodged them as she entered the darkened house. Upstairs, Grey was asleep.

Good for him, she thought. They could talk in the morning. But she was way too wired to follow him to bed.

He had been in the office at some point that evening, scattering folders on top of the filing cabinet. She flipped open one cover to find tax forms bound by binder clips, each stack with a sticky note declaring the year. A thick folder with house closing documents sat to one side. In a notebook, he'd made a list of the files and scribbles of things he'd been looking for.

Skimming through the house folder, she saw no statements of value. The only dollar figures mentioned were in the sale price. There was no documentary evidence at all to prove any allegation Grey knew the house was undervalued when he bought it. In fact, the sale papers said it was being sold *as is,* and the folder stuffed with house receipts for paint and wall patch and cleaning supplies would only support the argument that the house was in disrepair.

The IRS letter was there as well, tucked in a new folder labeled *Investigation* in Grey's steady, all-caps print. It was merely a notice of a document review. So far, there was no cause for alarm. Their defense, should they need to launch one, seemed easy, but it wasn't one she'd want to mount without a lawyer. If Meldrick wanted them out of their house that badly, and he found a way to make their lives hell, he could ruin them just with the cost of the lawyers alone. All for what?

Pacing fueled her thinking, but it made the floor creak. She came to a stop in front of the tube that Hannah Barnett delivered that morning. It sat on the floor next to the filing cabinet.

She unfurled the plans and traced the lines from room to room, following lengths of walls around curves and corners. Hannah Barnett's gift to the house was like a tour map, taking her on a guided expedition through dings in the trim, patches, and repairs. If not for the map she wouldn't have noticed the faint hint of a moved wall, where a partition had been pushed a few feet to one side to make room for more plumbing when showers were added to the bathroom.

She hadn't spent enough time in the large back bedroom to notice the trim around one window was newer than its twin. And she found an ironing board nestled in the wall between the bedrooms, right where the floor plan said it would be. When she pulled at a board in the wainscotting, it fell into her hands on well-rusted hinges. She winced at the sound, not wanting to wake Grey, and folded it back into the wall, holding it in place until she was sure it would stay.

The wall was cool beneath her hand, the wood polished to a deep, dark shine. It had to be a thick wall to contain an ironing board, but it also had room for the two built-in bookcases that faced the other way, into the den. According to the plans, there was a void between the walls too wide to account for just the depth of the bookcases. Guessing by the plans, it was about four feet wide. Back in the hall, she judged the length of the two rooms. How had they not noticed before?

Slipping into the den as quietly as she could, she spread the plans on the floor. The ironing board was there on the plans, as were the bookcases and the void between walls. A faint curved line seemed to indicate the swing of a door, just like the doors that led into the halls, but it was there, in front of the bookcase on the right.

She tugged the doors open, and glass rattled in the frame. She shushed it, holding it in place with her hand. Nothing seemed strange or unordinary about it. The shelves were held in place by nails or decades of paint, she couldn't tell which. The walls were solid.

Her heart drummed as she studied the plans and paced. Part of her wanted to wake Grey, but she'd only sound crazy if she woke him to say she thought the walls weren't right, and the rooms were too small.

She inspected the trim around the bookcase. There were no gaps, no place to put her hands to tug. She opened the door again, careful not to break the thin, rippled glass, and she tested her grip on a shelf. With increasing strength, she tugged on the shelf, and with a gentle crack, the case came away from the wall. A hot cloud of withering air escaped and hung at the dark opening as she pressed her hand to her mouth to muffle her gasp.

Holding her breath to muzzle her shriek, she inched from the door with her heart in her throat. Her imagination conjured images of massive spiders and poisonous beasts that lurk in the dark. Biting her lower lip, she used the flashlight from her phone to cut through the darkness.

The dark cavern was unfinished, with dried plaster dripping between the lathes. The pale raw floor was grayed, and traces of dust flittered in the flashlight beam that shook as her hand trembled. She slithered closer, craning her neck to see inside, taking shallow breaths. Hints of dark fabric, folded and stacked, drew her closer.

Ducking her head, though she didn't need to, she crept into the closet between the walls. It smelled like an attic, fifteen degrees warmer than the rest of the house, and stale. The thought crossed her mind that there could be a body in there, puddled and dried. If she died in there and the door swung shut, Grey might never find her.

She shined the flashlight through the space, about four feet wide and ten feet long. Knee-high stacks of dark -blue wool, brass buttons, and shorter stacks of lighter blue fabric rested on the floor in tidy rows. An old wood crate full of yellowed creased paper sat at her feet. She lifted one, careful not to let it crumble. It was crisp and brittle, like it might shatter if dropped.

The Confederacy it said in certificate script, arced across the top of the bill. Beneath the etching of a man she didn't recognize was a date. *Richmond. February 17, 1864.* It was a fifty-dollar bill.

"Confederate money?" She flipped it over and inspected the reverse. "This must have been worth a fortune back then." The whole crate was full of Confederate dollars, different sizes and denominations, sorted and stacked. What was all this Confederate money doing in a house in Maine?

Wooden crates stacked two and three high lined the walls, making a narrow aisle between them. And there were long things piled in the back where her flashlight wouldn't reach. She inched closer and peered around a stack of crates and the light fell on the wooden butt of a rifle with brass or bronze details. What was all of this doing in the walls?

With a hesitant hand, she reached down and touched a fold of dark blue wool, the brass button much colder than the air. Shining her light on the gathered fabric, she could make out the edge of a collar. With more confidence, she flipped back the lid of a crate. Its fragile metal hinges gave way, and the lid broke free. She caught it just before it hit the floor, her heart racing and mouth dry. Aiming her phone flashlight into the hollow, she found yellow papers folded and bundled, envelopes addressed in the brown ink of another time. To Anne Neal in Cassatt, South Carolina. To Roscoe Wolcott in Siloam, Georgia.

She rested her phone on the stack that crinkled under its weight and test-lifted the crate. Trusting its strength, she carried it out of the closet and into the room.

A buzzing pulsed from her phone through the letters, through the wood and up her arms. Setting the crate on the floor, she pressed the red button on her phone to silence it, but her trembling finger accepted the call instead. Her breath hitched in her throat.

"Christ. Hello?" She gasped, breathless, into the phone. It had to be a wrong number or a robocall about an extended warranty on a car she never owned. No one would call her at that hour.

"It's Meldrick."

She held the phone away from her face and tiptoed out of the crawlspace. "What do you want? And why do you have my phone number."

"Got it from Helen."

"It's a little late for scheming, don't you think? How do you know I'm not asleep? Or did you follow me home from work and peer in the windows?"

"I know you're awake because the bar just closed. I'm calling to ask you for a favor."

Eyes wide, it took all her strength to keep her voice down. "A favor? You think I'll do you a favor? You have got to be kidding me."

"Oh, you'll want to by the time I'm done. Let me tell you why. You broke the law when you used the bar's liquor license to get alcohol for your little party. And you earned yourself some prison time when you lied about your income to buy that house. With any luck on my part, you had some secret stash of your dad's laundered money lying around somewhere that you—"

"What is your point, Meldrick? What favor could you possibly want from me that you think you can only get by being such a total asshole? If you fell in the shower, I would call the fire department and tell them to turn on the hose. I've had a long day. Stop messing around and say what you have to say."

Grey snored and stirred in the other room. She congratulated herself on staying calm, not giving into the urge to scream at Meldrick. She wouldn't give him the satisfaction of arguing points. Whatever he sought to gain by catching her off guard when she was tired would have to go unsettled if he didn't get to the point.

"You have sixty seconds. What do you want from me?"

"I want you out of this town. Simple as that." His voice was flat, almost pleasant, but she knew better.

It wasn't about the house or mill or a conspiracy with Arvil, and it wasn't about Grey. It was about her.

"Why do you want to ruin people who've never even crossed your path? I've done nothing to you. Never said a word to you. I don't even give you a dirty look when you leave me pennies for tips on hundred-dollar bar tabs. If you really want this house, all you have to do is walk down the street and make an offer. It's that simple. Why are you hell-bent on ruining other people? I'm pretty sure I know; I just want to hear you say it."

"I'm not getting into a negotiating war with you over a house you have no right to."

"Oh." She said it like she'd just realized she forgot to butter her toast before she sat. "Well, if you think you're entitled to it, no wonder you're mad that Arvil sold it to Grey. He did sell it to *Grey*, you know. I'm not even on the deed. And he sold it for a pittance. I'm sure Arvil would have entertained other offers if you'd taken the time to make one."

The fact that Arvil intentionally kept Meldrick from hearing about the sale wasn't relevant. Not to Logan.

"Anyway," she said, "It seems to me that Arvil would have liked a little bidding war. And you still would have come out on top. It'll absolutely blow your mind when you find out what we paid for this place." Her mind wandered back into the closet, where at least one crate was flush with cash for an empire that wasn't meant to be. "Seems it doesn't matter how much money you have at your disposal. In the end, the chips fall where they ought to."

Meldrick clicked his tongue in a disapproving air that made its way through the phone. "Oh, the chips do fall. You'll see."

He didn't need a favor or have a question. He didn't even want to rile her. He was on a fishing expedition. She'd been on enough of her own to know. But this time she was the one holding all the fish.

"It won't be hard to prove our innocence, you know. Your made-up case is flimsy. But you must be desperate if you'd go to such lengths with lies that are easy to disprove. It may surprise you to learn that we're the ones with the chips this time."

Meldrick took a gasping breath of a pause and unleashed a tirade that made her pull her phone from her ear. She turned down the volume to keep from waking Grey. Half of what he said was garbled, and the half that came through wasn't worth listening to. She got his point. He was cornered, his efforts would fail, and he knew it.

When he quieted to a more reasonable tone, she tuned in again.

"You entitled people are all the same," he spat through the line. "You think the world revolves around you. You committed bank fraud and mortgage fraud, and I'll prove it."

"You can't prove a thing, and you know it. Because it didn't happen."

"Deny it," he demanded. "Out loud."

"You're absolutely insane. You know that, right?"

He let out a trickle of a laugh. "I have you on tape now, refusing to deny that you committed fraud. Maine is a one-party consent state, which you probably don't know. You bring no value to this town. Your father damaged the entire country, and all his investors and people like you, who think they can run the world, have no place in towns like Ramsbolt. This is *my* town. And it's about time you learn your place in it."

Logan sat on the floor next to the letters. They were tied in little bundles with ribbons and strings. She lifted one solitary envelope that sat apart from the rest, labeled To Whomever Finds This First.

"Meldrick, it's late. You'll grow tired of this game long before I do. I know just where my place is. It's at house number 628, at the end of the street on the right. And my favorite room in this gorgeous old house is the one I'm in right now. There's a little storage cubby hidden in the walls that's full of Civil War relics and Confederate cash that somehow is tied to your family. And it's the real reason you want this house so bad. It must be worth a damn fortune. I have to say, though, I do love this room. It has one hell of a closet. But all this stuff in it? I don't know. I'll destroy every piece of paper and every fiber in this room if you don't tell me the damn truth and leave us the hell alone."

CHAPTER THIRTY-TWO

"My family ran the mill outside of town."

Logan knew that, but she didn't want to interrupt Meldrick. Though his voice had a sharp edge, he sounded exhausted. Unlike her, he wasn't used to being up at this hour. Whether she'd worn him down emotionally or the late hour was catching up with him, in his tired state, he was likely to tell her even more than she bargained for. And there was no chance she would miss a word of it.

"Zeb's family bought that land sometime after the Civil War, when fabric was cheaper to buy from somewhere else. I wanted the land back from Zeb, to turn it into apartments, but Zeb sold it to Arvil instead, because he had cash in hand. Zeb didn't want apartments there, anyway, and Arvil knew it, too. He promised Zeb he could have a nice store to sell his food directly to consumers and that he already had some good leads to bring in retailers. He claimed he had meetings lined up with some national chains and some stores in Colby. It got Zeb all excited. A few days after Grey's truck started showing up at that house you bought, Arvil told Zeb he had cash and an investor with clout behind him. That clinched the deal for Zeb."

Logan sat on the floor and hugged her knees, eyes fixed on the letter addressed to her. Rather, it was addressed to whoever found that closet first, and she fit the bill. Her fingers itched to unfurl it, but there was no way she'd miss a moment of what Meldrick had to say.

His voice dripped with acidic resentment, but she recognized something in it. A ship lost at sea without a port. Meldrick's link to his lost past wasn't nearly as strong as hers, and maybe he was motivated more by greed than a yearning for home, but it stirred a hint of pity in her that was easy to quash.

"When Zeb sold that mill to Arvil, my chances to get that land back were ruined. And I lost the house at the same time. On top of it, the last thing Ramsbolt needs is you and your father getting your hands on this town."

"I have no connection to my father. But you and Arvil seem to have a lot of opinions about what Ramsbolt needs. Either one of you ever polled the town?"

"Is this your story or mine?" he snipped.

"By all means."

"You act like this place didn't exist before you showed up. That tavern was on its last legs when you got here, in case you hadn't noticed. Arvil was about to turn it into offices, and I finally had a shot to open apartments nearby. A fancy place for office workers to live. I had an agreement with him to open a business there. Between Arvil and Warren, my family's been locked out of real estate in this town for generations. You know what that's like, don't you? Oh, wait. No, you don't. Because you've lived a privileged life."

Meldrick's voice got louder and agitated. He gulped and ice rattled in a glass. His words slurred. "Everything you do works out. You should have lost that cocktail competition, but you won it because of someone else's blunders. That's how you always get ahead. On someone else's bad luck."

Arvil had said the same thing to her. It was the only weak attack a jealous man could wage. She took in a breath to fuel her argument, but she stopped herself from making it. "You weren't even there."

"I didn't need to be there. It was all over the commentary. Poor little rich girl, Logan Cole lost everything. You thought you were winning something on your own merit. That money was handed to you."

The mud stung more than she wanted to admit. She'd thought it herself at the time. It was half of the shame and fear that drove her to hide in her apartment when it was over. But she couldn't blame him for saying it, hurt as he was that he missed the chance to buy his ancestral home. Words were one thing, though. Turning them into the IRS for investigation was something else. That man might be human, but he was still scum.

"How or why I won that competition doesn't matter, Meldrick. I saved the tavern. I saved Helen. It's more than you've ever done for the town."

"Not true. My family ran that mill and made Union uniforms and tents during the Civil War, and we saved the North."

"Helped," she said. "If we're diminishing achievements here, let's be consistent."

"Screw you. When I found out from Zeb that Arvil sold a house in town to get the cash to buy the old mill, I knew which one. I'd seen Grey's truck up there. Both of them should have been mine, the mill and the house, and Arvil knew it."

"What about the HOA? All those signatures? Why bring that back up?"

"I've been trying to fix the chaos in this town for years. That house was grand once. The whole town was nice. Now it's just crumbling driveways. It doesn't live up to its potential, and people just need to be guided to the right way of doing things. You included. You'll ruin that house."

"Hardly. Years ago, you manipulated Jaleesa to get those signatures for your own gain, and then you tried to use them again for your own gain. And it never once occurred to you that any of those people would call you out on it?"

"Who cares if they did? They signed the petition to start an HOA. They each had their own reasons. Says more about them than it does about me if they go back on their desire for a better town just to spite the one person trying to make it happen."

"Whatever. If you wanted the house that badly, why didn't you just make an offer to Arvil years ago."

"It's revenge, sweetheart. Deep running revenge. Generations in the making." His light and airy tone made her skin prickle, and *sweetheart* was one of the few insults that made her blood boil. "My family money was tied up in Boroughs Textiles. You may have heard of it."

Logan's stomach dropped to the basement. She steadied her grip on the phone and planted her other hand on the floor. Boroughs

Textiles. Her voice was barely above a whisper. "The Boston Sewing Factory fire."

"Lord, you're slow. My great-great aunt and uncle built that house you're sitting in right now. But my great-great-grandfather moved to Boston and started a sewing factory. Boroughs. Your great something-or-other was the lawyer who represented the people who sued my family into oblivion. My family made things that helped people. Your family got its money by ruining people with lawsuits."

"We owned real estate. Those lawyers fought for worker protections, and you can't exactly say that your life would be better if your ancestors were allowed to get away with hurting people."

"Protecting people doesn't exactly run in your gene pool. Your father laundered money for a living, and there was no way in hell I would let a Cole sleep within my family's walls."

"That's rich, coming from someone who let the place rot. You had years of opportunity to buy it and fix it, now I'm the one scraping generations of cigar filth off the walls and peeling off nasty wallpaper."

She finally had a place she loved and a plot of land to call her own, and Meldrick Lacey was not going to make her feel bad about it.

"I was successful in the end, wasn't I? And you know how the government works. What do they say, you can indict a ham sandwich? Isn't that what your grandfather did to mine? I don't give a crap whether you committed fraud or not. All I care about is that it will cost you every penny you have and then some to defend yourselves. Even if they do find you innocent, you'll have to sell that house to pay for a lawyer, and by that time, it'll be a foreclosure. I won't have to have a bidding war with you. I'll have my home at pennies to the dollar, and with any luck, Ramsbolt will be rid of you."

"Hey, Meldrick?"

"Yeah."

"Fuck off." She hung up the phone.

Swiping the screen, she checked her voice call log app to make sure the call had been safely downloaded to her cloud account.

"What a moron. Like a girl who got death threats for two years would *ever* move to a two-party recording consent state."

CHAPTER THIRTY-THREE

2 June 1886.

If you are reading this letter it is because I am gone, off to the churchyard for the last time. My good fortune of living to see eighty and more years is great indeed, as both sides of the terrible war would find me treasonous, even all these years later, had they learned the truth.

If you are reading this, it is also because this missive has emerged from its cupboard and fallen into the light of day. Assuming it remains attached to my patriotic hoard, questions are sure to abound. Herein I will try to answer them, though my hand is unsteady, and my time is thin.

When I was a girl, it took near a day to get into town, but the roads got better, Norris's carriage wheels took the roads with increasing efficiency, and the mill was busy in those days. Worsted wool was fashionable. It was smooth and could be ironed flat and demand meant we could hire a manager to care for the mill and build a house closer to town away from the noise.

When my uncle designed the house for us, he included rooms for the kids. The large back bedroom was perfect for John Junior, who was just a baby in those days. The middle bedroom was for a daughter who wasn't meant to be. The hidden playroom behind a bookcase sat empty for many years.

It was as if wool and cotton were in their own war in those days. The sons of wool chose liberty for all for reasons both close to the heart and the economy. Cheap labor was not cheap in our eyes and our neighbors were not to be owned but loved as the good book says. But the sons of cotton kept pushing north. And as the first winter of battle drew near, the mill made jackets and pants and blankets for the militia.

John Junior took up the battle flag and marched on with the volunteer infantry, and we never saw him again. He died in a Confederate prison camp.

Dark days followed, and I shall not detail them here. It is as if a fog consumed everything after. My John died of a broken heart, and I lived on bitterness and fury alone in this house except for my cook and a housekeeper. I kept the mill running. How, I do not recall. It only began to lift when the minister came to call. With his hat in his hands, he sat in my sitting room and sought my willingness to aid Confederate soldiers in escaping their conscription.

A church across the border in New Brunswick was set to receive them, but the walk was too long, the journey too perilous to forge without a stop. My house was the largest, with room to spare. It sat away from prying eyes. Situated well, it would make the ideal respite before crossing the border to New Brunswick. The minister promised to give me aid.

I turned him out with no response, not eager to risk my life for a cause so distant. They who took my son had no right to my exposure. A fierce storm passed over that night, and I awoke, roamed the untouched rooms of my lost son and impossible daughter with the relief of one candle. The Lord spoke to me as only he can. Revenge, he said, is for the weak. It merely picks at a scab and leaves a scar. Justice and forgiveness cannot be detached from one another. To find one you must seek out the other. Before dawn, I made a plan.

For many months I welcomed deserting Southern soldiers to my home. I denied them to leave with that with which they came. Into my care they deposited monies, clothing, weapons, anything that identified themselves. I did this to protect myself, my intent to burn it all or bury it. At first, I replaced their garments with those from the mill, union volunteer army materials to give their likeness a friendly countenance. Later, with the minister's aid, I traded some of their weapons to locals in exchange for clothes I could give to our tenants.

They slept in the basement, away from daylight. Before departing on foot in the night, they would give me letters to pass on to family. I reluctantly took them at first, later with enthusiasm. I offered the gift they would not give my son. But I grew fearful.

I stored their items in the secret playroom until such a time as I could burn them in a fire, but the hoard grew and no time came that would permit me to dispose of them without arousing suspicion. If I were found out, I could be sent to prison. There were rumors in those days of deserters tortured with thumbscrews, flogged, or branded. I was terrified for my life. I only was able to burn the clothes they left behind in the last few years, in a pit in the yard, along with branches from ice storms. But I could not burn their letters. My heart was not that hard.

It is my wish that these letters find their way to good hands one day, to serve for the good of the country, should they survive their time in the playroom. Do what you will with the rest.

What time does with my intentions is not at my disposal.

Most sincerely,

Emma Barnett

* * *

Sunlight found its way into the little bedroom intended for a daughter that never happened. It snuck through the broken and twisted metal blinds and landed on the back of Logan's neck. She rubbed at it and shimmied clockwise a few degrees, squinting at the fine print of a man on the run, begging his mother's forgiveness for seeking solace in a foreign land. Scattered around her were their stories, spare coats from the mill that never graced a man's shoulders, muzzle loaders with bayonets abandoned by men who gave up their post. There were rusty revolvers and crates of cash and stacks of letters, bundled by state and never mailed.

"Logan?" Grey stirred and startled in the room next door. The floor creaked when his feet left the bed. She checked the time on her phone. It was nearly six thirty. How did time go so fast?

"I'm in the…den. Room. Whatever. Come over. You have to see what I found."

He appeared in the doorway, leaned against its frame, and rubbed sleep from his eyes. "I saw the floor plans when I was in here yesterday. Where did you get those? And what the hell is all this? Did you overthrow an armory on your walk home from work?"

Sleep was setting in, her eyes getting heavy. She hadn't realized how much time had passed. "It was all in that closet. I was looking at the floor plans and found a void in the walls. Did you know there's an ironing board in the walls in the other room?"

"No. I also don't know how to use an ironing board." Grey hopscotched over relics to inspect the cavern behind the bookcase. "This is like some CS Lewis thing. Minus the lions. You're sure there are no lions, right?"

"No lions. I wish I'd asked Meldrick more questions when he called."

Grey's questions were muffled by the wall that separated them. Her mind was too active and firing on too little sleep to make sense of her own questions, let alone his. Despite hours of research on her phone looking up relics and squinting at letters from another era in a primitive pen, she was no closer to grasping the depth of it all, but she was swallowed by it, lost in it. So many other things did make sense, though. The house never felt as young as it claimed to be. It was far too worn and loved.

She rested a hand on a worsted wool coat and locked eyes with Grey when he returned to the room.

"I'm a little tired, but here's what I know. All of these suits are unworn. They were made for the Union army. Most of those weapons are Confederate, as is the cash."

Grey lifted a revolver and tested the weight of it, bouncing it in his hand. He inspected the handle. "The etching is really elaborate."

"I've been trying to come up with dates for some of this stuff. It's just a slog, and I'm tired." She flapped a hand at a rifle. "That thing over there, that rifle. The one with carvings on the handles. It has initials carved in it. I was trying to match things like that up to the letters, but I ended up down a rabbit hole. I tried to figure out what military units used that kind of weapon. Then I looked on an ancestry site to figure out roster rolls. I guess a lot of people used their own weapons, so it's not easy. Anyway, this stuff belonged to Confederate soldiers, mostly, and a few Union guys who wanted to cross the border into Canada. Or what became Canada."

Grey tilted his head and rubbed at his hairline. "You need to be a little less intense in the mornings. I haven't had any coffee, and I don't think I'm following very well."

"I told you. All of this was in that closet cubby in the walls."

"There weren't any Civil War battles up here. There was one in Portland, but there were no prisoners in Maine. I don't think so, anyway. One of the guys from high school got super into reenactments, and I wasn't really listening in school, but…this doesn't make any sense."

"Here." She held out Emma's letter with a hand shaky for lack of sleep and in need of a cup of coffee. He grimaced at the yellowed page and handed it back.

"Interpret, please?"

"Meldrick's great-grandmother wrote this. They owned the mill."

"Arvil's mill?"

"Yeah. Meldrick's great-gran was mad at the war for killing her son. He died while being held in a Confederate prison. The anger was eating her alive, and one day the minister came by and asked if she'd help Southern soldiers who wanted to escape. She decided to help, so she turned her house into, like, an underground railroad stop and helped them flee into Canada."

"That explains the Confederate cash."

"She wouldn't let them take anything with them when they crossed the border. Not even their guns. She dressed some of them up in Union outfits, so they'd just look like locals or be less obvious or something."

"Why would Canada let Union soldiers cross the border, though?"

"I had the same question. I looked this up. It wasn't really Canada yet. It was a bunch of provinces, I guess you could say. And the borders were porous. The economies were tied together. And tens of thousands of future Canadians joined the Union army."

"All of these uniforms…"

She nodded. "Were made at the mill. This Emma Barnett…she stashed them here to give them to Confederate soldiers who didn't want to fight for that cause anymore. She burned the clothes they left behind years later. She traded some weapons with people from town, exchanging them for used clothes, too. Then she sealed it all away. She wrote this note before she died, back in the eighteen eighties, it seems. She left it on top of that crate of letters."

"This stuff must be worth a fortune."

"Some of it has value. It didn't to her, though. It was a huge liability. She was afraid of what would happen to her if anyone ever found it. Which reminds me, what's a thumbscrew?" She shook her head. "Never mind. I don't want to know before breakfast."

"This is crazy." He plopped down on the floor, cradling a revolver in his hands like a delicate flower. "Someone used this. It was fired at someone in the Civil War. That's insane."

"*Possibly* fired. It's also possible that its owner saw no conflict. I guess the right person could research all this and piece the letters to the weapons and possibly match them up to battles. Oh!" She leaned forward as far she could, arm outstretched, and tapped an old milk crate. It was half full of papers, some folded, some flat, their angular and looping letters all from different hands. Some were in envelopes pressed flat by the heaviness of the years. Others so brittle their corners had chipped and flaked to the bottom of the crate. "Some of the men left letters. They wanted her to send them on to their families. She never did. They're bundled by state. Here." She held out a bundle, and he declined with an outstretched palm.

"I don't want to touch anything. I'm afraid I'll destroy it."

"Me, too." she plucked a folded yellowed page from the top of a stack. "I read this one, though. This guy had a kid. He was going to send for his wife and son once he got to Canada. He had this dream that they'd buy a small farm. I wonder if he ever sent for her. Poor Emma had no idea how to get the letters out of town. She was afraid she'd get caught."

"Holy crap." Grey rubbed his eyes with the heels of his hands. "And all of this is because you found those plans."

"I didn't find them. Meldrick's distant cousin brought it by this morning, while you were working at the church."

"Man. Yesterday was a crazy day."

"You're telling me."

Grey ran a hand through his scraggly hair and blinked at the piles of letters and clothes and weapons. "And now all this is ours?"

"I figured we could sell it through Penny. She can make sure it goes to the right dealers and sell what she wants in her store. She's taking me to Colby today to get my stitches out. I can ask her about it on the way. Some of this is worth a lot, too." She woke her phone from its slumber and held it up. "This is the rifle over there with the etched metal handle thingy."

Grey's eyes widened, suddenly awake. "Fourteen thousand dollars?"

"Yeah. The weapons can be worth a ton of money."

"What's the rest of this stuff." Grey picked up a wooden case with metal hinges.

"That's a surgeon's kit. It has a bone saw in it and a bunch of stabby things."

"Ew." He wrinkled his nose and set it down.

"There's clothes and letters and tons of weapons. There are eight guns like that one."

"I can't believe this. We could be rich."

Logan had already settled for happiness. She'd settled for secure and comfortable. It was hardly settling at all to find herself in a house with a roof, with someone who loved her, in a town she was willing to fight for, surrounded by friends she wouldn't trade for the world.

She scooted closer. "Grey. I have to tell you something."

He leaned back. "You have uh-oh face. Do I need coffee for

this?"

"No. I screwed up. You were right. You said I didn't trust you, and that really hurt my feelings."

He shook his head, eyes wide, but she didn't want his explanation.

"That's not what I mean. It hurt because you were right, and you knew it before I did. It wasn't the house. It started a long time before that. And it wasn't anything you said or did. It was this voice in my ear that tells me the future will look like the past. Even if it's in a different box, the contents will be the same. You know?"

"You mean the way I expect you to start screaming sometimes. Or how I figure one day you'll get up and leave because that's what my mom did?"

"Totally different situations. We're nothing like our parents. I'm never gonna leave, and you're nothing like my father. I didn't trust you, and it wasn't your fault. I'm sorry."

Grey rubbed at his nose with the heel of his hand. "There's a lot of dust in here."

"Yeah. What do you say we close this door and walk to Marissa's for coffee and muffins?"

He reached across the floor and laced her fingers in his. His hands were warm. "I like it. We can talk about what we're going to do with all the money we make from selling this stuff."

"We can't keep it all, though. If you agree to it, I have a plan."

CHAPTER THIRTY-FOUR

"The best thing has happened." Logan's mother leaned in, beaming. Her face nearly filled Logan's cell phone screen. She wasn't in her kitchen this time, perched instead in a small living room. A Christmas tree twinkled in the background. "The hens got cold and stopped laying eggs."

One eye on the screen and the other on a tray of cookies, Logan raised the volume on her phone so she could hear above the laughter coming from the library. She bit into a wreath cookie. Her friends would never miss it.

"That's funny. And good for you."

"The timing is terrible. I was going to make eggnog. I found a recipe on the internet. It can wait, I suppose. I know you have friends over, and I do have to run myself, but I wanted you to know that I read the news about your letters all the way over her in France. They were picked up by one of those British tabloids that pretends to be all stiff upper lippy."

"Mmm. I know the type."

"Your friend Simon—"

"Stuart, Mom. His name is Stuart."

"His articles were very well written. It must have been quite the challenge finding the descendants of all those soldiers. If I had a heart, I would have felt something."

Logan couldn't help but laugh. "You said it, not me."

"Did you make any money off of all that junk?"

She rolled her eyes. "We sure did. A lot of it. Not by your standard, but a lot by mine. Most of it went into savings."

Her mother clapped, and Logan winced. There was a fine line between capitalizing on history for the sake of greed and ensuring the preservation of the past. With Penny's help, Logan had been certain that almost every item went to a good home, but she certainly wouldn't have given anything away for free.

"You've always been smart. I'm glad to hear you've set aside a little nest egg just in case. It makes your mother feel better."

"I didn't say that." Her eyes widened, defiance and offense colliding. "I've told you before, I don't need to protect myself from Grey. We put it into a joint account. To use for emergencies. And we put some into the house."

The doorbell rang. The last of their guests were arriving. She peered around the corner to see Grey scamper for the door.

"I should go, Mom. I have company."

"One last question." Propping her chin in her hands, her eyes full of longing, she gazed wistfully. "Did you buy anything fun?"

"You'll be disappointed in me." Logan smiled, her cheeks warm. "It was all furniture. We bought some chairs for the library and beds for the guest rooms. Nothing too exciting."

"You'll have to send me pictures." She waved Logan off as if she were boarding a train. "Now off with you. Have a good time. Talk to you soon."

The screen went dark. Logan popped the last of the wreath cookie in her mouth and carried the tray through the dining room and down the hall. Helen teetered on her cane in the doorway, Grey helping her shrug from her coat. Stuart and Sandy were in her wake, unfurling their scarves.

"We brought wine. Lots of it." Sandy held up two bottles and Stuart mimed.

"Red and white," he said.

Logan balanced the tray in one hand and gave Sandy a partial hug. "You two. You didn't have to do that."

"We wanted to." Stuart pointed the neck of a bottle toward the library, where Kyle sat neck craned, waving them in. "In there?"

"Yup. After you. There are glasses and open bottles on the bar cart. Help yourselves to whatever you'd like."

Grey took the cookies from her, holding them to his face and pretending to eat the platter. She swatted him.

"Oh, Logan." Helen gushed in the doorway, grasping Logan's forearm. "It's so refined. You've certainly done well."

"It's a trick. We hid all the clutter and dust in the drawers." Winking at Helen, she hid her pleasure at the approval.

For so long, she'd passed through that room on her way to other things. It had been a placeholder, a cardboard box storage room, and coat rack in the early days of autumn. Wallpaper removed and the walls painted dark green, the wood polished until it glowed, she'd convinced Grey to indulge her wishes for leather chairs and a mission style coffee table that made the room cozy. With a Christmas tree in the corner all lit up, a fire in the fireplace, and her friends gathered around, what the library lacked in books it had in warmth.

Helen radiated and clattered into the den, her face lit by the fire. Adelle and Kyle shuffled to make room for her, and she settled into a seat, her hands running over the leather arms.

"I've never sat in such luxury." She grinned up at Logan and accepted a snowflake cookie from the tray.

"I wasn't sure about these chairs." Grey refilled his glass of scotch from the bar cart and poured Logan a glass of wine. "I thought they'd be sticky in the summer. Like sitting in an old truck. Logan wanted them."

"He caved." She accepted her glass. "I wanted some adult furniture. Something we wouldn't have to replace in a few years."

Grey plopped into a chair, chin raised. "I like it. I feel like the lord of a manor. I need an ascot and a pipe."

"Stuart." Logan swirled her drink in her glass. "I almost forgot to tell you. My mom said she saw your articles all the way over in France."

A hand on Sandy's knee, he nodded and blinked up at her. "I still can't believe it. My little website crashed the day the *New York Times* ran the series. I met so many neat people trying to help those letters get home. I've been thinking about writing a book about my experience. I'd love your input, if you're interested. After the holidays, of course."

"That sounds neat. I'd help." Resting her wine glass on the mantel, she wiped cookie dust from her hands onto a red paper napkin with cartoon Santas and Rudolphs.

Penny raised her glass. "Me too. I can hook you up with some of the people who bought the clothes and guns and stuff. There were some historians who told me some really dry stories that you can probably turn into something interesting."

Helen perked up. "Has Arvil set an opening date yet?"

Logan sighed and swallowed her wine, lowering her glass to squint at the fading fire. "Not yet. But I have the first round of kits all boxed up and ready to go as soon as he does."

Adelle nodded. "Water and sewer were hooked up just before Thanksgiving. It's just little things now, and then his inspection. Shouldn't be long."

Grey poke at the fire. "Spring, probably. I imagine he'll wait until the thaw."

"Speaking of spring, that plan you drew for the yard looks great." Logan nudged Adelle's elbow and plopped down on the edge of the coffee table. "A lot of work went into that."

"Wait until we start digging holes." Kyle said. "I'm looking forward to helping. Not sure why."

"It does sound fun." Logan looked past Kyle to wink at Adelle. "The old plan translated really well."

"There were a lot of invasive plants in there that were trendy at the time. I swapped them out for native plants. It'll look a little silly how small things will be, but they'll grow. In a few years, it'll be amazing. I'm glad you let me play with it. I've been thinking about offering landscape design, and this gave me a push. I'm surprised you liked it the first round."

"Really? Why wouldn't I like it?"

"It's a lot of work."

Logan shrugged. "I'm not afraid of hard work. Besides, I'm ready to put down some roots. Pun intended."

Grey patted her leg, where the swollen scar had faded to dark pink months ago. "Do you want to give them the…you know?"

Logan jumped to her feet. All eyes followed as she skipped to the mantel and pulled envelopes from behind a cluster of candlesticks.

She handed the first to Penny, who gaped up at her. "We all agreed no presents."

Logan's hair whipped at her shoulders as she shook her head. "They're not presents. Open it. It's a finder's fee for hooking us up with that military collector guy. There are some happy museums and collectors now."

Peeking into the envelope and sealing it shut, Penny held it away as if it might bite. "This is a lot. Way too much."

"No. We are grateful to you guys. You're family. Here." She handed another envelope to Sandy. "I know this isn't much, but remember when we were at the bar, and I asked if you wanted any of those things for the library? You said you'd like to display Emma's letter and a Union Army jacket but didn't have the resources to care for them. This check should cover it."

Sandy peeked inside the envelope then clutched it to her chest. "This more than covers it. This is such a great gift to the town."

"Adelle." Logan whipped out another envelope. "This is to say thanks for the plants and helping bring Hannah Barnett's vision to life with me. And there's a second check in there. It's a donation to that town beautification fund. And you are not allowed to argue with me about either of them."

"You don't have to do this." Adelle shook her head. "The arts festival covers beautification, and you don't have to pay me for my help. That was a gift."

"The plan was a gift. The help was a gift. But all those shrubs and flowers are expensive. The way we see it, this is just Emma Barnett paying for her garden revival."

Grey handed an envelope to Kyle. "We're prepaying for some cooking classes. I really need those knife skills."

"And this is for you, Nate." Logan handed him an envelope. "I'd really like a new painting of the house someday, now that it's blue and cleaned up. If that's okay?"

Nate turned the envelope over in his hands. "I'd be happy to."

"And this one is for Helen." Logan passed her the last envelope. "I've been a real pain in the ass this year. I keep making stupid mistakes and being irresponsible. It's not even like I'm making bad choices. I've just been doing dumb things. The longer that IRS hassle went on, the more forgetful I got. It's all over now, and this is just my little way of saying I'm sorry. You're like a second mom to me. My Ramsbolt mom. Thanks for being understanding."

Helen pushed herself to her feet, and Logan returned a squeezing hug. "It's over now? Without a lawyer?"

The oven beeped in the kitchen. It was time to check the turkey. She waved a dismissive hand, brushing off the whole thing.

"Poof. It ended. Just like that. We got a letter saying the whole thing had been concluded with no evidence found. Meldrick's plan to sink us with legal bills never came to be. I have to check the bird. I'll be back."

Penny and Adelle were hot on her heels, drinks in their hands.

Logan flung open the stove door and steam escaped.

"That smells good." Adelle inflated with a gulp of air. "Like Thanksgiving as a kid."

Adelle agreed, and the two swapped stories of holiday culinary tragedies.

Logan had never smelled a Thanksgiving kitchen. Food showed up on the table, garnished. If her father were in a bad mood, the chef would have already carved it. It wasn't like she missed out on anything. Not when she could make so many new memories.

She stabbed the turkey in the thigh with a thermometer like the winner of her blog roulette contest suggested. It was done.

"You're saying that whole IRS thing just went away?" Penny leaned in the doorway.

"Yup." She put the turkey on the stove to rest and peeled off her yellow oven mitts.

"What are you going to do about Meldrick?" Adelle asked.

"Absolutely nothing." She slid the green bean casserole into the oven, grabbed the plastic tomato-shaped timer off the back of the stove and twisted it. "Forgiveness is the best revenge."